T0144263

# The Tickencote
# Treasure

# The Tickencote Treasure

William Le Queux

MINT EDITIONS

*The Tickencote Treasure* was first published in 1903.

This edition published by Mint Editions 2021.

ISBN 9781513280844 | E-ISBN 9781513285863

Published by Mint Editions®

 **MINT
EDITIONS**

minteditionbooks.com

Publishing Director: Jennifer Newens
Design & Production: Rachel Lopez Metzger
Project Manager: Micaela Clark
Typesetting: Westchester Publishing Services

# Contents

# I

## In which Job Seal Borrows a Fusee

If you are fond of a mystery I believe you will ponder over this curious narrative just as I have pondered.

Certain persons, having heard rumours of the strange adventures that once happened to me, have asked me to write them down in detail, so that they may be printed and given to the world in their proper sequence. Therefore, in obedience, and in order to set at rest for ever certain wild and unfounded reports which crept into the papers at the time, I do so without fear or favour, seeking to conceal no single thing, but merely to relate what I actually saw with my own eyes and heard with my own ears.

I read somewhere the other day the sweeping statement, written probably by one of our superior young gentlemen just down from Oxford, that Romance is dead. This allegation, however, I make so bold as to challenge—first, because in my own humble capacity I have actually been the unwilling actor in one of the most remarkable romances of modern times; and, secondly, because I believe with that sage old chronicler, Richard of Cirencester, that the man whose soul is filled with Greek has a heart of leather.

Fortunately I can lay claim to neither. Apart from my association with the present chain of curious events I am but an ordinary man, whose name is Paul Pickering, whose age is thirty-two, and whose profession at the time the romance befell me was the very prosaic one of a doctor without regular practice. You will therefore quickly discern that I was not overburdened either by fame, fortune, or fashionable foibles, and further that, as *locum tenens* for country doctors in ill-health or on holiday, I advertised regularly in the *Lancet*, and was glad enough to accept the fee of three guineas weekly.

Hard work in a big practice at Stepney and Poplar had resulted in a bad touch of influenza with its attendant debility; therefore, when one of my patients, a sun-tanned old salt named Seal, suggested that I should go a trip with him up the Mediterranean, I hailed the idea with delight.

Job Seal was quite a chance patient. He called one evening at the surgery in Commercial Road East, where I was acting as *locum* for a doctor named Bidwell, and consulted me about his rheumatism. A big, deep-chested, thick-set man, with grey hair, reddish uncut beard, big hands, shaggy brows, and a furrowed face browned by sea and sun; he spoke in a deep bass, interlarding his conversation with nautical expressions which were, to me, mostly unintelligible. The liniment I gave him apparently suited his ailment, for he came again and again, until one evening he called and declared that I had effected a cure as marvellous as that of Sequah.

"My boat, the *Thrush*, is layin' at Fresh Wharf, and I sail on Saturday for Cardiff, where we take in coal for Leghorn. Now, if you ain't got anything better to do, doctor, don't you sign on why as steward at a bob a day, and come with me for the round trip?" he suggested. "You told me the other night that you're bein' paid off from here on Saturday. My boat ain't exactly a liner, you know, but I daresay you could shake down comfortable like, and as the trip'll take a couple o' months, you'd see most of the ports up to Smyrna. Besides, this is just the right time o' year for a blow. It 'ud do you good."

The suggestion certainly appealed to me. I had never been afloat farther than Ramsgate by the *Marguerite*, and for years had longed to go abroad and see those wonderful paradises of the Sunny South of which, like other people, I had witnessed highly-coloured dissolving views. Therefore I accepted the bluff old captain's hospitality, signed the ship's papers in a back office off Leadenhall Street, and on Saturday evening boarded as black, grimy, and forbidding a craft as ever dropped down the Thames.

Job Seal was right. The *Thrush* was not by any means a liner, and its passenger accommodation was restricted. My cabin was very small, very stuffy, and very dirty; just as might be expected of a Mediterranean tramp steamer. As the outward cargo was invariably Cardiff steam coal consigned to the well-known firm of Messrs. Agius, of Naples, and Malta, there was over everything a layer of fine coal dust, while the faces of both officers and crew seemed ingrained with black.

The first day out I confess that I did not feel over well. A light vessel and a choppy sea are never pleasant to a landsman. Nevertheless, I very soon got my sea legs, and then the voyage down Channel was pleasant enough. It was the end of June, and the salt breezes were gratifying after the stuffy back streets of Stepney. Before my advent Job Seal was in the habit of eating alone in his cabin, because he was an omnivorous reader, and the chatter of his officers disturbed him. He welcomed me, however, as a companion. Max Pemberton, Conan Doyle, and Hyne he swore by, and in one corner of his cabin he had whole stacks of sixpenny reprints.

The first day out I rather regretted my hasty decision to sail with him, but ere we sighted Lundy Island and Penarth I was as merry and eager to smoke as any of the villainous-looking crew.

After four days loading in Cardiff the vessel was an inch deep in coal dust, and as the heavy-swearing hands in the forecastle began "cleaning up" we slowly glided out of the Bute Docks to the accompaniment of shouting, gesticulating, and strong language. At Seal's suggestion I had provided myself with certain articles of food to my taste, but as the grit of coal and the taste of tar were inseparable from the cuisine, and the cook's galley the most evil-smelling corner in the whole vessel, I enjoyed eating least of all. The weather was, however, perfect, even in the long roll of the Atlantic, and the greater part of each day I spent with the burly skipper on his bridge, lolling in an old deck-chair behind a screen of canvas lashed to the rail to keep off the wind. I had quite a cosy corner to myself, and there I smoked my pipe, breathed the salt ocean breezes, and yarned with my deep-chested friend.

"We don't carry forty-quid salooners on this 'ere boat," remarked Joe Thorpe, the first mate, when I mentioned casually that the rats gnawed my boots at night and scampered around my cabin and over my bunk. "When a passenger comes with us he has to rough it, but he sees a sight more than if he travelled by the P. and O. or the Orient. You'll see a lot, doctor, before you're back in London."

His words were prophetic. I did see a lot, as you will gather later on.

Craft and crew were, as I have said, as forbidding as can be well imagined. The vessel was black, save for a dirty red band around her funnel, old, ricketty, and much patched. On the second day out from Cardiff Mike Flanagan, the first engineer, imparted to me the disconcerting fact that the boilers were in such a state that he feared to work them at any undue pressure lest we might all take an unwelcome flight into space. Hence at night, when I lay in my bunk sleepless owing to the dirty weather in the Bay of Biscay, the jarring of the propeller caused my medical mind to revert to the instability of those boilers and the probability of catastrophe. I am not a seafaring man, but I have often since wondered in what class the *Thrush* might have been entered at Lloyd's.

Day followed day, and after we sighted Finisterre the weather became delightful again. Seal told me long yarns of his younger days in the Pacific trade, how he had been wrecked off the Tasmanian coast, and how on another occasion the steamer on which he sailed was burned at sea. The dreamy hours passed lazily. We ate together, laughed together, and at night drank big noggins of rum together. Cape St. Vincent loomed up in the haze one brilliant evening, and afterwards the great rock of Gibraltar; then, on entering the Mediterranean, we steered a straight course for that long, sun-blanched town with the high lighthouse lying at the foot of the blue Apennines, Leghorn, which port we at last entered with shrieking siren and flying our dirty red ensign.

But it is not with foreign towns that this narrative concerns. True, I went ashore with Seal and drank vermouth and seltzer at Nazi's, but during the weeks I sailed in company with the big-handed, big-hearted skipper and his villainous-looking crew we visited many ports in search of a cargo for London. Naples, Palermo, Smyrna, and Tunis were to me, an untravelled man, all interesting, while Job Seal was, I discovered, a most popular man ashore. Shipping agents welcomed him, and he drank vermouth at their expense; Customs officers were civil, with an eye to the glass of grog that would follow their inspection; and even British consuls were agreeable, unbending and joking with him in their private sanctums.

Yes, Job Seal was a typical Mediterranean skipper, a hard drinker in port, a hard swearer at sea, and a hard task-master at any time. In bad weather he put on his pluck with his oilskins. From the bridge he addressed his men as though speaking to dogs, and woe betide the unfortunate hand who did not execute an order just to his liking. He would roar like a bull, and conclude with an interminable cascade of imprecations until he became red in the face and breathless.

"I've done this round trip these nineteen years, doctor," he explained to me one night while we were having our grog together, "and I really believe I could take the old tub from the Gib. to Naples without a compass." And then in his deep bass tones he began to yarn as sailors will yarn, telling tales mostly of adventures ashore in foreign towns, adventures wherein Mike Flanagan—to whom he always referred as his "chief"— and alcoholic liquors played leading parts.

After leaving Tunis for Valencia, homeward bound, we experienced bad weather. The wind howled in the rigging, and the sea ran mountains high, as it often does in those parts at certain seasons of the year. One afternoon, attired in the suit of yellow oilskins I had purchased in Cardiff, I was seated on the bridge, notwithstanding the stiff breeze

WILLIAM LE QUEUX

and the heavy sea still running, for I preferred that to my stuffy, tarry cabin with its port-hole screwed down.

Seal, in ponderous sea-boots, black oilskins, and his sou-wester tied beneath his chin, had been chatting, laughing and pacing the deck, when of a sudden his quick eye observed something which to my unpractised vision was indistinguishable. He took his glass from its box, stood astride, and took steady sight of it.

"H'm," he grunted deeply, "that's durned funny!" and turning to the helmsman gave an order which caused the man to spin the wheel over, and slowly the bows of the *Thrush* swung round in the direction in which he had been gazing.

"Like to look, doctor?" he asked, at the same time handing me his glass.

I stood up, but the vessel rolling about like a bottle made it difficult for me to keep my feet, and more especially for me to focus the object. At last, however, after some effort I saw as I swept the horizon a curious-looking thing afloat. Indistinct in the grey haze, it looked to me like two square-built boxes floating high from the water, but close behind each other. I could not, however, see them well on account of the haze.

"That's curious!" I exclaimed. "What do you think they are, captain?"

"Haven't any idea, doctor. We're goin' to inspect 'em presently." And he again took sight for a long time, and then replaced his glass in its box with a puzzled air. "Queer lookin' craft, anyhow," he remarked. "They don't seem to be flying any signals of distress, either."

"Where are we now?" I inquired, much interested in the mysterious object in the distance.

"About midway between Fomentera and Algiers," was his answer, and then, impatient to overhaul the craft that had attracted his attention, he pulled over the brass handle of the electric signals and turned it back again, causing it to ring thrice. An instant later came the three answering rings, and a few moments afterwards the long cloud of dense black smoke whirling from the funnel told us that Mike Flanagan was about to get all the work out of his boilers that he dared.

Seal roared an order in the howling wind, and a tiny, coal-grimed flag ran up to the mast-head and fluttered in the breeze, while with eyes glued to his glass he watched if any response were given to his signal.

But there was none.

News of something unusual had spread among the crew, and a few moments later the first mate, Thorpe, whose watch had ended an hour before, sprang up the ladder to the skipper's side.

"Look, Joe!" exclaimed Seal. "What the dickens do you make out o' that?"

Thorpe swung his body with the motion of the vessel and took a long look at the object of mystery.

"Thunder, cap'n!" he cried. "Looks like Noah's Ark, sir."

By this time the smutty-faced crew, in their dirty blue trousers and sea-boots, had emerged from the forecastle and stood gazing in the direction of the mystery, heedless of the waves that now and then swept the deck from stem to stern. Some of the men shaded their eyes with horny hands, and the opinions expressed were both forcible and various.

Job Seal borrowed a fusee from me and lit his foul-smelling pipe, a habit of his when puzzled. With his blackened clay between his teeth he talked to Thorpe, while the spray showered in our faces and the vessel rose and fell in the long trough of the sea.

Again and again he sighted the object which his sea-trained eyes had so quickly detected, and each time growled in dissatisfaction.

At length, in a voice quite unusual to him, and with all the brown gone out of his face, he said:—

"There's something very uncanny about that blessed craft, doctor! I've been afloat these thirty-three years come August, but I never saw such a tarnation funny thing as that before! I believe it's the *Flyin' Dutchman*, as true as I'm here on my own bridge!"

He handed me the binocular again, and steadying myself carefully I managed to focus it.

Sailors are nothing if not superstitious, and I could see that the unusual sight had sent a stir of consternation through the ship.

"What do you make her out to be?" roared Seal to the look-out man.

"Never saw such a thing before, sir," responded the man in oilskins; "maybe she's one o' them secret submarine inventions of the French what's come to the surface"—a suggestion which pleased the crew mightily, and was greeted with a chorus of laughter.

"Submarine be hanged!" exclaimed one old seaman whom I had heard addressed as Dicky Dunn. "It's old Noah a-making for Marseilles! Can't yer see the big square port in the stern where he lets his bloomin' pigeons out?"

And so the suggestions went on, and while the *Thrush* rapidly bore down with full steam ahead, with the salt spray flying across her bows, the mystery of our discovery increased.

WILLIAM LE QUEUX

# II

## What We Saw and What We Heard

"Well, I'm blowed!"

The simple exclaimation was Seal's, but the words of the sentence were most expressive.

The strange object was now but a few cable lengths of us, and certainly the skipper's surprise was shared by every one of us. Even the blackened, half-naked stokers had emerged on deck and stood gazing at it with wide-open eyes.

Job Seal, the big, roaring man, dauntless of every thing, stood leaning over the bridge and glaring aghast at his discovery. And well he might, for surely no similar object sailed the sea in these modern days.

In the sea, close behind one another, rode two wooden houses, three-storeyed, and having big square windows of thick glass. So near were we to it that now, for the first time, I could distinguish that there was a submerged connexion between the two objects above the surface. Then, in a flash, the astounding truth dawned upon me. It was an ancient ship of that curious Elizabethan build, like those I had seen in pictures of the Spanish Armada!

From the high bows there projected a battered figure-head, shaped like some marine monstrosity, while beyond the submerged deck rose the high stern, from which jutted three projections, each farther over the water than the others. At such close quarters I could see that out of the roof of both houses stood the stumps of masts, but there was not a vestige of cordage.

The strangest fact of all, however, was that everywhere, even over the roof of the high bow and stern, were barnacles, sponges, and shell-fish of all descriptions, while enormous bands of brown seaweed streamed and flapped with the wind. A tangle of marine plants was everywhere, matted, brown and green for the most part, and so luxurious that almost every part of the mysterious vessel was completely covered. The shells, slime, and seaweed certainly indicated that the strange ship had reposed at the bottom of the sea for many a long year, and the uncanny sight caused considerable misgivings among the forecastle hands.

The barnacles and shell-fish had not attached themselves to the windows, hence the outline of the latter was still preserved, but over everything else was a dense slimy tangle a foot or so thick, the higher parts half-dried by the wind, while a quantity of seaweed floated around the hull in long waving masses. Water-logged, she rolled and pitched helplessly in the troubled waters, so that to me, unaccustomed to the sea, it seemed as though she must topple over. Surely it was one of the strangest sights that any eye had witnessed.

A derelict is always of interest alike to sailor and to landsman, but it assuredly does not happen to many to discover a craft that has been lost to human ken for at least three hundred years.

"She's a beauty, she is!" laughed Seal, although I could see that his discovery somewhat troubled him, for, like all his class, he was full of superstition. "Wonder what her cargo is?"

"Corpses," suggested Thorpe. "She's only bobbed up lately, I should say, from her lovely shroud of weeds."

"Perhaps there may be something on board worth having," remarked the captain reflectively. "She's a mystery, anyway, and we ought to solve it."

"Yes," I said eagerly. "I'm ready to go on board and investigate. Lower a boat, captain, and let's see what's inside."

Seal glanced at the high sea and shook his head dubiously.

"Beg pardon, sir!" shouted the man Dicky Dunn up to the captain, speaking between his hands. "There's a face at one o' them attic windows in the stern. It only showed for a moment, and then disappeared—an awful white face!"

"Dicky's got another touch of his old complaint," remarked one of the stokers philosophically; but the statement caused all eyes to be turned to the row of small square windows.

"Ghosts aboard!" remarked Thorpe. "If I were you, cap'n, I'd have nothing to do with that hulking craft. She's a floatin' coffin, that's what she is."

"You're a white-livered coward, sonny," roared Seal. "I've discovered Noah's Ark, and I mean to see what's aboard her." Then he shouted an order for a boat to be lowered, adding in a meaning tone: "If any man's too chicken-hearted to board her let him stay here."

The effect was magical. Sailors hate to be dubbed cowards, and every man was in an instant eager to face the tempestuous sea and explore.

"Dunn!" cried the skipper. "Are you certain you saw a face, or is it your groggy imagination?"

"I saw a face quite distinct, sir. It was grinning at us like, and then vanished. I'll bet my month's pay that there's somebody aboard—or else it's spirits."

"Alcohol, more like," grunted Seal, beneath his breath, as he turned to the helmsman and ordered him to keep a circular course round the water-logged hulk. The propeller had stopped, and we were now rising and falling in the long sweep of the green water.

"Come on, doctor," Seal said, after he had ordered Thorpe to take command, and added a chaffing remark about Davy Jones and his proverbial locker; "let's go and see for ourselves."

So together we descended to the deck, and after several unsuccessful efforts to enter the boat, I at last found myself being tossed helplessly towards the high seaweed-covered walls that rolled ever and anon at a most fearsome angle.

The excitement was intense, for the boarding of the mysterious vessel was an extremely perilous undertaking, and it was a long time before one of the men could obtain a foothold on the slippery weeds. At last, however, the boat was made fast, and one by one we clambered up a patch of barnacles on to the roof of the stern. At that height, and rolling as we were, our position was by no means an enviable one. We sank to our knees in the brown, slimy seaweed that covered the roof, and at Seal's order the men, with axes, began chopping away the growth and digging down to the timbers in search of hatches.

At last we found them, but they seemed to have been hermetically closed, and it was a long time before saw and hatchet made any impression on the teak. Still the six of us worked with a will, and in half an hour we succeeded in breaking our way into the vessel.

As we peered down into the gloom of the interior there arose a dank odour of mustiness, and I noticed that even the fearless Seal himself hesitated to descend and explore. When, however, I announced an intention of making the attempt, the others with one accord quickly volunteered to accompany me.

Through the hole I lowered myself, expecting to discover some stairway, but my legs only swung in air with the rolling of the hulk. My head being below the roof, however, I soon discovered in the dim light that the place was a large, wide cabin with a long oaken table down the centre. My feet were only a foot from the table, so I dropped and shouted to the others above to follow.

The place, with its panelled walls and deep window-seats, was more like an old-fashioned dining-room in a country house than a ship's saloon. The table, a big heavy one, was handsomely carved, and there were high seats with twisted backs, covered with faded velvet, while as I moved I stumbled over some pieces of armour—helmets, breastplates, and swords, all red with rust. There were a few bones, too, which at a glance I saw belonged to a human skeleton.

The place had evidently been air and water tight, for although submerged for years the water had not entered. On the contrary, the bodies of those confined therein had crumbled into dust.

Seal and his men, who joined me one after the other, stood aghast, giving vent to exclamations of surprise, mingled, of course, with strong language.

Knowing something of antiquities, I made an examination of the furniture and armour. On the rusted sword-blades was stamped the name "Tomas," with the sign of the cross, by which I knew them to be the best-tempered steel of Toledo, and the date of the armour I put at about the end of the sixteenth century.

"Strike me if it ain't like a bloomin' museum, doctor!" Seal remarked, pressing the point of a sword to the floor to try its temper.

"A most remarkable find," I said. "As far as I can see at present it's an old Spanish ship, but where it's been all these years no one can tell."

"It's been down below, doctor, you can bet your boots on that," Seal replied. "Been a mermaid's palace, perhaps!"

The place wherein we stood was evidently the chief saloon. The ghastly bones on the floor interested me, as a medical man, the more so because one of the skeletons—and there were three—was certainly that of a man, who, when alive, must have stood over six feet high.

I gave that as my opinion, whereupon one of the horny-handed men hazarded the remark that it was "a giant's Sunday-going yacht."

One of the men who had sailed in the *Seahorse*—for such we afterwards discovered her name to be—had assuredly been a giant in stature, for I discovered his breastplate and sword, and certainly they were the most formidable I had ever seen. He was no doubt the commander, judging from the inlaid gold upon the armour, which still glistened, notwithstanding the rust.

Wooden platters, rusty knives, and leathern mugs, lay on the floor, having evidently been swept from the table when the vessel had heeled over and sunk, while there were the remains of high-backed chairs, decayed and broken, sliding on the floor with each roll of the unsteady craft.

At the farther end of the curious old cabin was a heavy oaken door, and passing beyond it we entered a smaller cabin projecting over the stern with three little square windows. On the panelled wall hung a helmet and sword, together with a time-mellowed portrait of a sour-faced man with fair pointed beard and ruffle. On the floor lay an old blunderbuss, and at one side, fixed against the wall, was a small oak desk for writing; while on the other, secured to the floor with huge clamps, were three great iron-bound and iron-studded chests, securely locked and heavily bolted.

"Treasure!" gasped Seal. "By Christopher! there may be gold ducats in them there boxes! Let's have 'em open. Now lads," he cried, bustling up the men, "'er's your chance to go a-gold finding! Get to work, quick."

The order to open the boxes was easier given than executed. One man searched in vain for the keys, while the others worked away till the perspiration rolled off their brows, and yet the strong boxes resisted all their efforts. Presently, however, Dicky Dunn discovered a long bar of iron, and the four men, using it as a lever, managed to wrench the lid of the first box off its hinges. To our utter disgust, however, we found it empty.

The second chest did not take quite so long as the first to force open, and as the lid was raised loud cries of joy broke from all our lips.

It was filled to the brim with golden coin!

I examined some and found them to be old Italian, Spanish, and English pieces—the latter mostly bearing the effigies of Queen Elizabeth and King Edward VI.

The excitement had now risen to fever heat. The men would have filled their pockets with the gold, there and then, had not Job Seal drawn a revolver and in a roaring voice threatened to shoot the first man dead who touched a coin.

But the gluttony of gold was upon them, and they attacked the third box with such violence that it was open in a jiffy.

No gold was, however, within—only a big bag of thick hide heavily riveted with copper, and securely fastened with bolt and lock.

"Bank-notes in that, perhaps!" remarked the skipper excitedly, ignorant of the fact that there were no bank-notes in the days when that curious craft had sailed the ocean. "Break it open, boys. Look alive!"

"Be-low!" cried old Dicky Dunn, and as his shipmates drew aside he raised his axe and with one well-directed blow broke off the rusted bolt and in an instant half-a-dozen hands were plunged into the leathern sack.

What they brought forth was certainly disappointing—merely two folded pieces of yellow, time-stained parchment, one having a big seal of lead hanging to it by a cord, and the other a small seal of yellow wax attached to a strip of the parchment itself.

The skipper glanced at them in disgust, and then handed them to me, as a man of some book-learning, to decipher.

I had steadied myself with my back fixed to the panelling and was examining the first of the documents, when of a sudden we were all of us startled by hearing a weird sound which sent through us a thrill of alarm.

It was plain and unmistakable—a deep, cavernous human voice!

Every man of us stood silent, looked at each other, and held his breath.

"Hark! Why, that's the ghost wot Dicky Dunn saw!" gasped one of the men with scared face. "I've had about enough of this, mates. It ain't no place for us here."

I stood listening. There was undoubtedly yet another mystery on board that strange, uncanny vessel that the sea had so unaccountably given up.

# III

## The Mysterious Man

Again the strange deep voice sounded.

It seemed to come from below the small cabin in which we stood—a snarling noise as though of a man enraged.

Neither Seal nor his men liked the situation. I could see by their faces that they were thoroughly scared. They had found gold, it was true, but below was the owner of it.

"Come on, lads," urged Dicky Dunn courageously, "I'm going below to make the acquaintance of the skipper of this 'ere craft. The way is down that hatchway at the end of the big saloon."

Encouraged by the old seaman the men moved back into the cabin we had first entered, and with Dunn I descended the dark stairs to explore, Seal following close behind us armed with his revolver.

I struck a match and, by its light, saw a quantity of ancient arms and armour lying with several skulls and bones. Apparently the men were below when the ship went down, and, the hatches being closed so tightly, neither air nor water reached them, so that they had been asphyxiated.

The passage led along to a bulkhead, where it took a turn at right angles and ended with a closed door.

This Seal opened boldly, and we found ourselves in a small cabin, quite light—for the big square window had been broken out—and furnished in the same antique style as the big saloon above.

It had an occupant—the strangest-looking creature I ever saw.

He was an old man with long white hair and white beard, a man with a thin, haggard face and black, deep-sunken eyes. On first entering he escaped our notice, but we saw him crouching beneath the table, hiding from us in terror.

His dress, ragged and tattered, was of three centuries ago—short breeches, a doublet of faded crimson velvet, and an old coat with puffed sleeves, while in his hand he carried a rusty poniard and seemed prepared to spring out upon us.

I shall never forget the ghastly look of hatred and terror upon the queer old fellow's countenance as he faced us. We all three stood absolutely dumfounded. It was very interesting to discover a ship lost for three centuries, but to find a survivor still on board was incredible.

Yet there was a human being actually in the flesh; a weird old fellow who, for aught we could tell, had lived on board that vessel for ages.

"Come out, sonny," cried Seal, when he found tongue; "we won't eat you."

In response the weird individual gave vent to that same shrill cry of rage that had first attracted our attention, brandishing his knife threateningly, but not budging an inch from his hiding-place.

"Enough of that, my man," exclaimed the captain, authoritatively. "Come out and talk like a Christian. Where are you bound for? and how many days are you out?"

"The bloomin' ship's about three 'undred years overdue, I should fancy," remarked Dicky Dunn, who was the ship's humorist.

"Come along," Seal urged persuasively, placing his hands on his knees and bending down to him. "Come out of it, old chap, and let's have a yarn. I ain't got any time to spare."

But the old fellow only gnashed his gums and brandished his knife, for he appeared to entertain the greatest antipathy towards our skipper.

Presently, after some further coaxing, but receiving no word in reply, I succeeded in reassuring him that we meant him no harm, and he came forth from his hiding-place and with a savage grin stood before us. He was tall and gaunt, about six feet in height and as thin as a lath. But when we came to question him he steadily refused to answer one single question.

All the skipper's queries he resented with marked hostility, and with me alone was he tractable.

Before long, however, I discerned the true state of affairs. This strange individual, whoever he was, was dumb, and, further, he was not in his right mind. Privation and solitude were probably the cause of it; but whatever the reason, the fact remained that the queer old fellow was unable to utter one single intelligible word, and he was also not responsible for his actions.

Now and then he burst into peals of laughter, grinning hideously, with all the characteristic symptoms of the maniac, and then he would suddenly strike an attitude as though to attack our skipper.

Fortunately I induced him to put his knife aside, for although rusty it was still very sharp. By all the means I could think of I endeavoured to extract some word from him, but in vain. The sounds that escaped him were deep, gutteral, and utterly unintelligible. By dumb show I tried to inquire who and what he was, but insanity asserted itself, for he only gave vent to a demoniacal shriek and cut some absurd capers that caused all three of us to laugh heartily.

I took out my pocket-book and handed it to him, together with a pencil, but instead of writing, as I hoped to induce him, he only looked to see what was contained in the pockets of the book and handed it back to me.

"Well!" cried Seal, "this chap beats everything! Who in the name of fortune can he be?"

"He's a mystery," I answered, utterly puzzled.

"He looks as old as Methuselah," remarked the skipper. "He's just as though he walked out o' one of them old pictures."

"He's a lunatic, ain't he, doctor?" asked Dunn.

"Most decidedly," I responded; "and judging from the manner he received us, he is a rather dangerous one."

"Well," said Seal, "we'd better take him on board with us. Perhaps when he's had a bit of grub and some rest we'll be able to make him out. This mystery is a first-class one—better than any I've ever read in books. How old is he, doctor?"

"Impossible to tell," I replied. "A good age certainly."

"As old as this ship?" asked the seaman.

"I think not," I responded, laughing.

"Well, we must find out something about him," declared Seal, decisively.

"And what about that chestful of gold, sir?"

"Oh, we'll ship that, of course," answered the skipper. "It perhaps belongs to him, but we may as well hold it till he proves his right to it," and he grinned meaningly.

The ancient mariner had turned, and was gazing out through the big open window to where the *Thrush* was lying awaiting our return. He seemed quite calm now, and no longer resented our intrusion upon his privacy. Indeed, with me he became quite friendly, and when I spoke again appeared to make an effort to understand me. He pointed to his mouth, which only emitted unintelligible sounds.

That he was insane there was no doubt. The strange look in his eyes was sufficient proof of it, but I entertained a hope that his mind was only unhinged by privation and solitude, and that by careful treatment his mental balance might become restored.

While we were questioning him the three men we had left above were rummaging the ship. One of them, it seems, managed by the aid of a rope to cross the wave-swept deck to the other cabin in the high bows and with an axe effect an entry. His report was that there were a number of skeletons there, most of them still in armour, together with old-fashioned cannon, and he brought back with him a fine banner of purple silk bearing a golden Maltese cross.

Below where we stood, the waves thundered ever and anon, and the heavy rolling told us that the wind was increasing.

"We'd better be getting aboard," Seal remarked anxiously. "If we don't make a start we shan't be able to ship that there gold. You take charge of the old boy, doctor. What shall we call him, eh?"

"The Mysterious Man would be a good name, sir," suggested Dunn.

"All right," responded the skipper. "We'll put him on the papers as Old Mr. Mystery. Go above and get the lads to shift that box of gold. Be careful with it, and mind it don't go to the bottom."

"Aye, aye, sir," responded the grey-bearded seaman; and he went above, shouting to his shipmates to start work on the removal of the treasure.

He must have made some signal to Thorpe on the *Thrush*, for a few minutes later we heard the siren blowing, while the men in the small cabin were working away with a strong will stowing the gold coins into anything they could find, for with such a sea running it was impossible to remove the great chest entire, besides which it was heavily bolted to the floor.

The Mysterious Man accompanied me above, and in silence stood watching the coin being removed. Sight of it produced no impression upon him whatever. His agility and fierce antipathy had given place to apathy, as it so often does in certain phases of insanity.

The old portrait of the thin-faced man in ruffle and doublet caught his eye, and he faced it and shook his fist at it, as though the original were his enemy. Then he went through into the main saloon, and, picking up one of the rusty swords, returned and slashed the picture until the canvas hung in its frame in ribbons.

The two parchments that we had found in the old leather bag were secure in my pocket, and the bag was used for the transport of part of the treasure. While the work of removing the coins was in progress, however, I seized the opportunity of searching further in the small cabin, and discovered in the oak panelling a small cupboard, wherein were several big parchment-bound books looking almost like commercial ledgers.

One of them I opened, and found it to be in manuscript in a crabbed hand that I could not decipher, but on certain pages were drawn rough plans. A second volume proved to be a printed book in Latin; and a third a rare old Book of Hours, printed by Pasquali, of Venice, in 1588. I took possession of half-a-dozen, but the others seemed to me to be of no account—one a Latin lexicon, and another a book in which certain household recipes had been written. All were, as far as I could judge, books written or printed in the first half of the sixteenth century, although I knew nothing of the mysteries of palæography or bibliography. Some of the writing was even and well executed, while the other was execrable, with long loops and curious dashes and flourishes above certain letters.

I gave the books I wanted into the hands of one of the sailors, who lashed them together and lowered them to the boat after the gold had been safely shipped.

Every moment the gale was increasing, so Seal thought fit to send the boat back to the steamer with its precious freight before we proceeded, as the gold weighed heavily, and he feared that if we went with it we might be swamped.

Through the square window of the big saloon, very like the window of an old-fashioned house, we watched the boat rise and fall on the long, green waves as it toiled towards the steamer. We watched one of the men shout through his hands, and could see the excitement his news created on board.

Thorpe bent over from the bridge and shouted back, while a dozen willing hands were ready to haul up the gold.

It was half an hour before they returned for us, and Seal expressed some doubts about the vessel weathering the storm. The pitching was terrible, and it was impossible to stand without clinging hold of something.

I occupied the time in searching every nook and crevice in the big saloon, but I discovered practically nothing, save in a cupboard some old pewter, over which a collector of such stuff would probably have gone into raptures, and an old silver tankard, which I took as part of my share of the loot, together with a helmet, sword, and breastplate.

But at length my search was brought to a conclusion by the boat hailing us from below, and we lowered the Mysterious Man by means of a rope around his waist, for he was too decrepit to spring, and the sight of his skinny legs dangling over the sea was certainly ludicrous. Then, when we were all clear, the men pulled us through the boiling waves back to the steamer, and as we looked behind we saw the weird seaweed-covered craft rocking and rolling as though every minute she must heel over.

# IV

## In which I Examine the Parchments

The advent of the stranger on board the *Thrush* caused an outburst of surprise and consternation among the men, who stood in a group around him, addressing him and making remarks upon his personal appearance and his clothes.

"'E looks like old Father Christmas been starved to death!" I heard one seaman remark. "Look at his shoes. Them buckles are silver, mates!"

And then for the first time I noticed that the buckles on his shoes were very beautiful ones.

"There's something confoundedly mysterious about both the craft and the man," declared a seaman who had accompanied us. "There's lots of skeletons on board, and old armour, cannon, and things. She was a battleship, I believe. At any rate, the men on board her were soldiers."

"If they were, then the old fossil's a good specimen," one of them said, to which the old seaman who had rowed our boat replied:—

"Well, we collared over a thousand quid in gold, sonny. It was in them heavy bags that are stowed in the skipper's quarters. Besides, the doctor's got a few things—books, bits of parchment, and the like."

They asked for a description of the craft, and we gave it to them, explaining the circumstances in which we discovered the Mysterious Man. The latter was seated on a coil of rope, glancing at us but utterly apathetic to the fact that he was the centre of attraction. We told them how the old fellow was both dumb and insane, whereupon their interest in him was increased fourfold. Their jeering remarks regarding his gorilla-like countenance and his quaintness of attire were quickly turned into expressions of sympathy and even the roughest man among them was ready to render the afflicted stranger any little service.

The armour and books had been placed in my cabin, and when Seal had related our experiences to Thorpe, the latter suggested that we should stand by the *Seahorse* and take her in tow when the gale abated. It would mean a day or two overdue in London, but we should nevertheless secure a prize such as no living man had ever before seen. Apart from the interest in the old vessel and the mystery of how it had come to the surface after being so long submerged, there were on board many things of value from an antiquarian point of view.

And so it was arranged that we should lay to that night, and if the wind went down next day, as Seal believed it would because the morrow was the fourth day of continued bad weather, we should tow the extraordinary craft to Valencia, and, if possible, round to London.

The Mysterious Man, after eating ravenously of food set before him, curled himself up in one of the men's bunks in the forecastle and soon went to sleep. One man, a well-spoken, middle-aged sailor named Harding, was told off to take care of the madman and to see that he did not get into mischief, while the cure of his intellect was left in my charge.

Together with Seal I proceeded to examine our find. As the sun sank crimson and stormy, flooding the skipper's cabin with a blood-red glow, he and I carefully counted the gold. There were 1,783 pieces, large and small, and of great variety. The English ones mostly bore the effigies of Edward VI and Elizabeth. There were none of James I., but many were of Henry IV of France, together with a variety of Spanish doubloons and Italian pieces. I found none of a later reign than Elizabeth, therefore I put down the date of the *Seahorse* as about 1603, or a few years earlier.

"I wonder whether Old Mystery will claim the coin?" Seal reflected, as he slowly filled his pipe, having finished the counting.

"As the sole survivor, it most probably belongs to him," I said.

"But if he's a lunatic, what claim can he make to it? There'll be some job to find the vessel's owner, I reckon."

His remark caused me to remember the two parchments I had in my pocket, and I drew them out, opened them, and examined them carefully.

The first was beautifully and clearly written, about a foot square, and headed "Cosmvs." It was in Latin, and I must admit that although I had passed in Latin up at Edinburgh, I was very rusty in it. The document at commencement read as follows:—

Cosmus Dei Gratia Magnus Dux Etruriæ, etc. et sacræ Religionis, et Militiæ Militum S. Stephani Papæ, et Martyris Magnus Magister et Custos, etc., Dilecto Nobis Pompæo Marie a Paule, Nobili Pisano et S. Stephani Militi, gratiam uram, et omne bonum.

Then, after a screed of twenty long lines, the document ended:—

Datum Florentiæ die pa. Februarij anno ab incarn. MDCI.
Nostri Magni Ducatus Etruriæ anno VI.

Below were three signatures in ink that had long ago faded yellow, but so badly written were they that I could not decipher them. At the foot of the document was threaded a hempen cord, and to it was attached a heavy leaded seal, a trifle bigger than half a crown. On the obverse was a Maltese cross, the same as upon the faded silken banner at my side, and on the reverse a shield bearing six balls, the arms of the Florentine house of the Medici. Around the cross was the legend "Sancti Stephani Signum Religioni," while around the armorial bearings were the words: "Cosmvs Mag. Dux Etr. Magn. Magis."

So insufficient was my knowledge of Latin that all I could make out of the writing was that it was some diploma or deed concerning some one named Paule, a noble of Pisa. But what honour it conferred upon him I could not decipher, so I turned my attention to the second parchment.

It was yellower, and penned in a hand so crabbed that for a long time I could not make out in what language it was written.

At last I decided that the first portion was in the abbreviated Latin of old documents, for after much puzzling I deciphered that the first words read "In Dei Nomine, Amen." At foot was an endorsement in old English, which I deciphered, making a covenant between certain parties, and below were seven scrawly signatures in that strange old Elizabethan hand, namely of Geo. Greene, Gilbert Kanadale, John Ffreeman, Alex. Stephen Wyon, John Dollington, Clement Wollerton, and George A. Dafte, hys mark.

The bottom of the parchment had been cut until a short strip an inch wide hung from it, and upon this the round seal of yellow wax had been impressed, the device upon it being a shield with a leopard rampant, together with a fleur-de-lys. That is how best I can describe it, not being versed in heraldic terms.

That the two documents were precious ones could not for a moment be doubted when I recollected how carefully they had been preserved: first in that leathern bag and secondly in the treasure-chest. To me, however, they presented no appearance of value.

"What are they all about, doctor?" inquired the skipper, puffing at his pipe.

"At present I can't tell. They're both in Latin," I answered, "and we must wait until we get a proper translation. This"—and I held the second document in my hand—"was written in the time of Queen Elizabeth, and seems to be a covenant, or something of the sort."

"I suppose we can get some lawyer chap to puzzle 'em out?" Seal said.

"Oh, I don't anticipate any difficulty," I answered. "Only if there is any secret attached to them we don't want to give it away."

"Ah! I never thought of that," remarked the skipper. "It is, as you say, very probable that some secret is contained there, and for that reason they were so carefully preserved and hidden away. No, doctor, we'd better not employ a lawyer. He'd want to know too much."

Then I turned my attention to the books. The first I opened was of fine white parchment, thick, heavily bound, and written in a bold hand with many flourishes. A glance through it showed that it was an inventory of some kind, but it was all in Italian and much beyond me. The only part I could translate was the commencement, which, as far as I was able to decipher, read as follows:—

In The Name Of Almighty God *and of His Holy Mother, Saint Mary, and of St. Peter, and of St. Paul, of St. John the Baptist, and of all the Celestial Court of Paradise, who have conceded to me the benefit that I should commence this book sound of body and of mind. Amen.*

In This Book *written by me, Bartholomew di Simon da Schorno, I have set down certain things that all men should know, as well as a certain Secret that one alone may discover to his advantage hereafter.*

And then followed about 150 pages of manuscript and memoranda.

Through an hour I diligently endeavoured to decipher correctly regarding the secret mentioned, but it was in old Italian, with long l's and s's, and therefore extremely difficult to understand.

The date of the conclusion of the book I discovered to be August 16, 1591, on a Friday; while here and there I discovered the name of Paule, evidently the same family as the Pompæo Marie a Paule, the Pisan noble mentioned in the document with the leaden seal of Cosimo di Medici.

The author, Bartholomew da Schorno, whoever he was, had certainly produced a very respectable volume as regards size, and Job Seal and myself were extremely anxious to learn the secret which, in the introduction, was said to be contained therein.

The other books were not of great interest save perhaps to a bibliophile. They, however, showed that their owner was a scholar. The first, a thin manuscript on paper, and written in a neat Gothic hand, which I afterwards discovered was of the early fifteenth century, bore the title, "Trithemius, Liber de Triplici Regione." The others were a well-written book of monastic law on vellum, with red and blue capitals of about the same date, and a kind of old pocket-book, in which was a treatise entitled "Loci Communes Theologici per Dominicas et Festes Totius Anni."

It was the secret of old Bartholomew da Schorno—an Italian, evidently—that we were eager to discover, for both Seal and I felt confident that it would reveal to us the name of the dead owner of the *Seahorse* and the history of that remarkable resurrection.

In that heavy parchment book was a secret which old Bartholomew declared "one alone may discover to his advantage hereafter."

What could it be?

Job Seal and I sat smoking our pipes and wondering what strange things were hidden within that yellow old volume that emitted so musty a smell.

Little, however, did we dream of the remarkable consequences that were to follow upon our startling discovery. It is, indeed, well sometimes that the Book of Fate is ever closed to us.

# V

## With a Story to Tell

At daybreak next morning I was called up to the Mysterious Man, whom I found standing in a corner of the forecastle holding a loaded revolver in his hand and pointing it threateningly at anyone who approached him.

He had awoke, I was told, made a tour of the ship, and, gaining possession of the weapon belonging to the second engineer, proceeded to fire one chamber point-blank at Thorpe, who was on duty on the bridge. Then, when pursued, he took refuge in the forecastle, where I found him.

On my approach he calmed down immediately, and handed me the revolver as obediently as a child. Somehow I seemed to possess an influence over him which no one else could exercise, and very quickly induced him to return to his bunk, greatly to the satisfaction of the man who had been told off to be his keeper, and who had no doubt slept on duty.

The storm showed no sign of abatement, and laying to as we were we received the full force of the sweeping gale. The skipper was asleep, snoring loudly, as was his wont, therefore I returned to my berth, and for a couple of hours watched the capers of the rats, until the motion of the boat rising and rolling lulled me again to unconsciousness.

Through the whole of the following day we lay off the seaweed-covered relic of the past until, in the red sundown, the wind dropped, and after several attempts the men secured a wire hawser to the battered prow, and when Seal rang, "Full steam ahead," the *Seahorse* began slowly to follow in our wake, amid the loud cheering of those on board.

The Mysterious Man stood on the bridge at my side and watched the operation with an expression of complete satisfaction, although more than once, when he believed I was not looking, he would turn and shake his skinny fist at the curious old craft at our stern.

Our progress was slow, for the *Thrush* was never at any time a fast boat. And with such a dead weight behind her the engineer had to be careful at what pressure he worked our unsafe boilers.

The skipper, after consultation with Thorpe and myself, decided not to make for Valencia but to tow his prize straight to Gibraltar and on to

London. As the great black hull with its shroud of marine plants rose and fell behind us it certainly presented more the appearance of Noah's Ark, as pictorially represented, than of a sea-going vessel. One fact I now discovered that I had not before noticed was that on the bows above the broken figure-head representing a seahorse was a wooden crucifix perhaps two feet high; broken it was true, but still bearing an effigy of the crucifixion, while upon the breast of the seahorse was carved a Maltese cross of similar design to that upon the old silken banner.

The mystery of it all was the sole topic of conversation both on the bridge and in the forecastle. Every man on board tried to obtain some word from the castaway, but in vain. He became tractable, ate well, would not touch grog, but remained always silent. He would stand erect by the capstan in the stern for hours, and with folded arms watch the rolling hulk ploughing her way slowly in the long streak of foam left by our propeller. He still wore his faded velvet breeches, but his bare legs were now covered by a pair of woollen stockings, while in place of his ragged doublet he wore an old pea-jacket, and sometimes an oilskin coat and peaked cap. He still, however, clung to the rusty sword which he had chosen, a blunt but finely-tempered weapon, and often it would be seen poking from beneath his oilskin as he walked the deck.

Once an attempt had been made to trim his long white hair and flowing beard, but this he had resented so vigorously, threatening to spit the man who held the scissors, that the effort had to be abandoned. He thus gave them to understand that although he might accept their modern dress as a loan he would brook no interference with his personal appearance.

Who was he? That was the question which all of us, from Job Seal down to the apprentices, were anxious to solve.

The mystery of the *Seahorse* was great enough, but that surrounding the unknown man was greater. My own theory regarding the vessel was that in the early seventeenth century she had gone down or aground in shallow water, perhaps in one of the many coves on the Moroccan or Algerian coast, but the high prow and stern being closed down so tight both air and water were excluded. Those on board—fighting men, it seemed—had perished, but the buoyancy of the ship had been preserved, and by some submarine disturbance—volcanic, most probably—it had become released and risen to the surface.

The growth of barnacles, mussels, and weeds over the whole of the vessel from the stumps of her masts caused Seal to believe that she could only have been covered at high tide, and that she must have lain hidden in some well-sheltered spot where the force of the waves had been broken, otherwise she must have been beaten to pieces. He pointed out to me how some of the weed on her was only to be found on rocks covered at high water, yet if the theory were a correct one then she could not have been hidden in the Mediterranean, as it is an almost tideless sea.

Seal suggested that she might have been aground on the coast of Western Morocco, a country but little known to the civilized world although so near one of the greatest trade routes, and that she might have drifted from the Atlantic to the spot where we had discovered her.

This theory seemed the most likely one, although the presence of the Mysterious Man was utterly unaccountable.

The main point which puzzled Seal, I think, was what he should do with the gold. He regarded the poor old fellow as a gibbering idiot, and had but little to do with him. Customs officers and lunatics were the bluff old seaman's pet abominations. He would probably have liked to claim the hoard of gold himself if it were not for the existence of one with a prior claim to it, and once or twice he expressed to me an anxiety as to what his owners would say to it all. They were skinflints of the worst type, and would, I expected, probably lay claim to it themselves.

Steaming slowly we passed the Gib. and made a straight course for Cape St. Vincent, which we sighted at dawn one rainy morning, then hugging the Portuguese coast we safely passed the mouth of the Tagus, being hailed more than once by other craft, the skippers all asking us with humorous banter what we had in tow.

Fortunately the weather had improved greatly, and even as we traversed the Bay of Biscay we had no reason to complain, for the old *Seahorse* rode proudly in our wake, rocking a good deal on account of its house-like shape, but nevertheless giving Seal the greatest satisfaction.

"It'll make 'em open their eyes, doctor, when we tow 'er up the Thames," he often said, as he paced his bridge and looked at her straining on the hawser.

Never a day passed but I occupied myself diligently with the documents and manuscripts that had fallen into my hands, but I am fain to confess that beyond what I have already explained to the reader I discovered absolutely nothing. Although I had passed my final examination and could write M.D. after my name, my book-learning was not sufficiently deep that I could decipher and understand those crabbed old screeds.

I showed them to the Mysterious Man, hoping that they would attract his attention and give me some clue to their meaning, but he remained quite passive when he saw them, and turning upon his heel looked out through the round port-hole.

I certainly was very anxious to get back to London to obtain some opinion upon the big vellum book in which Bartholomew da Schorno declared there was a secret that would be discovered hereafter. My voyage, besides being a pleasant one, had been full of excitement, for we had found an object the like of which no living eye had seen, together with an individual who was a complete and profound mystery.

The weather was all that could be desired when we entered the Channel, keeping close in to the coast of Normandy as far as Dieppe, and then taking a direct course across to Beachy Head, where we were signalled as homeward bound. When, however, we were off Folkestone, about nine o'clock one night, a squall struck us so suddenly that even Job Seal was unprepared for it. The glass had fallen rapidly, he had noticed, but such a heavy squall as it proved to be was not to be expected at that season of the year. Within a quarter of an hour a terrific sea was running, and the *Thrush* seemed ever and anon thrown almost on her beam-ends. I noticed that Seal's face for the first time during our trip betrayed some anxiety, and not without cause, for he suddenly exclaimed:—

"Ah! just as I expected. Blister my kidneys, doctor, but we've no bloomin' luck. That hawser's parted!"

I turned quickly to look astern, and there, sure enough, the *Seahorse* was adrift and out of our wake. Until that moment the strain on the hawser had kept her comparatively steady, but the instant the steel cable had broken she pitched upon her beam-ends, burying her nose deep into the angry waves.

We both stood gripping a rail and watching, neither of us uttering a word.

For perhaps five minutes the antique vessel strove again and again to right herself, until one wave greater than the others crashed over her high stern. From where we stood we could hear the breaking of glass and the shivering of the heavy timbers that, half rotten, now broke up like matchwood.

Then almost immediately the saloon which we had explored began to fill, and slowly before our eyes she went down stern first.

The men, watching like ourselves, set up a howl of disappointment, and Seal gave vent to a volley of nautical expressions which need not here be repeated; but the Mysterious Man, who had also noticed the disaster, began dancing joyously and cutting capers on the deck, heedless of the storm raging about him. It was evident that the final disappearance of the *Seahorse* gave him the utmost satisfaction.

As for ourselves, we gazed with regret upon the mass of floating timbers that were swept around us. It was to our bitter chagrin that, after towing that relic of a bygone age all those miles at a cost of fuel and time, we had lost her almost at the mouth of the Thames.

But regret was useless. The *Seahorse*, with its freight of crumbling skeletons, had gone down again, and would certainly never reappear. So Job Seal drew his oilskin closer around him, lamented his infernal luck, and, recollecting the thousand odd pieces of gold in his cabin, turned and gave an order to the helmsman which caused the bows of the *Thrush* to run nearer towards the dark line of England's cliffs between Folkestone and Dover.

Lights white and green were beginning to show in the distance, those of other ships passing up and down Channel, and as I stood by his side in my dripping oilskins I congratulated myself that if we weathered the squall I should be safely back in London in a very few hours, with as strange a story to tell as any man had related.

# VI

## AN EXPERT OPINION

On the night following the regrettable disaster to the *Seahorse* I was back again in the cheap and rather comfortable rooms I had occupied for a couple of years or so in Keppel Street, Chelsea. It is a thoroughfare in which nearly every house exhibits the enticing legend, "Apartments to Let," mostly in permanent, neatly-framed signs of black and gold.

Mrs. Richardson, my landlady, was "full" and had been for a year past, so No. 83, where I had diggings, was a quiet, eminently respectable house, a fitting, residence for a man of my serious calling. When, however, I returned with the Mysterious Man in a well-worn seaman's suit, unkempt head, and his sword in hand instead of a cane, Mrs. Richardson looked askance at me.

I explained that my friend had come to live with me for a few weeks, and that I should want an extra room; when she, good soul, looked him up and down, noticed the big cracks in his sea-boots and the slit in the sleeve of his pea-jacket, and rather reluctantly replied that she would turn one of the servants out and prepare the room for my friend.

Presently, however, I took her aside and explained the curious facts, whereupon she said:—

"Lor', doctor! Only fancy! The old gentleman may be two hundred years old!"

"Ah!" I remarked, "his age is only one of the minor mysteries connected with the affair. It is in order to solve them that I've decided that he shall remain under my care and treatment. He's just a little wrong in his head, you know. Nothing at all serious."

"He didn't answer me when I spoke to him."

"No, for a very good reason. He's dumb."

"Two hundred years old, insane, and dumb! Lawk a mercy! He is a strange old gentleman."

"Well, Mrs. Richardson," I said, "you've been very kind to me for the past two years, and I hope that you will do me the favour of looking after my friend."

"Of course I will, doctor. But what's his name?"

"He has no name. We call him the Mysterious Man."

"Old Mister Mystery the girls will call him, I expect. But it don't matter what they nickname him if he's wrong in his head."

I laughed and, leaving her, returned to my sitting-room, where the old castaway was engaged in examining all the objects in the room. He had opened the back of my small American timepiece and was watching the movement as though he had never hitherto seen any such mechanical contrivance.

The day had been a busy one for me. I had arranged with Seal that the old fellow should remain with me while the mystery of the *Seahorse* was solved, and as regards the gold we had placed the whole of it in a big sea chest, sealed it, and that afternoon had deposited it in the care of the manager of the Tottenham Court Road branch of the London and South-Western Bank, where I had a small account.

The documents, manuscripts, armour, and silver tankard which I had secured from the ancient vessel I had carried to Keppel Street. The skipper was, of course, busy on the first day of landing, but his chagrin was intense that he had lost the *Seahorse*. That we had really discovered it could, of course, be proved by those vessels that had spoken us in the Channel, but proof of that sort was not like towing the remarkable relic up the Thames.

His owners, it appeared, were extremely angry at his being nearly a fortnight overdue, and that he had wasted time and fuel upon what they declared was a worthless derelict. According to what he afterwards told me, he had a bad half-hour with the senior partner of his firm, and very nearly got his notice of dismissal. He pointed out to the smug, go-to-meeting old gentleman, who was a churchwarden down at Chislehurst, that the boilers of the *Thrush* were in such a state that he dare not steam at any pressure, whereupon the senior partner replied:—

"That matters nothing whatever to us, Seal. The boat's insured, and we should lose nothing."

"No; but myself and the crew may lose our lives," observed the skipper.

"If your berth does not suit you, Seal, there are many other men quite ready to sail in your place," was the calm rejoinder.

And after that Seal left the office as quickly as he could, in order to give vent outside to his private opinion of the firm and their line of ships. This he did very forcibly, in language that only a Mediterranean skipper is in the habit of using.

WILLIAM LE QUEUX

Now that I was back again, enjoying the comfort of my own shabby little sitting-room after the small, stuffy cabin of the *Thrush*, one rather curious incident caused me to reflect.

It occurred on the morning after the loss of the *Seahorse*. The squall had gone down. We had passed the Nore and were steaming full ahead into the mouth of the Thames. I had been seated on the bridge with Seal and Thorpe for a couple of hours or so when I had occasion to descend to my cabin.

On entering I found an intruder in the person of Harding, the seaman who had been told off as the keeper of the Mysterious Man. He did not notice my approach, for I had on a pair of tennis shoes with rubber soles, therefore I stood in the doorway for a few moments watching him.

He had spread open that document with the seven signatures that had so puzzled me, and with paper and pencil seemed to be scribbling some notes as to its purport. Strange, I thought, that a common seaman could decipher those ill-written lines of Latin where I had so entirely failed. So I watched and saw how, with his head bent to the open port-hole in order to obtain a good light, he was carefully deciphering the words contained there, and I detected by the expression on his countenance that what he found entirely satisfied him. Upon the small piece of paper in his palm he scribbled something now and then, and was just slipping it into his pocket, when I asked in a hard voice:—

"Well, what are you doing here?"

He turned with a start, his face flushed in confusion, and stammered:—

"Nothing, doctor. I—I was only looking at this old parchment you got out of Noah's Ark."

"You've been reading it," I said. "I've watched you making some extracts from it. Give me that paper."

He made a movement to place it in his pocket, but at the same moment I snatched the old document from his other hand and arrested his effort to conceal the scrap of paper.

"You have no right here," I said angrily, "and I demand that paper whereon you have made notes of an affair that does not concern you."

"I shall not give it you," he responded defiantly.

"Then I shall call the captain."

"You can do so if you wish. I shall be paid off to-day, so it doesn't matter."

"Give it to me," I cried, incensed at the fellow's insolence, and made a swift movement to seize his wrist. He was, however, too quick for me, for, grasping my arm with his left hand, he screwed up the paper with his right and dropped it through the porthole into the sea.

I saw it flutter for a moment in the air and drop into the surging water ten yards away.

"Leave this place at once," I commanded. "You have no right here, and have evidently entered for some dishonest purpose. I shall inform Captain Seal at once."

"All right," he answered, shrugging his shoulders as he went through the doorway, "you needn't get your wool off, doctor. I was doing no harm, surely, having a look at that old scribble."

But the truth was patent. That man, an ordinary seaman, had read and understood what was written there. That look of supreme satisfaction on his face was sufficient to tell me that he had gained knowledge of some secret hidden from me.

Benjamin Harding was a seaman of exemplary conduct, it was true. He drank little, seldom swore, and was much more careful of his personal appearance than the rest of the grimy crew. His speech betokened a somewhat better education than the others, and I had more than once detected beneath his rough exterior traces of refinement. More than once, too, I had overheard him repress a too expressive imprecation from the mouth of one or other of his shipmates. Tall, lean, and muscular, his age I judged to be about forty, his beard and hair sandy, and his eyes a washed-out grey. His cheeks showed marks of smallpox, and under his left eye was a long white scar. I returned to the bridge and told Seal of the incident, but the pilot not yet being aboard he was too much occupied with the navigation of the ship to be able to reprimand the man there and then.

So I went again to my cabin and counted over my treasures, finding to my satisfaction that none were missing.

I saw but little more of the man Harding. The skipper later on told me that he had given the fellow a good talking too, and that he had expressed his regret at his insolence. He had, however, only shipped for the voyage, and would be paid off that day, therefore it was useless to do more than remonstrate.

Nevertheless, the incident disturbed me. I had a strange, indescribable intuition that the man Harding had obtained possession of some secret hidden from me; that the apparently ignorant seaman was acquainted with the Latin script and with those puzzling abbreviations which had so utterly floored me. Before my eyes he had deciphered line after line, reading it off almost as easily as the copies of *Lloyd's* and the *Dispatch*, that found so much favour in the forecastle. Yet why had he taken such precaution to destroy the memoranda he had written if the facts did not relate to some secret from which he expected to receive benefit?

Thus, while the Mysterious Man slept soundly in the room prepared for him, I sat for a long time over my pipe trying to decipher the uneven scribble and pondering over what might be written on that time-stained parchment.

Next day Seal came to see me, dressed in his shore-going toggery—a neat navy blue suit and a peaked cap a size too small for his ponderous head. The Mysterious Man so far demonstrated that his senses were returning that he expressed pleasure at meeting the skipper by holding out his hand to him, a fact which gave both of us satisfaction.

"I'm busy unloading now, you know, doctor," the captain said, in his deep, cheery voice, "so I must leave it all to you. Act just as you think fit. For my own part I think we ought to get them parchments deciphered. They might tell us something interesting."

"And the gold?"

"For the present we'll stick to that," was his prompt reply. "If anybody claims it we'll investigate their claim, as the insurance people say, but as far as I can see the only person entitled to it is that lunatic over there," and he jerked his thumb in the direction of the Mysterious Man.

He drank deeply of my whisky, and pronounced it good. We chatted for an hour or more, and when I asked about Harding he merely answered:—

"Oh, the fellow was paid off last night. I'm quite your way of thinking—there was some mystery about that chap. I've made inquiries and find that he hadn't been many voyages before, because he betrayed ignorance of many common terms at sea, and gave himself away in lots of details."

"He was an educated man," I remarked.

"Yes, I believe he was. He's left one or two books about the forecastle which are not the sort that sailors read."

"What class of books?" I inquired.

"Oh, one was a Latin dictionary, another an odd volume of *Chambers' Encyclopædia*, and a third book called *Old English Chronicles*, whatever they are."

The latter was certainly not a work in which a sailor would be interested. I had known it at college, the mediaeval chronicles of Geoffrey of Monmouth and other monks, a volume of the driest and most uninteresting kind, save to an antiquarian student. Yes, I felt more convinced than ever that Benjamin Harding was not what he had pretended to be.

The Mysterious Man had taken to smoking. I had purchased for him a shilling briar at a tobacconist's in King's Road, and while we talked he sat puffing at it and looking aimlessly down on the street. The pity of it all was that the poor old fellow was dumb. Even though a lunatic he might, if he could have spoken, have given us some clue to his past. But up to the present we were just as ignorant as to who or what he was as in that first moment when we had discovered him in the dark cabin of that death-ship.

To his old rusty sword he clung, as though it were a mascot. Even now he wore it suspended from his waist by a piece of cord that had come from off my trunk, and at night it reposed with him in his room. Once it had no doubt been the sharp, ready weapon of some swaggering elegant, but it was now blunt, rusted, and scabbardless, only its maker's name and the remarkable temper of its blade showed what it once had been.

A week later I set about to discover some one who could decipher the parchments and the book containing the hidden secret of Bartholomew da Schorno, for therein I anticipated I should discover some clue to the mystery of the *Seahorse*. In the Manuscript Department of the British Museum I obtained the address of a certain Charles Staffurth, who, I was told, was an expert upon the court and commercial hands of the sixteenth and seventeenth centuries.

So to his address in the Clapham Park Road, I carried my precious book and documents, and sought an interview. A prim old gentleman in steel-rimmed spectacles received me in a back room fitted as a study, and after the first half dozen words I recognized that he was a scholar.

I told the story of my discovery, to which he listened with breathless interest, and when I undid the brown paper parcel and revealed the parchments his eyes fairly danced with expectation and delight. He was an enthusiast.

He bent over them, handling them with a reverence and fondness which showed him to be a true palaeographist. He ran quickly through the pages of the vellum book and remarked:—

"Ah! they are not numbered, I see. Sixteenth century hand of Central Italy!"

He recognized it at once, without looking for dates.

"Really doctor—Doctor Pickering," he exclaimed, glancing at my card, "this is a most remarkable story. I'm sure it will give me the greatest pleasure to look through these papers, and I will do so if you will leave them with me for a day or two. The book, you see, is voluminous, and will require a good deal of deciphering. They have many such at the Museum, so I have experience of the difficulties in reading them. Let's see, to-day is Tuesday. Will you call on Thursday afternoon? By that time I hope to have read the greater portion of what is contained here. If, however, I discover anything of very great importance I will telegraph to you."

And so it was arranged. I remained chatting with him for nearly half an hour, and then returned to my strangely silent companion, the Mysterious Man.

The old expert had evidently been much impressed by my story, and had commenced to decipher the documents as soon as I took leave of him, for at eleven o'clock next morning I received a telegram from him, worded as follows:—

"Please call here at once. Most important discovery.
                                                            Staffurth

# VII

## What was Written in the Vellum Book

As soon as I entered Mr. Staffurth's little study I saw by his manner that the discovery he had made filled him with interest.

"I have lost no time in going through your documents," he said calmly, when I was seated by his table. "Your story of the finding of the strange ship with the mysterious survivor on board was most interesting, and last night, after you had gone, I turned my attention at once to this book, written by Bartholomew da Schorno."

"And you have discovered the secret?" I asked eagerly.

"Not entirely," he responded. "But I have deciphered sufficient to tell us a curious narrative, and to explain to some degree the mystery of the *Seahorse*. Are you acquainted with the history of Tuscany?"

I replied in the negative. I knew my history of England fairly well, but had never cared for the study of the history of other countries.

"In that case I must first explain to you a few historical facts, in order that you may rightly understand the situation," he said. "During the late fifteenth century the southern coasts of France, and especially of Italy, from the Var mouth along to Leghorn, were continually raided by the Corsairs of Barbary, who ravaged the towns and villages and carried thousands of Christians into slavery, in Algera and Tunis. The great breakwater at Algiers was constructed by them, and at one of the gates of the city are still preserved the hooks upon which the unfortunate captives were hung to die if they offended their cruel taskmasters. So bold were these pirates and so terrible their depredations, especially in the country between Savona and the mouth of the Arno, that in the year 1561, by a privilege granted by Pius IV, an order of chivalry was founded, called the Knights of St. Stephen, the members being all of the Italian aristocracy, and the object to construct armed ships to sweep these Corsairs from the sea.

"The headquarters of the Order were in Pisa, then an important city, where they constructed a church which still remains to this day hung with banners taken from the Corsairs, a magnificent relic of Italy's departed glory. The founder of the Order was Cosimo di Medici, who, according to the volume here"—and he placed his hand upon a folio bound in yellow parchment—"took the habit in the Cathedral of Pisa on March 15, 1561, of Monsignor Georgio Cornaro, the Papal Nuncio."

"I fear," he continued, "that these are rather dry details of a chapter of the forgotten history of Italy, but if you will bear with me for a few minutes I think I shall be able to explain the mystery to a certain extent. These extremely rare volumes I have obtained from the library of my friend, Sir Arthur Bond, the great Italian historian, in order that you may examine them." And opening the first at the title page he placed it before me. Printed in big rough capitals on the damp-stained page were the words:—

*I pregj della Toscana nel' Imprese piv 'segnalate de' Cavalieri di Santo Stefano. Opera data in Lvce da Fulvo Fontana della Compagnia di Gesù. In Firenze MDCCI.*

The other was a somewhat thicker but smaller volume, parchment bound like the first, its title being *Statuti dell' Ordine de Cavalieri di Stefano* and contained in Italian a complete history of the Order, the bulls of the Popes concerning it, the regulations of its church and administration of its funds.

It was evident that Mr. Staffurth, although an elderly man, was not one to let grass grow beneath his feet. He pored over the books, blinking through his spectacles, and then continued his explanations, saying:—

"It seems that the first admiral of this primitive fleet was Guilio di Medici, and although the knights rowed in galleys against the stronger ships of the Turks they succeeded in capturing three of the latter on their first voyage in 1573. From that year down to 1688 they waged continuous war against the Corsairs, until they had burned most of the strongholds of the latter, and entirely broken their power on the sea. Now," he added, "you told me something of a banner with a cross upon it." And opening the bigger volume he showed me a large copper-plate engraving of one of the battles wherein vessels exactly similar in build to the *Seahorse* were engaged, and each was flying a flag similar to the one I had discovered.

"The Maltese cross," he explained, "was the distinguishing badge of the Knights of St. Stephen who fought for Christianity against the Mohammedans, and succeeded in liberating so many of the white slaves. No movement was perhaps more humane, and none so completely forgotten, for even the Order itself is now discontinued, and all that remains is that grand old church in Pisa, nowadays visited by gaping tourists. From my investigations, however, it seems quite plain that the *Seahorse* was one of the ships of the Order, and although of English name, and probably of English build, its commander was the noble Bartholomew da Schorno, who had as lieutenant Pompæo Marie a Paule. The latter, as stated in the document with the leaden seal, was appointed commendatore by Cosimo the Second."

"Then the fact is established that the reason cannon and armed men were aboard the *Seahorse* was because she was engaged in the suppression of piracy?" I said.

"Exactly. Your remark regarding the banner with the Maltese cross gave me the cue, and I have, I think, successfully cleared up the first point. And, furthermore, you have recognized in this picture vessels built on the same lines. This picture, as you will see, represents the taking of the fortress of Elimano from the Corsairs in the year 1613."

"Then do you fix the date of the loss of the *Seahorse* about that period?"

"I cannot say," he responded. "It might have been ten, or even twenty years later."

"Not more?"

"No; not more. In these later pictures you will see that the vessels were of somewhat different build," and the old expert turned over folio after folio of the rare and interesting volume.

"All this, however," he remarked, "must be very dry to you. But you have sought my aid in this curious affair, and I am giving it to the best of my ability. We men who make a special study of history, or of palæography, are apt to believe that the general public are as absorbed in the gradual transition of the charter hands, or the vagaries of the Anglo-Norman scribes of the twelfth century, as we are ourselves. Therefore, I hope you will forgive me if I have bored you, Dr. Pickering. I will promise," he added, with a laugh, "not to offend again."

"No apology is needed, my dear sir," I hastened to reassure him; "I am so terribly ignorant of all these things, and all that you discover is to me of most intense interest, having regard to my own adventures, and to the existence of a survivor from the *Seahorse*."

"Very well then," he answered, apparently much gratified; "let us proceed yet another step." And he placed aside the two borrowed volumes. "Of course, I have not yet had sufficient time to decipher the whole of this volume written by Bartholomew da Schorno, but so far as I have gone I find that the writer, although of Italian birth, lived in England, and it is with certain things in England that occurred in 1589 and 1590 that he deals—matters which are mysterious and certainly require investigation."

From between the parchment leaves of the heavy book he drew several sheets of paper, which I saw were covered with pencil memoranda in his own handwriting, and these he spread before him to refresh his memory and make certain of his facts.

"From what is written here in old Italian—which, by the way, is not the easiest language to decipher—it seems that Bartholomew, the commander of the *Seahorse*, was also a Commendatore of the Order of St. Stephen, and a wealthy man who had forsaken the luxuries of ease to fight the Corsairs and release their slaves. Most probably he was owner of the vessel of which his compatriot Paule was second in command. This, however, must be mere conjecture on our part for the present. What is chronicled here is most important, and it was in order to consult you at once that I telegraphed."

Then he paused, slowly turned over the vellum pages with his thin white hand, glancing for a few moments in silence at his memoranda. He had worked for hours over that crabbed yellow handwriting; indeed, he afterwards confessed to me that he had not been to bed at all, preferring, as a true palaeographist, to decipher the documents in the quiet hours instead of retiring to rest.

"It seems that this Bartholomew da Schorno was an Italian noble who, falling into disgrace with the Grand Duke of Ferrara, sold his estates and came to live in England during Elizabeth's reign," he said. "As far as I have yet been able to gather, it appears that he purchased a house and lands at a place called Caldecott. In my gazetteer I find there is a village of that name near Kettering. The main portion of the manuscript consists of a long history of his family and the cause of the quarrel with the Grand Duke, written in a kind of wearisome diary. When, however, he comes to his visit to England, his audience with Queen Elizabeth, and his decision to settle at Caldecott, he reveals himself as a man aggrieved at the treatment he has received in his own country, and yet fond of a life of excitement and adventure. It was the latter, he declares, that after a few years' residence in England induced him to become a Knight of St. Stephen and to sail the seas in search of the Corsairs in company with 'the dear friend of his youth, the noble Pompæo a Paule, of Pisa.'"

"But the secret," I said interrupting him.

"As far as I have yet deciphered the manuscript I can discover nothing of it, only the mention that you have seen in the commencement. The book ends abruptly. Perhaps he intended to explain some secret, but was prevented from so doing by the sinking of his ship."

Such seemed a most likely theory.

"The reason I called you here was to suggest that you should go to this place, Caldecott, and see whether any descendants of this Italian nobleman are still existing. They may possess family papers, and be able to throw some further lights on these documents. The place is near Rockingham and not far from Market Harborough."

This suggestion did not at that moment appeal to me. We were still too much in the dark.

"Have you read the other document?" I inquired. "I mean the one with the seven signatures and the seal with the leopard."

"Yes," he responded, and I noticed a strange expression pass across his grey countenance; "I have made a rough translation of it. The Latin is much abbreviated, but its purport is a very remarkable one. At the present moment it is, perhaps, sufficient for me to briefly explain the contents without giving you the long and rather wearisome translation."

Then, taking up his pencilled notes again, he continued: "It is nothing else than a statement by this same Bartholomew da Schorno relating a very romantic circumstance. On a date which he gives as August 14, in the thirty-first year of Elizabeth's reign—which must be 1588—he was sailing in a ship called *The Great Unicorn*, and when off the Cornish coast encountered a Spanish ship which vigorously attacked them. This vessel proved to belong to the defeated Armada, and had escaped the chase by Howard, but by clever manoeuvring of *The Great Unicorn*—presumably a ship used to fight the pirates of Barbary—the Spanish galleon was captured after a terrible encounter with great loss on both sides. On board was found a quantity of gold and silver, jewelled ornaments, and other treasure worth a great sum, and this being transferred to *The Great Unicorn*, together with the survivors of the crew, the vessel itself was scuttled and sent adrift. Our friend Bartholomew was evidently commander of the victorious vessel, for he weathered the storm which practically destroyed the remnant of the Spanish fleet, sailed up Channel, and landed his treasure secretly at Great Yarmouth, afterwards concealing it in a place of safety. As his was not an English warship and he had merely assumed a hostile attitude and fought fair and square in self-defence, he claims that he was entitled to the gold and jewels that had fallen into his hands.

"The persons who knew the place of concealment numbered seven, all of whom signed a covenant of secrecy. They were Englishmen, all of them, and evidently the trusted followers of Bartholomew. The covenant enacts that the treasure shall remain untouched under the guardianship of one Richard Knutton, who was left 'at the place of concealment' for that purpose. The seven men each swore a sacred oath to make no attempt to seize any part of the gold or jewels, they having each received from their master an equal amount as prize-money. The remainder was to lie hidden until such time as the Order of St. Stephen should require funds for the prosecution of their good work of rescuing Christian slaves, when it was to be carried to Italy. This, of course, seems rather a romantic decision, but there is added a clause which shows that this Bartholomew was not only a chivalrous man, but was also fully alive to the wants of posterity.

"The second covenant provides that if the Order of St. Stephen never required funds, the secret of the existence of the treasure is to descend in the family of Richard Knutton alone, but two-thirds of the treasure itself is to become the property of the youngest surviving child of the family of Clement Wollerton, whom Bartholomew names as 'my esteemed lieutenant, who has twice been the means of saving my life,' and 'the remaining third to its guardian, the descendant of the said Richard Knutton, seaman, of the Port of Sandwich.'"

"A very curious arrangement," I said. "How do you understand it?"

"Well," the old man remarked, fingering the yellow parchment with its faded scribble, "it seems quite plain that a large amount of treasure was seized from a Spanish galleon, brought ashore at Yarmouth, and concealed somewhere under the care of three persons—Richard Knutton, George A. Dafte, and Robert Dafte. If the Knights of St. Stephen have never claimed it, as most probably they have not, for they were a very wealthy association right up to the time of their extinction at the end of the seventeenth century, then the gold and jewels still remain concealed, the secret still being in the hands of the lineal descendants of Richard Knutton alone, and the heir to it, the youngest child of this Wollerton family."

"But have you discovered the place of concealment?" I asked anxiously.

"No. I expect the secret mentioned in this volume written at a later date has something to do with it, but I have not yet deciphered the whole. On the other hand, however, I cannot help thinking that if seven persons were aware of the secret hiding-place, and had signed the covenant, old Bartholomew would scarcely write it down on parchment that might fall into an enemy's hands."

# VIII

## The Seven Dead Men

H is argument was quite logical. There was no doubt that the Italian had at first intended to make a permanent record of the secret, but had afterwards thought better of it. He was evidently no fool, as shown by the testamentary disposition of the Spanish loot.

I took up the parchment, with its dangling seal, and noticed a dark smear across it. The old expert told me that the stain was a smear of blood.

"Then the secret is in the hands of some one named Knutton, and the right owner of two-thirds of the concealed property is a Wollerton?"

"Exactly."

"Is there any accurate description of the treasure?"

"Yes. It is contained in an appendix in Bartholomew's handwriting; a careful inventory of the numbers of 'pieces of eight,' the ornaments, bars of gold, and other objects of value. One gold cup alone is set down as weighing five hundred ounces." And he turned over the leaves of vellum and showed me the inventory written there in Italian, a long list occupying nearly eighteen pages.

"The family of Knutton, knowing the secret, may have seized the treasure long ago," I remarked.

"No, I think not," was his reply. "In the document it is distinctly stated that a certain deed had been prepared and handed to Richard Knutton in order that it should be given to his eldest son and then descend in the family, and that so guarded was it in wording that it was impossible for any one to learn the place of concealment. Therefore, even if it still exists in the family of Knutton—which is an old Kentish name, by the way, as well as the name Dafte on the document, it would be impossible for the family to make any use of it."

"Then where is the key plan of the place where the gold is hidden?" I queried.

"Ah, that, my dear sir, is a question I cannot answer," he replied, shaking his head. "We may, however, hazard a surmise. We have gathered from Bartholomew's own writings that he lived at a place called Caldecott, which would be about a hundred miles from Great Yarmouth, as the crow flies. Now, my theory is that he most probably transported the treasure by road to his own property as the most secure place for its concealment."

"Most likely," I cried, eagerly accepting his idea. "He would be much more prone to place it in his own house or bury it on his own lands than on property belonging to some one else."

"Exactly. That is the reason why I suggest that you should take a journey to Caldecott and make inquiries if any of the names of the present inhabitants coincide with any of the nine names mentioned in this document."

"Well," I said, excitedly, "the affair is growing in interest. A treasure hunt here in England is rather unusual in these days. I hope, Mr. Staffurth, you can find time to accompany me for a couple of days down there."

"No," he declared, "go down yourself and see whether you can discover anything regarding persons bearing any of these names."

Then taking a slip of paper he copied the seven signatures, together with those of Richard Knutton and Bartholomew da Schorno himself, afterwards handing it to me.

"The treasure may, of course, be concealed at Caldecott," he said. "Indeed, if it is still in existence and intact, it is, I conjecture, hidden there. At any rate, if you make careful investigation, and at the same time avoid attracting undue attention, we may discover something that will give us a clue. The treasure, you must recollect, was placed in hiding about three hundred years ago, and it may have been discovered by some prying person during those three centuries."

"Well," I said, "it is quite evident that these documents themselves have fallen into no other hands except our own."

"True; but seven persons, in addition to this Richard Knutton, knew the place where the loot was hidden. One or other of them may have broken their oath."

"They might all have been on board the *Seahorse* when she was lost," I suggested. "From the rough manner in which the agreement was prepared it seems as though it were written while at sea."

"Exactly. It was certainly never prepared by a public notary. The men evidently did not think fit to expose their secret to any outsider—they were far too wary for that, knowing that the English Government would in all probability lay claim to it."

"So they will now, even if we discover it. It will be treasure-trove, and belong to the Crown."

"Not if it is claimed by its rightful owner—the youngest child of the Wollertons."

"You don't believe that this book contains the secret of the hiding-place after all?" I suggested.

"No. Unless my theory is correct that it was transferred from Yarmouth to Caldecott. Why should he have sailed in the teeth of that great gale from the Cornish coast right round to Yarmouth if he had not some object in so doing?"

"Well," I said, "it forms a curious story in any case."

"Very curious. This old Italian seems to have been an adventurer as well as a noble, judging from his own statements. The Turkish ships he seized in the Mediterranean he sold and pocketed the money, and more than once in the capture of the Corsair strongholds a big share of valuable loot fell to him. So it was not altogether from motives of humanity that he had become a Knight of St. Stephen, but rather from a love of profitable adventure."

I recollected how I had stood beside a skeleton that was undoubtedly his, a man of unusual stature still wearing a portion of finely inlaid Italian armour such as I had seen in museums.

"He must have been a wealthy man," I remarked.

"Undoubtedly. And, furthermore, if we discover the spot where the treasure is hidden, we may also discover the loot that he most probably secured and brought to England for concealment."

"Is anything stated regarding his family?"

"He had one son, but his wife died of the plague in Italy two years after her marriage. The son he names as Robert, but no doubt he was not on good terms with him, otherwise he would have left the secret to him, and the treasure as an inheritance."

I slowly turned over in my mind the whole of the strange circumstances. It hardly seemed credible that Richard Knutton, the guardian of the treasure, should die without revealing its whereabouts to any one, especially as his family was to profit one-third on its distribution.

This I mentioned to Staffurth, but the latter pointed out that the secret was probably transmitted in some unintelligible form, and would therefore be useless without the key. Besides, the family of Knutton were most probably in ignorance of what was contained in those documents, considering that they had been always at sea for the past three centuries.

Leaving old Mr. Staffurth to continue the deciphering of the Italian manuscript, I returned to Chelsea.

The Mysterious Man was seated at the window, his sword against his chair, covering sheet after sheet of paper with grotesque arabesques, wherein the Evil One seemed to be constantly represented. He took no notice of my return, therefore I awaited the coming of Dr. Gordon Macfarlane, the great lunacy specialist of Hanwell Asylum, who shortly arrived.

I introduced my patient, but the latter only grasped his sword and fixed the specialist with a stony stare.

Macfarlane tried to humour him, and asked him a few questions. To the latter, of course, he received no response. We both examined the quaint drawings, and the more we looked into them the more marvellous seemed the execution—the work of a madman, certainly, but such an intricate design that few first-class artists could imitate.

Macfarlane was, I could see, much interested in the case, and was quite an hour making his diagnosis. Presently, however, he took me aside into the adjoining room and said:—

"A very remarkable case, Pickering. I have only met with one which at all bore resemblance to it. Now, my own opinion is that the old fellow is at certain brief moments quite sane—a sign that he will, in all probability, recover. I should be inclined to think that his mental aberration has not been of very long duration, six months perhaps. He has certain fixed ideas, one of them being the habitual carrying of his sword. He also, I noticed, is interested in any mechanical contrivance—my watch, for instance, attracted his attention. That is a symptom of a phase of insanity of which a cure is hopeful. And as regards his dumbness, I believe that it is due to some sudden and terrible fright combined, of course, with his unbalanced mind. Do you notice his eyes? At times there is a look of unspeakable terror in them. With a cure, or even partial cure, of his insanity, speech will, I believe, return to him."

This favourable opinion delighted me, and I thanked the great specialist for his visit, whereupon he admitted his interest in the unusual case, and said that if I would allow him he would take it under his charge in his own private asylum down at Ealing.

So next day I conveyed the Mysterious Man to "High Elms," as the place was called, and, having left him in charge of the superintendent, packed my bag, and set out on the first stage of my journey to discover the whereabouts of the hidden loot.

I undertook it with a light heart, now that the responsibility of keeping the Mysterious Man in safety had been lifted from my shoulders, but so many were the mysteries which crowded one upon the other, and so many the secrets which circumstances alone unravelled, that I think you, my reader, will agree with me, when you know all, that the pains old Bartholomew da Schorno took to conceal the whereabouts of his treasure betrayed a cleverness which almost surpasses comprehension.

Well, I went to Caldecott about a month after landing in England, for a family matter occupied me in the meantime, and if you will bear with me I will tell you what I discovered there.

# IX

## One Point is Made Clear

Caldecott was, I found, a very out-of-the-way little place. The pretty village of Rockingham, with its long, broad street leading up the hill and the old castle crowning it, was its nearest neighbour, for at that station I alighted from the train and walked through the noonday heat along the short, shadeless road pointed out by the railway porter.

The country in that district is of park-like aspect, mostly rich pastures with spinneys here and there, and running brooks; but on that blazing summer's day, with the road shining white before me, I was glad enough when I got under the shadow of the cottages of Caldecott.

My first impression of the place was that the village was both remote and comfortable. The cottages were mostly well kept and nearly all thatched, with quaint little attic windows peeping forth here and there and strange old gable ends. Every house was built of stone, solidly and well, and every cottage garden seemed to be gay with jasmine, hollyhocks, sunflowers, and other old-world flowers. Not a soul was in the village street, for in that great heat the very dogs were sleeping.

Behind, on a slight eminence, stood a fine old church of Early English architecture, with narrow, pointed lancet-shaped windows similar to those in the choir of Westminster Abbey, and as I passed, the sweet-toned bell from the square ivy-clad tower struck two o'clock. Walking on a short distance I came to a small open space which in olden days was, I suppose the village green, and seeing an inn called the Plough I entered the little bar parlour and called for some ale. The place seemed scrupulously clean and comfortable, very old-fashioned, but well-kept, therefore I decided to make it my headquarters, and engaged a room for at least one night.

The young woman who waited upon me having explained that she and her brother kept the place, I at once commenced to make some inquiries. It was, I knew, most necessary that I should avoid attracting any undue attention in the gossiping little place, therefore I had to exercise the greatest caution. I gave her a card and explained my presence there to the fact that I was taking a holiday and photographing.

"By the way," I said, standing at the bow window which gave a view on to the church, "whose house is that away among the trees?"

"The Vicarage, sir. Mr. Pocock lives there, a very-nice gentleman."

"Has he been vicar long?" I inquired.

"Oh, he's been here these five years, I think, or perhaps a little more."

"And is there an old Manor House here?"

"Yes, sir. Right up the top end of the village. Mr. and Mrs. Kenway live there. They're new tenants, and have only been there about a year."

"Is it a large house?"

"One of the largest here—a very old-fashioned place."

"Is it the oldest house?"

"Oh, yes, I think so, but I wouldn't care to live in it myself," and the young woman shrugged her shoulders.

"Why?" I inquired, at once interested and hoping to learn some local legend.

"Well, they say that all sorts of strange noises are heard there at night. I'm no believer in ghosts, you know, but even rats are not pleasant companions in a house."

"Who does the place belong to?"

"To a Jew, I think, who lives in Ireland. Years ago, I've heard, the place was mortgaged, and the mortgagee foreclosed. But lots of people have rented it since then, and nobody within my recollection has lived there longer than about three years."

What the young woman told me caused me to jump to the conclusion that the house in question was once the residence of Bartholomew da Schorno, and after finishing my ale I lit a cigarette and sauntered forth to have a look at the place.

I need not tell you how eagerly I walked to the top of the village, but on arrival there I saw no sign of the house in question. I inquired of a lad, who directed me into a farmyard gate, whence I found a short, ill-kept road which ended in a *cul-de-sac*, leading into a field. On my right was a clump of elms, and hidden among them was the quaint and charmingly old-world Manor House.

First sight of the place was sufficient to tell me that it had been allowed to fall into decay, and certainly it was, even in that summer sunshine, a rather dismal and depressing place of abode.

The old cobbled courtyard was overgrown with moss and weeds, and some of the outbuildings had ugly holes in the roofs. The house itself was long, low, and rambling, of Elizabethan architecture, with old mullioned windows, built entirely of stone, now, however, grey with lichens and green with moss on the parts which the clinging ivy had failed to cover. The outside woodwork, weather-beaten and rotting, had not been painted for a century, while upon one of the high square chimneys stood forth the rusty iron angle of a sundial, from which, however, most of the graven numerals had long ago disappeared.

The high beech hedge which formed one of the boundaries was sufficient proof of the antiquity of the place, but the trees of the broad pleasure grounds, which had no doubt once extended far away down to the river, had been cut down and the land turned into pastures, so that only a small, neglected kitchen garden now remained. The place, even in its present decay, spoke mutely of a departed magnificence. As I stood gazing upon it, I could imagine it as the residence of the lord of the manor in the days when peacocks strutted in the grounds, when that moss-grown courtyard had echoed to the hoofs of armed horsemen, and the talk was of the prowess of Drake, of Walsingham's astuteness, of the martyrdom of Mary at Fotheringhay, and the fickleness of the Queen's favour.

Determined to make the acquaintance of the present occupiers, even though it might or might not be the former residence of old Bartholomew, I went up to the blistered door and pulled a bell, which clanged dismally within, and made such an echo that I wondered if the place were devoid of furniture.

My summons was answered by a rather stout, middle-aged woman, who, in response to my inquiry, informed me that she was Mrs. Kenway. I was somewhat taken aback at this, for I had believed her to be a servant, but the moment she opened her mouth I knew her to be a countrywoman.

I was compelled to make an excuse for my call, so I invented what I conceived to be an ingenious untruth.

"I have called to ask you a favour," I said, "My mother was born in this house, and being in the neighbourhood I am most anxious to see the old place. Have you any objection?"

"Oh, no, sir," was the kindly woman's prompt response. "Come in; you're very welcome to look round, I'm sure. No, keep your hat on, there are so many draughts."

"Is it draughty, then?"

"Oh, sir," she said, shaking her head and sighing; "I don't know what the place used to be in days gone by, but me and my husband are truly sorry we ever took it. In winter it's a reg'ler ice-well. We can't keep ourselves warm anyhow. It's so lonely, and full of strange noises o' nights. I'm not nervous, but all the same they're not nice."

"Rats, perhaps."

"Yes, I suppose so." And she led me along the narrow passage where the stones were worn hollow by the tread of generations, and ushered me into a small, low room where black beams ran across the ceiling. But, oh! the incongruity of that interior. Over the old panelling was pasted common wall-paper of hideous design in green and yellow, while the furniture was of modern description, quite out of keeping with the antiquity of the house. As she led me through room after room I noticed how successive tenants had, by papering and white-washing, endeavoured to turn the place into a kind of modern cottage home. Much of the old woodwork had been removed, and even the oaken doors were actually painted and grained! The staircase was still, however, in its original state of dark oak, and handsomely carved, and the stone balustrade which ran round the landing was a splendid example of Elizabethan construction. Half the rooms were unfurnished, but the good woman took me along the echoing, carpetless corridors and showed me the various chambers above as well as below.

Could that ruinous place be the one which the noble adventurer had chosen for the concealment of the loot?

The place certainly coincided in date with the written statement, but I had nothing to connect it with the name of da Schorno. Perhaps, however, some of the title-deeds connected with the place might tell me something, so I obtained from Mrs. Kenway the name and address of the landlord, a man named Cohen, living in Dublin.

"This isn't at all the house me and my husband wanted," she declared. "Our idea when we took it was to take paying guests, because I'm used to lodgers. I let apartments for six years in Hunstanton, and our idea in coming here was to take paying guests, as they call 'em nowadays. We advertised in the London papers and got two ladies, but they only stayed a fortnight. It was too quiet for them, they said. Since then several people have been, but I haven't let once."

I was certainly not surprised. If I were paying guest in that house I should go melancholy mad within a week. Besides, as far as I could see, the place was comfortless. An appearance of freshness was lent it by the new paper in execrable taste in the hall, and a gaudy new linoleum upon the beautiful old polished stairs, but beyond that the interior was just as dingy and cold-looking as the outside.

Indeed, so depressing was my visit that I was rather glad when it was over. One or two of the upstair rooms were panelled, with oak evidently, but the woodwork had been painted a uniform white, while the floors were rickety and suggestive of dry-rot.

She had another two years' lease of the place, Mrs. Kenway regretted to say. They were trying to re-let it, for if compelled to keep it on until the end of the term it would swallow up all their slender savings.

"You see, we are earning nothing, except a little that my husband gets out of canvassing for an insurance company. But it takes him out so much, and I am left alone here from morning till night."

I was secretly glad to hear of this state of things, because if I could prove that the house had belonged to old Bartholomew, it might become necessary for us to rent it and make some investigations.

Through the lattice window of the long, low room wherein I stood a wide view could be obtained across the neglected garden and the pastures beyond away down to the river, and as I looked forth it occurred to me to ask what rent was required.

"We pay forty-five pounds a year," was her reply.

"Well," I said reflectively, "I know some one who wants a quiet house in the country, and I'll mention it to him if you like."

"Oh, I'd be most thankful, sir," she cried, enthusiastically. "The gentleman would be quiet enough here. There are no neighbours, and not even a passer-by, for, as you see, the road leads to nowhere."

Again I wondered whether, concealed in that weird, tumble-down old place were the gold and jewels from the Spanish galleon and the spoils from the Corsairs of Barbary. Behind that panelling upstairs might be concealed treasure worth a fortune. As far as my cursory observations went, there was no likely place downstairs, unless, as in many old houses of that character, there was a "priest's hole" cunningly concealed.

I went forth accompanied by the lady who was waiting in vain for paying guests, and examined the front of the house, which faced south towards the sloping pastures.

Walking a little way back into the wilderness of weeds which was once a garden, I looked up to the row of long mullioned windows, and saw in the centre of the dark grey wall a large square sculptured stone bearing the date 1584. Above was a coat-of-arms cut in the crumbling stone, a device that was in an instant familiar to me.

As my eyes fell on it I could not repress a cry of satisfaction, for there was the leopard rampant with the fleur-de-lys, the very same device that was upon the seal of the document with the seven signatures I had found on board the *Seahorse*!

Thus was it proved most conclusively that it was the actual house mentioned by Bartholomew da Schorno, for it bore his arms, with the date of either its construction or restoration.

I talked with Mrs. Kenway for some little time as an excuse to linger there, and when I left I held out strong hopes to her that I might induce my friend to take the remainder of the lease off her hands.

# X

## The Guardian of the Secret

I had some tea at the Plough, with fresh butter and cream which, after those weeks on board the *Thrush*, were delicious.

Much gratified that I had at last discovered the house of the noble freebooter, I set to work to make inquiries regarding the family of Knutton, the hereditary guardians of the treasure, and of the descendants of Clement Wollerton, who, it appeared, had been Bartholomew's lieutenant, and whose skeleton I had most probably seen on board the *Seahorse*.

The innkeeper's sister was still communicative, so I asked her if she knew any one of either name in the village.

"No, sir, I don't know any one of such name in Caldecott," she answered, after reflecting a few moments. "There's old Ben Knutton, who lives in Rockingham."

"What kind of a man is he?"

"Well, his character's not of the best," she answered; "he's a labouring man, but he's a lazy, good-for-nothing old fellow, who frequents every inn in the district."

"Married?"

"No, a widower. He lives in a cottage close to the Sonde Arms, in the main street of Rockingham."

The description she gave was certainly not that of the hereditary guardian of the Italian noble's treasure. Nevertheless, as he was the only person of that name in the district, I decided to walk back past the station and on to Rockingham, a distance of about a mile, and make his acquaintance.

It was a lovely summer's evening, and the walk through the cornfields was delightful, although my head was filled with the strange, old-world romance which within the past few weeks had been revealed to me. The main point which occupied my attention was whether the treasure was still hidden—or had it ever been hidden?—in that tumble-down old Manor House. In order to make secret investigation it would be necessary to rent the place and carefully search every hole and corner. Some of those panelled, low-ceilinged rooms above were, to me, attractive. A good deal might be hidden there, or in the roof.

After some inquiries I found the man Knutton's cottage, small, poorly-furnished, close-smelling, and not over clean. A slatternly girl of fourteen called "Uncle! You're wanted." And a gruff voice responded from the upstairs room. He came heavily down the narrow, uncarpeted stairs, a rough-looking type of agricultural labourer, in drab moleskin. His age was about sixty-five, with beery face, grey eyes, round-shouldered, and wearing his trousers tied beneath the knee, and boots that had never known blacking.

"Your name's Ben Knutton, isn't it?" I asked.

"Yes, sir. That's my name."

"Well, Mr. Knutton," I said, "I want to have a few minutes' chat with you alone."

I noticed that he looked somewhat aghast. Afterwards I learnt that he was an expert poacher, and he probably believed me to be a detective. Through a decade or so he had had a good deal of the Marquis of Exeter's and Mr. Watson's game, and the major part of it had found its way by an irregular route to Northampton market.

He first went very red, then white, his hand trembled, and he had to steady himself for a moment.

"Just go out for a minute or two, Annie," he said to his niece. "I want to speak to this gentleman. Take a seat, sir." He pulled forward one of the rush-bottomed chairs from beside the rickety old bureau.

"Don't think, Mr. Knutton, that I've come here with any hostile intent," I said, in order to reassure him. "I've come to Rockingham expressly to ask you one or two questions regarding your family. I am making some investigations about the Knuttons, and perhaps you can assist me. Have you any brothers or sisters living?"

"No, sir, I haven't. My brother Dick died this ten years ago."

Dick! Then that man's name was Richard Knutton!

"Did he leave any sons?" I inquired.

"Only one—young Dick. He enlisted, and was killed in Afghanistan."

"He enlisted after his father's death?"

"Yes, sir," he answered, more at his ease.

"Your family is a very old one in this neighbourhood, isn't it?"

"One o' the oldest, they says. The Knuttons lived at the Manor Farm up at Caldecott for more'n a hundred years. But we've come down in the world since then."

"The Manor Farm is the one attached to the Manor of Caldecott, eh?"

"It's close to Caldecott Manor House. There's fifteen hundred acres o' land with it. And nowadays, sir, I often works on that self-same land for Mr. Banks, what owns it now."

"Are you the oldest of your family?"

"No, sir, Dick was. I was the second. Dick was the lucky'un, and was old Mr. Banks' foreman for years; that was in the present Mr. Banks' father's time, when farmin' was a lot better than what it is now. Lor', sir, in this district three-quarters of the farms scarcely pay their rents. All the landlords ought to be generous like the Duke o' Bedford; but they ain't, and we labourers have to suffer."

"More work and less beer," I remarked, with a laugh.

"Well, sir, when you mention beer, I'd be pleased to drink a pint at your expense." A remark which showed the rustic cadger.

"And so you shall when we've finished our talk," I said. "Tell me, have you ever heard or known of any person called Wollerton?"

"Wollerton!" he repeated. "Why, now that I remember, that's the very question the gentleman asked me the day before yesterday."

"What gentleman?" I gasped.

"A gentleman I met in the Sonde Arms. He said he knew me, but I didn't remember ever having set eyes on him before. He treated me and then asked me a whole lot of questions, some of'em very similar to what you've asked me. I don't understand what he or you—beggin' your pardon, sir—are driving' at."

"But this person who was so inquisitive? What kind of man was he?"

"A middle-aged gentleman from London. He stayed the night at the Sonde Arms, and left in the morning. He was a tall, fair man, and funnily enough seemed to know a lot about my relations."

"You don't know his name?"

"No, he didn't tell me."

This fact was certainly strange. Was it possible that some other person was in possession of the secret of the hoard and had forestalled me in making inquiries?

This beery labourer seemed, without doubt, a descendant of the Richard Knutton whose signature was written upon the faded parchment. As guardians of the treasure, the Knuttons had apparently been given the Manor Farm in order to be constantly near the spot where the spoils of war were concealed. Their residence at the farm through generations appeared to show that instructions had passed from father to son, and had, until seventy years ago, been strictly observed. Then the family had fallen upon evil times, and the descendants had degenerated into labourers, the youngest enlisting as a private soldier.

"I suppose you told this gentleman you met all about your family, just as you've told me—eh?"

"Pretty well the same story."

"What else did he ask you?"

"Well, he wanted to know one or two rather queer things about my family history—things I'd never heard nothing about. My father always did used to say that we were entitled to a big fortune, and he'd heard it from his father. Only that fortune ain't come, and I don't suppose it ever will. But both you gentlemen coming to me and asking the same questions has aroused my curiosity."

"Ah!" I said. "Fortunes that are talked of in families are usually phantom ones. Why, there's scarcely a family in England who don't believe that they've been done out of their rightful inheritance."

"I know that, sir. I could name twenty people in Rockingham who believe themselves the rightful heirs to property. That's why I never believed the story about our fortune. My poor old father had to go on the parish before he died—a shilling a week and two loaves. So the idea of the fortune didn't benefit him much."

"But what was the story which your father told you?" I inquired.

"Oh, it was quite a romance. Half the people in Rockingham know about it, because when the old man used to get a drop o' beer he always boasted of the great wealth that would be his some day."

"But what was the story? Tell it to me as nearly as you can remember it."

"Well, he used to say that long ago—hundreds of years, I think—the Knuttons were rich, but one son turned an adventurer, and accumulated a big treasure of gold and silver. This he hid away very carefully, because in those times there was no banks and places like there is now; but he left the secret in the hands of the head of the family, to be handed down for a certain number of years."

"Then has it come down to you?" I asked quickly.

"No, sir, I only wish it had," he laughed. Although a hard drinker, as I could tell from his puffed cheeks and unsteady hand, I was fortunate in finding him on that occasion quite sober.

"Perhaps the term of years ended and the fortune was realized," I suggested, for to me it seemed more than probable that the secret of the hiding-place had been discovered long ago.

"No, sir, I think not," was the old man's prompt reply. "If it had, we should have all been in a better position. No, I believe the whole thing is a fable, as every one has declared it to be. Why here, in Rockingham, they used to call my father 'Secret Sammy,' because when he was drunk he always spoke mysteriously of what he called 'The Secret.'"

"Have you any idea of the reason your family left the Manor Farm?"

"Owing to several bad seasons on top of each other. They were ruined, like hundreds of others. I've heard say that the last of the Knuttons who had the place used very often to go up to London by the coach, and he was fond of gambling. That was what really ruined him."

"Do you know anything about the Manor House—who lived there when you were a boy?"

"Why that's one of the questions the stranger asked me in the Sonde Arms," he exclaimed.

Very curious certainly, I thought. Who could possibly be aware of the secret given up by the sea except myself, Mr. Staffurth, and Job Seal?

"And you told him, I suppose?"

"I told him that old Squire Blacker lived there with his wife and two daughters from my early recollection. They all died, except the elder daughter, who didn't marry, and lived there for over twenty years, an old maid. When she died the place was bought by a Jew living in Ireland, and there's been lots o' tenants since. They never stay long because o' the damp and the rats. I worked there seven years ago, helpin' to do a drain, and the rats were something awful. I never saw such monsters in all my life. Young Jack Sharpe's terrier killed nearly a couple of hundred of 'em in one day. The stackyard is so close, you see."

"As far as you know, your family has never had any connection with the Manor itself?" I asked.

"I never heard it," he replied. "We were at the Manor Farm for generations, as I've told you—but never at the Manor House."

"And you don't believe the story about the fortune awaiting you somewhere?"

"Well, sir, I wish I could believe it," was the old man's answer. "We've been awaiting for it long enough, ain't we?"

I laughed, as though I shared his view with regard to the legend. At that juncture it was not my intention to tell him the object of my inquiries, and when he pressed me I turned the conversation into a different channel.

As I had promised, I went with him across to the Sonde Arms and regaled him with beer. Then when he saw the tangible reward for his communicativeness he endeavoured to assist me further.

"I say, missus, what was the name o' that there gentleman who stayed 'ere the night afore last? You know—the gentleman who talked such a lot to me in yon little parlour?"

"Oh, he gave his name as Purvis—Charles Purvis, of London, is what he wrote in the book," answered the landlady. "But I think you were a fool, Ben—a big fool. I didn't like that man at all. He wanted to know too much about everybody's business."

"Yes, he was a bit curious like," and the old man glanced meaningly at me. "But why was I a fool, missus?"

"Why to sell him that old bit of parchment. If nobody could make it out in Rockingham, there were lots of people up in London who could have read it. Perhaps it has to do with your fortune—you don't know."

"What!" I cried, starting to my feet; "did you sell the stranger a parchment? What kind was it?"

"It looked like a deed, or something of the sort," explained the landlady, "and it's been in Ben's family for years and years, they say."

"Young Dick gave it to me before 'e went a soldierin'. His father had given it to him, telling him to be sure and not part with it. So he gave it to me for fear he might lose it. It had a yellow seal a-hanging to it, and a whole lot o' scrawly signatures. I showed it to lots of people, but nobody could make head nor tail of it."

"And you sold it—the night before last?" I cried, in utter dismay.

"What was the good o' keepin' it? The stranger offered me half a sovereign for it, and I wasn't the one to refuse that for a bit o' dirty old parchment what nobody could read."

# XI

## Forestalled

M ere words fail to express my chagrin. Job Seal could perhaps have uttered remarks sufficiently pointed and appropriate, but for myself I could only reflect that this unknown man who called himself Mr. Purvis, of London, had forestalled me.

The parchment he had purchased of this drink-sodden old yokel might, for aught I knew, give a clue to the spot of which I was in search. We had more than a thousand golden guineas locked up safely in the bank in London, but both Seal, Mr. Staffurth, and myself felt certain that the great bulk of the treasure still remained undiscovered.

But what was the explanation of these inquiries by the mysterious Purvis? He evidently knew that the family of Knutton had been appointed hereditary guardians of the Italian's hoard, and he, like myself, was investigating the possibility of securing it.

I asked the old labourer, Ben Knutton, to describe the parchment he had sold, but owing to the landlady's sharp and well-meant remonstrance he was not communicative.

"It was all stained and faded so that you could hardly see there was any writin' on it at all," he said vaguely.

"But there was a seal on it. What was it like?"

"Oh, it was a thick, round bit o' wax what had been put on to a narrow piece of parchment and threaded through at the bottom so that it hung down."

"Did you ever notice the device on the seal?" I inquired eagerly.

"There was a lion, or summat—it were very much like what's on the stone in front o' Caldecott Manor."

That decided me. The document the foolish old simpleton had sold for half a sovereign was the one that had been in his family since the days of Queen Elizabeth, and in all probability gave some clue, if a guarded one, to the secret.

"This stranger knew all about the Knuttons?" I hazarded.

"Lor' bless you yes. He knew more about my family than I do myself. Been studying 'em, he said."

I smiled within myself. Whoever this man Purvis was he was certainly no fool.

"Well," observed the landlady, addressing me, "my own opinion is, sir, that Ben has made a very great mistake in selling the paper to a stranger. He don't know what it might not be worth."

"I quite agree," I said. "The thing should have been examined first."

"Oh," said the old man, "Mr. Beresford, who was the parson before Mr. Pocock, borrowed it from my brother Dick and kept it a long time, but couldn't make head nor tail of the thing. He said it was written in some kind of secret writing."

"In cipher, perhaps," I remarked. And it then occurred to me what Mr. Staffurth had told me, that at the end of the sixteenth century a great many private documents were so written that only those in possession of a key could decipher them. It might be so in the case of the one in question.

"How big was it?" I inquired.

"Oh, when it wor spread out, it measured about a foot square. It folded up, and there was some scribbling on the back. I remember that my father, just afore he died, called Dick to him and told him to look in the bottom of the old chest—the one I've got at home now. He did so, and brought the faded old thing out. I'd never seen it before, but my father told Dick to keep it all his life, and give it to his eldest son. He made Dick promise that."

"And before your brother Dick died he carried out his father's wish?"

"Yes, sir. Then young Dick gave it to me. I thought half a sovereign for it was a good bargain."

"It all depends upon what it contained. It might have been of great importance to your family," I said; "it might have had to do with the fortune which it is supposed to be yours by right."

"Ah, sir!" the landlady exclaimed, smiling. "We've heard a lot about that great fortune of the Knuttons. I used to hear all about it when I was a girl, how that if they had their own they'd be as rich as the Marquis of Exeter. It's an old story in Rockingham."

"It was foolish in the extreme to sell a document of the contents of which he was ignorant," I declared. "But he's parted with it, and it's gone, so, as far as I can see, nothing can be done."

"Where's the half-sovereign?" asked the landlady sharply of the old fellow.

"Spent it."

"Yes, on drink," she said. "You know very well you treated all your friends out of it, both here and at the other inns, and that you haven't been sober these two days till to-night. If you didn't have so much beer, Ben Knutton, it would be better for you, and for us too, I can tell you that."

"That's enough, missus," the old man said, "you're always grumbling, you are."

I left the old yokel sitting on a bench over a big mug of beer and chatted with the landlady. In the course of conversation I asked if she knew any one of the name of Woollerton, but she was unaware of any person bearing that cognomen. Then in the summer twilight I strolled back to my headquarters in Caldecott, much puzzled over the curious manner in which I had been checkmated by this mysterious Purvis.

As far as it went my visit there had been satisfactory, because I had established the fact that there was truth in the story of Bartholomew da Schorno's property at Caldecott, and that in the family of Knutton there had been, until two days ago, a document similar in form to that I had found on board the *Seahorse*. We had in the bank tangible proof that the owner of the *Seahorse* was a man of wealth; therefore I could not help believing that there was treasure stored somewhere ashore. Besides, the local legend of the fortune of the Knuttons added greatly to its possibility.

I smoked with a couple of farmers that evening, and learnt what I could from them. It was not much, only that a few years ago some one had taken the Manor House with an idea of turning it into a private lunatic asylum.

"Did it answer?" I asked of one.

"No. They had only three gentlemen, so I suppose it didn't pay."

Neither of the men knew anything regarding the facts I desired to prove. They were not natives of the place, one being from Orton, in Huntingdonshire, and the other from Islip, near Thrapston. So they were not versed in the legendary lore of the place.

I ate my plain supper alone, and went to bed when the house closed at ten. But betimes I was up, and before noon next day was sitting in Mr. Staffurth's little back study.

He had before him a big pile of valuable manuscripts which he was deciphering and investigating, part of his profession being to catalogue and value manuscripts for certain well-known dealers and auctioneers. This is a profession in itself, and requires the most erudite knowledge of the mediaeval literature of Europe, as well as an acquaintance with the rarity of any particular manuscript. Piled on the table was a batch just sent from one of the West-end firms who employed him. Most of the bindings were the original ones—oaken boards covered with leather, some were of purple velvet mostly faded, while the manuscripts themselves were of a varied character, Latin Bibles of the twelfth and thirteenth centuries, an exquisite fifteenth century *Horæ* with splendid illuminations and miniatures, a rare copy of what is known as *La Bible de Herman*, a fine Gothic copy of Du Guesclin, with miniatures in *camaïeu gris* heightened with gold, a tenth century Hieronymus, and a dozen other smaller manuscripts, the value of none being below fifty pounds apiece.

"Ah!" cried the old gentleman, pushing his spectacles to his forehead as I entered, "I'm very glad to see you, doctor," and he moved aside a wonderfully illuminated *Horæ* that he had been examining, counting the number of leaves, the number of lines to a column, the number of miniatures, and determining its date and where it was written.

"So you've been down to Caldecott. Well, what did you discover?"

I took the cigarette he offered and, flinging myself in the old arm-chair, related all that had transpired and all that I had discovered.

As I did so he drew towards him the old vellum volume that I had discovered on board the *Seahorse*—the book written by Bartholomew da Schorno—and opened it at the place where he had put in a slip of paper as mark.

"You certainly have not been idle," he remarked. "Neither have I. To be brief, doctor, I have, after spending the whole of yesterday upon this manuscript, at last discovered the secret referred to in the beginning."

"You have!" I gasped excitedly. "What is it? The secret of the treasure?"

"No, not exactly that," was his answer, calm and slow as befitted an expert in such a dry-as-dust subject as faded parchments. "But there is given here the key to a certain cipher which may assist us in a very great degree. There is, or rather was, in the possession of Richard Knutton and his family a certain document written in cipher explaining how and where the Italian had disposed of his secret hoard. It was written in cryptic writing in order that the Knuttons themselves, although guardians of the secret, should not be able to seize the treasure. Only by means of this book can the document entrusted to them by old Bartholomew be deciphered. Here is a full description of it. Let me read in English what it says:—

WILLIAM LE QUEUX

I Have This Day, The Fourth Of May, 1590, given into the hands of my trusted lieutenant, Richard Knutton, a parchment wherein is explained the hiding-place of all I possess, including all that I took from the Spanish galleon two years ago. I have presented unto this same Richard Knutton the Manor Farm of Caldecott as a free gift to him and to his heirs for ever, while he has sworn before God to hand down the sealed parchment to his eldest son, and so on until the gold shall be wanted for the treasury of the noble Knights of St. Stephen. The document is in cipher that no man can read, but hereunto I attach a key to it by which the secret of the treasure-house may at the proper time be revealed and its contents handed over, either to the Knights at Pisa or to the youngest representative of the house of Wollerton, as I have already willed.

"Then," remarked the old expert, "there follows an alphabet to which he has fortunately placed the cipher equivalent, and by means of which we should be enabled to make out the document in the hands of the Knuttons."

"Mr. Staffurth," I said gravely, interrupting him, "I much regret to tell you that we have been forestalled."

"Forestalled! How?" he cried, starting and turning to look at me full in the face.

I explained my meeting with the besotted Ben Knutton of Rockingham, and of how, only two days ago, he had sold for half a sovereign the actual document we wanted, and had been drunk for a couple of days afterwards.

"What bad luck!" exclaimed the old man. "What infernal luck! If we had got hold of that the secret would have been ours within an hour or two. But as the thing has passed into other hands—well, as far as I can see at present, we must remain utterly in the dark."

"Yes. But there's a great mystery surrounding the identity of the person who has so cleverly forestalled us," I said. "Who can he be? And how can he be aware of the existence of the treasure?"

The old man shook his head.

"My dear doctor," he said, "the whole affair is a very romantic and mysterious one. It certainly increases our difficulties a hundredfold, now that the last of the Knuttons has sold the parchment that has been in his family for three centuries or so. Still, we have at least one satisfaction, that of knowing that the person into whose hands it has passed can make nothing out of it without the key contained here." And he smiled with evident satisfaction.

"We must discover the identity of this man who calls himself Purvis," I said firmly. "Perhaps we can obtain it from him."

"We must—by fair means or foul," remarked Mr. Staffurth calmly, taking off his spectacles and wiping them carefully. "I agree with you entirely. We *must* recover possession of that parchment."

# XII

## Job Seal Makes a Proposal

Can you, my reader, imagine a more tantalizing position than the one in which I now found myself? It took a great deal to arouse enthusiasm in the breast of old Mr. Staffurth, whose interest in the world had seemed to me as dried up as those musty parchments he was so constantly examining. But the mystery of it all had certainly awakened him, and he was as keen as myself to get to the bottom of it—and to the treasure, of which I had promised him a small portion as repayment for his services.

Next day I went down to Fresh Wharf and found the *Thrush*, with cranes creaking over her, looking more grimy and forbidding than ever. As I went on board the men one and all saluted me, and when I knocked at the door of the captain's cabin there came a low gruff growl—

"Well, what is it now?"

I announced who I was, and was of course at once admitted. Job Seal, in shirt and trousers, had been lying in his bunk smoking, taking his ease after a full night ashore in company with his "chief." He had been reading the paper, and a big glass of brandy and soda at his elbow told its own tale.

"Come in, come in, doctor," he cried cheerily, holding out his enormous hand; "I intended to come over and see you to-night. Well, what's the latest news of Old Mystery?"

"As I told you, he's in the hands of the first specialist in lunacy in London, and under treatment at a private asylum."

"Will he get better?"

"Nobody can tell that. The doctor, however, anticipates that he will."

"Well, I hope by the time I get back from this next trip he'll have told you his story. We sail to-morrow on our usual round—Cardiff, Leghorn, Naples, Valencia, and home. But I don't suppose we'll be picking up any Noah's Arks this trip—eh?"

"No," I laughed. "I see that a paragraph has crept into the papers about our discovery, and it is discredited. One paper heads it 'A Seaman's Yarn.' I suppose some of the men have been talking about it on shore."

"Suppose so. One o' them chaps from the newspapers came aboard yesterday and began asking all about it, but I blessed him for his inquisitiveness, and sent him about his business. What the dickens has it to do with him?"

"Quite right," I said approvingly. "We ought to keep our knowledge to ourselves. People can believe or disbelieve, just as they like. If, however, they saw those bags of gold at the bank, I fancy it would convince them."

"Or if they saw Old Mister Mystery with his red velvet jacket and sword," he laughed. "Lor', doctor, I'll never forget the funny figure that chap cut when we hauled him out. He was real scared at first, wasn't he?"

His words brought back to my memory that never-to-be-forgotten evening of our discovery. The mystery of how the cumbersome old vessel had got afloat again was not one of the least connected with it.

The reason of my visit was to tell him the result of my inquiries and the neat manner in which we had been foiled. Therefore, after some preliminaries, I explained to him all that I have set down in the previous chapter. He heard me through, blowing vigorously at his pipe and grunting, as was his habit. The amount of smoke his pipe emitted was an index to his thoughts. If pleased, his pipe burned slowly, the smoke rising in a tiny thin column; but if the contrary, the smoke came forth from pipe and mouth in clouds. The cabin was now so full that I could scarcely see across it, and when I arrived at the critical point and told him how I had been forestalled, he jumped up, exclaiming—

"The son of a gun! He actually sold it for 'arf a quid!"

"He has," I answered sadly. "If we could only get it back it might be the means of bringing wealth to all of us."

"Then you really believe in all this yarn what's written in the parchments, doctor?" he asked.

"How can I do otherwise?" I said. "There are signatures and seals. Besides, I have, I think, sufficiently proved that Bartholomew da Schorno, whoever he was, lived once at Caldecott Manor, and further, that the Knuttons were owners of the Manor Farm. You must remember, too, that Mr. Staffurth is an expert, and not likely to mislead us."

"Well, doctor," he said, "the whole thing makes a queer yarn, an' that's a fact. Sometimes I almost feel as though the overhauling of Noah's Ark was a dream, only you see we've already got about a thousand quid to go shares in. Now, what I've been thinkin', doctor, is that you'll want a fair understandin' if you're goin' to follow this thing up. I'll be away, and shall have to leave it all in your hands. Now, I'm a plain-spoken man—that you know. For my own part, I'm content with the thousand quid we hauled aboard, and if you like to forego your claim to the half of it, I'll forego my claim to whatever you may find ashore. Forgive me for speakin' plain, doctor, won't you?—for it's no good a-beating about the bush."

"Well," I said, "if you are ready to accept such an agreement, I also am ready, although I think, captain, that you may be doing an injustice to yourself."

But Job Seal did not see it in that light. He was a hard-headed British skipper, and regarded a safe thousand pounds better than an imaginary million. For that nobody could blame him. On the one hand I felt regret at giving up my share of the gold, but on the other it left me open to share the treasure, if found, with the unknown descendant of the Wollertons.

So we drew out together an agreement by which I relinquished all claim to the gold in the bank, and he, on his part, withdrew any claim upon any treasure discovered by means of the parchments found on board the *Seahorse*.

I could see that after I had signed the paper Job Seal was greatly relieved. He was but human, not avaricious, he declared, but urged to the suggestion by the knowledge that he must be absent, and would be unable to assist in the search ashore.

And it so happened that for five hundred pounds I bought out my friend the skipper. Who had the best of the bargain will be seen later in this curious chapter of exciting events.

I wrote an order to the bank to deliver up the gold at Seal's order at any time, and after a final drink shook hands and left.

"I may be over to see you before we sail, doctor," were his parting words; "but if not, you'll see me, all being well, back in London in about five weeks. Good-bye," he said, heartily gripping my hand; "and good luck to you in your search."

At home in Chelsea I sat calmly reflecting, smoking the while and lazily turning over the leaves of the old fifteenth-century manuscripts, the *Decretales Summa*, the *Trithemius*, and others that I had found with the documents on board the *Seahorse*. They were evidently Bartholomew da Schorno's favourite reading, which showed that though he might have been a fierce sea-dog he was nevertheless a studious man, who preferred the old writers in their ancient manuscripts to the printed editions. They smelt musty now, but showed how well and diligently they had been studied. He must have been a devout Catholic, surely, to have studied the *Decretales* of the Friar Henry so assiduously. It was his property, for on the last leaf of vellum, in faded ink, was written his name: "Bartholomew da Schorno, Cavaliere di Santo Stefano, Maggio 5, 1579."

I tried to conjure up what manner of man he was. Probably that giant in stature whose skeleton had laid heaped in the big saloon of the *Seahorse*. If so, he had surely been a magnificent successor to the Crusaders of olden days—a powerful friend and a formidable foe. The latter he must certainly have been to tackle and capture one of the Spanish galleons sent against England. But probably no ships ever saw such fierce and sanguinary frays as those of the Knights of St. Stephen. Every man on board was a picked fighter, and against them even the dreaded power of the Barbary pirates was insufficient, for the latter were gradually crushed, not, however, without enormous bloodshed on both sides.

The power of the Corsairs at one time was so great that they constantly landed at points along what is now known as the Corniche road, between the Var mouth and Genoa, and took whole villages captive, sacking and burning the houses, and laying desolate great tracts of country. Thousands of Christians were carried into slavery to North Africa, and a veritable reign of terror existed along the Mediterranean shore.

It took nearly a hundred years for the Knights of St. Stephen to crush the robbers, but they did so, owing to their indomitable pluck and hard and relentless fighting.

I recollected the old Elizabethan portrait of the hard-faced man that hung upon the panelled wall, but could not believe that that was a picture of old Bartholomew. No, I pictured him as a merry, round-faced, easy-going type, tall to notoriety, a giant in strength, a very demon in war, and a clever and ingenious administrator where his own personal affairs were concerned.

His independence in his quarrel with the Duke of Ferrara was shown by the manner in which he sold his estates and shook the dust of the province from his feet, and his religious fervour by the fact that although a wealthy man he braved the perils of the sea and of the fight to aid and release the Christian slaves.

I could only think of him as a grand type of the past, a dandy in dress, and even in armour, a patrician in his food, and a sad dog where women were concerned. He was Italian by birth, so it was to be presumed that he loved easily, and forgot with similar facility.

But reverie would not uplift the veil of mystery that surrounded the present situation.

Now I, like you, my reader, had read all sorts of stories about hidden treasure, mostly imaginary, and all in more or less degree exciting. Treasure exists, it seems, mostly on islands the exact latitude and longitude of which is a secret, or else in caves in Guatemala or beneath the earth in Mexico—all far afield. But here I had tangible proof of a treasure deposited in rural England in the days of Good Queen Bess at some spot between the port of Yarmouth and the village of Caldecott. Therefore, if you had been in my place, would you not have searched for that mysterious Mr. Purvis who bought the missing document from a half-drunken labourer for half a sovereign?

I carefully reviewed the situation, and after due consideration could only hope for one thing—namely, that the purchaser of that parchment, finding it useless to him, might sell it to one or other of the London booksellers who deal in manuscripts—Quaritch, Maggs, Tregaskis, Bumpas, Dobell, and the others. The market for such things as codexes and interesting documents on vellum is limited, and in the hands of very few dealers; therefore, I later on wrote a letter to all of them from the list given me by Mr. Staffurth, saying that, if any document answering to the description which I gave should be offered for sale, they were commissioned to purchase it at any price up to fifty pounds.

This was, I thought, a step in the right direction. Mr. Purvis, when he found that the document he had purchased was useless, would probably dispose of it at a profit, and if he did so through any of the recognized channels, it must certainly fall into my hands.

Job Seal did not call, but three days later I received a much-smeared post-card, sent from Cardiff, regretting that he had not been able to wish me good-bye as he had intended. He ended by an inquiry after Old Mister Mystery, and asking me to send any important news to him at the Poste Restante at Leghorn.

A fortnight went by. I went one day to Ealing to see the Mysterious Man, but he was just the same, and knew me not. The weather was still hot in London, those blazing days when the very pavements seem aglow, but old Mr. Staffurth, whenever I called upon him, still sat in his back parlour poring over the codexes and valuable manuscripts submitted to him. Often I consulted him, but, like me, he could see no way by which we could advance farther. Things were at an absolute deadlock.

I believe that he rather blamed me for my settlement with Seal, feeling that, after all, the continued existence of the treasure was still uncertain, for it might have been discovered and carried away years ago. Still, towards me he was always the same courteous, low-spoken, if dry-as-dust old gentleman.

I went ever in search of the man who called himself Purvis, but although there were many persons of that name in the *London Directory* I was unable to discover the identical one who had tempted the drunken labourer with half a sovereign.

After three weeks of going hither and thither it became necessary to reflect upon matters more material, and, compelled to work at my profession for a living, I became *locum tenens* for a doctor who had a dispensary in the Walworth Road, near Camberwell Gate. Probably that part of London is well known to you, the great wide thoroughfare that is one of the main arteries of South London, but dull, grey, and overcrowded; a depressing place for a man who like myself had so recently come from weeks of the open sea and sunshine.

I still bore the bronze of the sun and salt upon my cheeks, according to the remarks of my friends, but although well in health and with an appetite like the proverbial horse, my mind was full of the mystery of the *Seahorse* and the ingenious purchase of the missing parchment.

The practice in the Walworth Road was a big and a poor one. The majority of the patients were hoarse-voiced costermongers from East Street and its purlieus, seamstresses, labourers, and factory hands. There is nothing mean in "the Road" itself, as it is called in the neighbourhood, but alas! many of the streets that run off it towards the Old Kent Road are full of squalid poverty.

It was not my duty to be at the dispensary at night, the night calls being attended to by a medical friend of the man whose practice I was taking charge of; therefore at ten o'clock each night the boy closed the door, put out the red light, and I took the omnibus for Chelsea.

One night just as the last patient, a garrulous old man with gout, had taken his departure and the cheap American timepiece on the mantelshelf was chiming ten, the signal for Siddons, the boy, to turn off the gas in the red lamp, I heard voices in the shop that had been turned into a waiting-room. It was after hours, and Siddons had his

WILLIAM LE QUEUX

orders, therefore I did not anticipate that he would disobey them. But he did, for he entered, saying:—

"There's a lady just come, sir. Must see you, sir—very urgent, she says."

"Do you know her?"

"No, sir—stranger," replied the sharp Cockney youth.

I groaned within myself, and announced my readiness to see her. She entered, and as she did so and our eyes met I rose to my feet, open-mouthed, utterly dumb.

# XIII

## A Call, and its Consequence

My visitor evidently noticed my stupefaction. She must have done, or she would not have been a woman.

The reason of my sudden surprise was not because I recognized her, but on account of her perfect and amazing beauty. Every doctor sees some pretty faces in the course of practise, but having been asked to set down the chief details of this romance, I must here confess that never in all my life had I set eyes upon such a sweet and charming countenance.

I judged her to be about twenty, and the manner in which she entered the dingy consulting-room that reeked with the pungent odour of iodoform showed that, although not well dressed, she was nevertheless modest and well bred. She wore a plain, black tailor-made skirt, a trifle the worse for wear, a white cotton blouse, a small black hat, and black gloves. But her face held me fascinated; I could not take my eyes off it. It was oval, regular, with beautifully-moulded cheeks, a small, well-formed mouth, and fine arched brows, while the eyes, dark and sparkling, looked out at me half in wonder, half in fear. Hers was a kind of half-tragic beauty, a face intensely sweet in its expression, yet with a distinct touch of sadness in its composition, as though her heart were burdened by some secret.

This latter fact seemed patent to me from the very first instant of our meeting.

"Is Dr. Whitworth in?" she inquired, in a soft, rather musical voice, when I bowed and indicated a chair.

"No," I responded, "he's not. My name is Pickering, and I am acting for the doctor, who is away on a holiday."

"Oh!" she exclaimed, and I thought I detected that her jaw dropped slightly, as though she were disappointed. "Will Dr. Whitworth be away long?"

"Another fortnight, I believe. He is not very well, and has gone to Cornwall. Are you one of his patients? If so, I shall be delighted to do what I can for you."

"No," she responded; "but my brother is, and, being taken worse, wanted to consult him."

"I shall be very pleased to see him, if you think he would care for it," I said rather eagerly, I believe, if the truth were told.

She seemed undecided. When a person is in the habit of being attended by one medical man, a fresh one is always at a disadvantage. People have such faith in their "own doctor," a faith that is almost a religion, often misplaced, and sometimes fatal. The old-fashioned family doctor with his out-of-date methods, his white waistcoat, and his cultivated gravity still flourishes, even in these enlightened days of serums and light cures. And in order to impress their patients, they sometimes prescribe unheard of medicines that are not to be found even in "Squire."

"Dr. Whitworth has attended my brother for several years, and has taken a great interest in his case," she said reflectively.

"What is his ailment?" I inquired.

"An internal one. All the doctors he has seen appear to disagree as to its actual cause. He suffers great pain at times. It is because he is worse that I have come here."

"Perhaps I can prescribe something to relieve it," I suggested. "Would you like me to see him? I am entirely at your disposal."

"You are extremely kind, doctor," she replied. "But we live rather a long way off, and I am afraid at this time of night—"

"Oh, the hour is nothing, I assure you," I laughed, interrupting her. "If I can do anything to make your brother more comfortable, I'll do so."

She was still undecided. Somehow I could not help thinking that she regarded me with a strange fixed look—a glance which indeed surprised me. Having regard to the strange *dénouement* of the interview, I now recollect every detail of it, and can follow accurately the working of her mind.

"Well," she said at last, rather reluctantly it seemed, "if you are quite sure the distance is not too far, it would be most kind of you to come. I'm sure you could give Frank something to allay his pain. We live at Dartmouth Hill, Blackheath."

"Oh, that's not so very far," I exclaimed, eager to be her companion. "A cab will soon take us there."

"Dr. Whitworth usually comes over to visit my brother once a week— every Thursday. Did he tell you nothing of his case?"

"No. Probably he considers him a private patient, while I am left in charge of the poorer people who come to the dispensary."

"Ah! I understand," she said, drawing the black boa tighter around her throat, as though ready for departure.

I made some inquiries regarding the region where her brother's pain was situated, and, placing a morphia case and bottles of various narcotics in my well-worn black bag, put on my hat and announced my readiness to accompany her.

As I turned again to her I could not fail to notice that the colour in her face a moment before had all gone out of it. She was ashen pale, almost to the lips. The change in her had been sudden, and I saw that as she stood she gripped the back of her chair, swaying to and fro as though every moment she might collapse in a faint.

"You are unwell," I said quickly.

"A—a little faintness. That is all," she gasped.

Without a moment's delay I got her seated, and rushing into the dispensary obtained restoratives, which in a few minutes brought her back to her former self.

"How foolish!" she remarked, as though disgusted with herself. "Forgive me, doctor; I suppose it is because I have been up two nights with my brother and am tired out."

"Of course; that accounts for it. You have over-taxed your strength. Have you no one who can take your place?"

"No," she responded, with a strange sadness which seemed an index to her character; "I have, unfortunately, no one. Frank is rather irritable, and will have nobody about him except myself."

Brother and sister appeared devoted to each other.

She spoke of him in a tone betraying that deep fraternal affection which nowadays is not common.

I waited while the boy Siddons closed the surgery and put out the lights, and then, having locked the outer door, we walked together to the cab-stand at the top of Beresford Street and entered a hansom, giving directions to drive to Blackheath.

The man seemed rather surprised at such an order at such an hour, but nevertheless, nothing loth to take a fare outside the radius, he whipped up, and drove straight down the Boyson Road, through into Albany Road, one of the decayed relics of bygone Camberwell when the suburb was fashionable in the days of George the Third, and on into that straight, never-ending thoroughfare, the Old Kent Road.

Seated side by side our conversation naturally turned upon conversational subjects, and presently she remarked upon the great heat of the day just closed, whereupon I told her how oppressed I had been by it, because of my recent voyage where the sea breeze was always fresh and the spray combined with the brilliant sunshine.

"Ah!" she sighed, "I would so much like to go abroad. I've never been farther than Paris, and, after all, that's so much like London. I would dearly like a voyage up the Mediterranean. The ports you put into must have been a perfect panorama of the various phases of life."

"Yes," I said, "the Italian is so different from the Syrian, the Syrian from the African, and the African from the Spanish. It is all so fresh and new. You would be charmed with it. The only disagreeable part is the return to hot and overcrowded London."

"Myself, I hate London," was her remark. "The fresh open country always appeals to me, and Blackheath, you know, is better than nothing at all."

I had to confess that I was not acquainted with Blackheath. Apart from my term at the hospital and a year or two doing *locum tenens* work in London I knew more of the country than of the Metropolis. Unless one is a London-born man one never knows and never in his heart loves London. He may delight in its attractions, its social advantages, and its pecuniary possibilities, but at heart he shudders at the greyness of its streets, the grime of the houses, and the hustling, whirling, selfish crowds. To the man country-born, be he peer or commoner, London is always intolerable for any length of time; he sighs for the open air, the green of Nature, the gay songs of the birds, and the freedom of everything. Unfortunately, however, the country is not fashionable, save in autumn for shooting and in winter for hunting, even though the London season may be, to the great majority, an ordeal only to be borne in order to sustain the social status.

I ask of you, my readers—who perhaps work in the City and go to and from the suburbs with clock-work regularity—whether you would not be prepared to accept a lower wage if you could carry on that same profession in the country and live in a house with a real garden instead of one of a row of jerry-built "desirable residences" so crowded together that what was once a healthy and splendid suburb is nowadays as cramped as any street in Central London? You know your house, a place that was run up in six weeks by a speculative builder; you know your garden, a dried-up, stony strip of back yard, where even the wallflowers have a difficulty in taking root; you know your daily scramble to get into a train for the City—nay, the hard fight to keep a roof over your head and the vulpine animal from the door. Yes, you would move into the country if you only could, for your wife and children would then be strong and well, instead of always sickly and ailing. But what is the use of moralizing? There is no work for you in the country, so you are one of millions of victims who, like yourself, are compelled to stifle and scramble in London, or to starve.

All this we discussed quite philosophically as we rode together through that hot summer's night, first past shops and barrows where lights still burned, and then away down the broad road, dark save for the long row of street-lamps stretching away into the distance.

I found her a bright and interesting companion. She seemed of a rather reflective turn of mind, but through all her conversation ran that vein of sadness which from the first had impressed itself upon me. From what she led me to believe, her brother and she were in rather straitened circumstances, owing to the former's long illness. He had been head cashier with a firm in Cannon Street, but had been compelled to resign three years ago and had not earned a penny since. I wondered whether she worked at something, typewriting or millinery, in order to assist the household, but she told me nothing and I did not presume to ask.

It is enough to say that I found myself charmed by her, even on this first acquaintance. Although so modest and engaging, she seemed to possess wonderful tact. But after all, now that I reflect, tact is in the fair sex inborn, and it takes a clever man to outwit a woman when she is bent upon accomplishing an object.

She told me very little about herself. In fact, now I recall the curious circumstances, I see that she purposely refrained from doing so. To my leading questions she responded so naïvely that I was entirely misled.

How is it, I wonder, that every man of every age will run his head against a wall for the sake of a pretty woman? Given a face out of the ordinary rut of English beauty, a woman in London can command anything, no matter what her station. It has always been so the whole world over, even from the old days of Troy and Rome—a fair face rules the roost.

We had crossed a bridge over a canal—Deptford Bridge I think it is called—and began to ascend a long hill which she told me led on to Blackheath. She had grown of a sudden thoughtful, making few responses to my observations. Perhaps I had presumed too much, I thought; perhaps I had made some injudicious inquiry which annoyed her. But she was so charming, so sweet of temperament, and so bright

WILLIAM LE QUEUX

in conversation, that my natural desire to know all about her had led me into being a trifle more inquisitive than the circumstances warranted.

"Doctor," she exclaimed suddenly, in a strange voice; "I hope you will not take as an offence what I am about to say," and as she turned to me the light of a street lamp flashing full on her face revealed to me how white and anxious it had suddenly become.

"Certainly not," I answered, not without surprise.

"Well, I have reconsidered my decision, and I think that in the circumstances you had better not see my brother, after all."

"Not see your brother!" I exclaimed, surprised.

"No. I—I'm awfully sorry to have brought you out here so far, but if you will allow me to get out I can walk home and you can drive back."

"Certainly not," I answered. "Now I'm so close to your house I'll see your brother. I can no doubt relieve his pain, and for that he would probably be thankful."

"No," she said, involuntarily laying her hand upon my sleeve, "I cannot allow you to accompany me farther;" and I felt her hand tremble.

Surely there is no accounting for the working of a woman's mind, but I certainly believed her to be devoid of any such caprice as this.

I argued with her that if her brother were in pain it was only right that I should do what I could to relieve him. But she firmly shook her head.

"Forgive me, doctor," she urged anxiously. "I know you must think me absurdly whimsical, but this decision is not the outcome of any mere whim, I assure you. I have a reason why I absolutely insist upon us parting here."

"Well, of course, if you really deny me the privilege of accompanying you as far as your house I can do nothing but submit," I said very disappointedly. "I shall tell Dr. Whitworth of your call. What name shall I give him?"

"Miss Bristowe."

"And are you quite determined that I shall go no farther?" I asked earnestly.

"Quite."

I saw some hidden reason in this decision, but what it was I failed to make out. She was certainly most determined, and, further, she seemed to have been suddenly filled with an unusual excitement, betrayed in her white, almost haggard, face.

So I stopped the cab at last, just as we reached the dark Heath.

"I must say that I am very disappointed at this abrupt ending to our brief acquaintanceship," I said, taking her hand and helping her out.

"Ah! doctor," she sighed. Then, in a voice full of strange meaning, she added: "Perhaps one day you will learn the real reason of this decision. I thank you very much for accompanying me so far. Good-night."

She allowed her hand to rest in mine for a moment; then turned and was lost in the darkness, leaving me standing beside the cab.

# XIV

## Requires Explanation

The pretty Miss Bristowe was certainly an enigma.

In that dingy consulting-room in the Walworth Road I often sat during the days that followed, musing over that curious and fruitless journey. I felt rather piqued than disappointed, for to put it bluntly I had been fooled, and left to pay nearly a sovereign to a cabman.

Her parting words to me: "Perhaps one day you will learn the real reason of this decision," seemed ominous ones, while her agitation was strange in such circumstances. She parted from me so hastily that it seemed almost as though she held me in fear. But why? I am sure I acted towards her with all the gallantry in my rather rough nature. No; the more I thought over it the more remarkable seemed the incident.

But a few days later I discovered yet a stranger circumstance. In order to find out something regarding my pretty companion on that long cab drive, I wrote to Dr. Whitworth at Bude, telling him that she had called, and inquiring the nature of her brother's complaint. To this I received a brief note saying that he had never heard of "Miss Bristowe" in his life.

Then the truth was rudely forced upon me that the woman who had held me fascinated by her beauty was actually an impostor.

What, however, could have been her object in inducing me to accompany her upon such a vain errand? Doctors see some queer things and meet with strange adventures in the course of their practice, but surely her motive in fooling me was utterly unintelligible.

Through the remaining fortnight I continued to treat the crowd of poor suffering humanity that seemed to greet me ever in the waiting-room; for Whitworth was a kindly man, hence all the poor came to him. Night after night I sat listening to the ills of costermongers and their wives, labourers, factory hands, cabmen, tram-men, and all that hard-working class that makes up lower London "over the water." Sometimes they told me their symptoms with quaint directness, using scientific terms wrongly or atrociously pronounced—the result of School Board education in elementary physiology, I suppose. But, as in every neighbourhood of that class, drink was accountable for, or aggravated, at least two-thirds of the cases that I saw. Surely it would open the eyes of the social reformer or the temperance advocate if he spent one evening in the consulting-room of a dispensary in lower London.

At last Whitworth returned, fresh and bronzed, from the Cornish coast, and as I sat handing back to him the keys of the place and receiving a cheque for my services, I mentioned the subject of Miss Bristowe.

"Ah!" he laughed, "what did you mean by that letter? I don't know any such person, nor even anyone who lives at Blackheath."

"And she said that you had attended her brother for nearly two years for some internal ailment. She came here one night to fetch you. I told her you were away, and after some persuasion she allowed me to accompany her. Then, when we got to Blackheath, she suddenly changed her mind and sent me back."

"You never saw the brother?"

"Never went to the house. She wouldn't let me."

"But you yourself suggested going with her, you say?"

"Yes," I replied, "I did."

"Pretty?"

"Very much so."

"And you were struck with her, eh?" he laughed, for he was a prosaic married man with a couple of children.

"Just a trifle," I admitted.

"Well," he said, "the girl possibly saw that you were gone on her, so she had a lark with you. You paid her cab home, and she had no objection."

"But her story was so plausible."

"Every woman can be plausible when she pleases," he said. "But are you sure she asked for me?"

"Quite certain. She first inquired for you, telling me that you were an old friend."

He laughed heartily at what he termed the woman's audacity; then, after some further discussion of the subject, we dropped it as one of those little mysteries of life that are beyond solution.

On relinquishing my position at the dispensary I wandered heedlessly hither and thither in London. The weather was still hot, more oppressive even than I had felt it at Naples or at Leghorn, and all seemed dull because my friends were away in the country or at the seaside. Through the *Lancet* I was offered a three months' engagement as assistant to a doctor in Northumberland, but I declined it, as it was too far from London. Somehow I felt it necessary, for the elucidation of the mystery of the *Seahorse*, to remain in town—why I cannot tell.

One day in response to a note, I called upon Macfarlane, the specialist in lunacy, and found him seated in his consulting-room, a fine apartment furnished in old oak, of which he was an ardent collector, and surrounded by a number of fine old clocks of various periods.

"Well, Pickering," he exclaimed cheerily, rising to greet me, "I've got some news for you about your—what shall we call him—foundling, eh?"

"That's a good description," I laughed. "Captain Seal used to call him 'Old Mister Mystery.' But what is the news?"

"Well, he's taken a decided turn for the better. I see him every day, and although at first he was bitterly hostile towards me because I wouldn't allow him to wear his sword, he has now become quite mild and tractable. And what's more, he's taken to writing, which is one of the best signs of impending recovery that we could have. Here are some of his efforts," he added, taking from a drawer a quantity of scraps of paper, from half-sheets of foolscap to bits torn from newspapers, and placing them before me. "I don't suppose you can make anything more out of them than I can. His brain is clearing, but is not yet rightly balanced. Now and then his ideas run in the direction of a design made up of creepy-looking demons and imps. There's no doubt about it, that whoever he is, he's a man of some talent. Did you see what was in the *Telegraph* the other day?"

"I saw a distorted story about the *Seahorse*," I answered.

"But on the following day there was a short statement regarding this nameless patient of ours. They sent a reporter to me to obtain further details, but I did not consider myself justified in giving them. The less the public knows about the affair the better—that's my opinion."

"Certainly," I said. "I'm very glad you did not allow yourself to be interviewed."

Then I turned myself to the uneven scribble, mostly in pencil, which had been executed by the lunatic. My hopes were quickly dashed, for I found it poor stuff. Sometimes it appeared as though he wished to write a letter, for there were the preliminary words, "Dear sister," "Dear Harry," and "My dear sir." Once he started to write a nautical song, whether of his own composition or not I am unaware. The lines, written quite distinctly, although in a shaky old-fashioned hand, were:—

*There's nothing like rum on a windy night,*
*Sing hey, my lads, sing hey!*
*When the rigging howls and you're battened tight,*
*Yo ho! my lads, Yo ho!*

On a dirty piece of newspaper was written: "Jimmy Jobson, 1st mate, went to Davy Jones's locker May 16." Another bore the statement: "Pugfaced Willie ought to have been a tub-thumper instead of sailing under the black flag. That is Andy Anderson's opinion."

The last piece I examined was half a sheet of note-paper bearing the heading, "High Elms," the paper given to patients for their correspondence. It was covered with scribble, just as a child scribbles before it can write, but in a small blank space near the bottom were the strange words: "Beware of Black Bennett! He means mischief!"

The latter had been written as a warning, but to whom addressed it was impossible to tell.

"All are, of course, the wanderings of the patient's mind," remarked Macfarlane. "Those names may possibly help us to establish his identity."

"Have you determined his age?"

"Not more than seventy, if as much," was the reply. "But I feel certain that he'll recover, if not at once, within, say, a year. This writing is a very hopeful sign. Of course, I can't say that he'll recover his speech too—probably he won't. But he can write, and by that means tell us something of how he came on board the ancient ship."

I remained with the great specialist for half an hour longer, then taking possession of the curious evidence of the old fellow's returning sanity I went back to Chelsea.

Time after time I examined that strange warning regarding "Black Bennett." Who could he be?

There was one remark about the black flag, which meant piracy. Possibly, then, this man Bennett had been a pirate at some time or other.

Anyhow, I was greatly gratified to think that ere long the Mysterious Man might be able to give us an intelligible account of himself, and although the meaning of the warning regarding "Black Bennett" was an enigma, I quickly forgot all about it.

The one point upon which all my energies were concentrated was the recovery of that cryptic document which the drunken old labourer at Rockingham had disposed of. I called at all the chief dealers in manuscripts in London and made inquiry if anything like the parchment I described had been offered for sale, but was informed that sixteenth-century parchments of that character were too common to be of sufficient value for them to consider. Codexes or charters of any century down to the fifteenth would always be looked at, but a notarial deed of so late a date as the end of the sixteenth century was beneath the notice of any of the dealers.

Early one morning I received a telegram from Mr. Staffurth, and, in response, went to Clapham Park Road in hot haste.

I found, to my surprise, a strange, black-bearded man in his study, and the old gentleman was greatly excited and alarmed. A pane of glass in the window was, I noticed, missing, and it was accounted for by his breathless statement that during the night his house had been broken into by burglars.

The black-bearded man, who was a detective, chimed in, saying:—

"It seems, sir, as though they were after some of the valuable books the gentleman has. They didn't go further into the house than this room, although the door was unlocked."

"You see what they've done, doctor—cut out a pane of glass, opened the window, forced the shutters, and got in. Look at the place! They've turned everything topsy-turvy!"

They certainly had, for papers and books were strewn all over the floor.

"Have you missed anything?" I asked quickly.

"One thing only. It is, I regret to say, that parchment deed of yours with the seven signatures. They've taken nothing else but that, although here, as you see, is an illuminated *Horæ* worth at least £300, and the twelfth-century St. Bernardus that Quaritch bid £200 for at Sotheby's last week."

"They were expert thieves," the detective remarked, "and were evidently in search of something which they knew the gentleman had in his possession."

"But the book—the book containing the cipher!" I cried, dismayed, the truth dawning upon me that the burglars had been in search of those documents of mine.

"Fortunately, they were unable to secure it," was old Mr. Staffurth's reply. "I had locked it in the safe here as a precaution against its destruction by fire." And he indicated the good-sized safe that stood in the opposite corner of the room. "You see upon it marks of their desperate efforts to open it, but with all their drills, chisels, wedges, and such-like things they were not successful. The secret of the cipher is still ours."

"Then they were hired burglars?" I said.

"That seems most probable, sir," replied the detective. "Such a thing is not by any means unusual. They were professionals at the game, whoever they were."

# XV

## Reveals Something of Importance

The thieves had made a thorough search of old Mr. Staffurth's study. Every hole and corner had been methodically examined, an operation which must have occupied considerable time.

Neither Mr. Staffurth, his housekeeper, nor the servant girl had heard a sound. It seemed that only after searching the study thoroughly had the burglars turned their attention to the safe. There were three of them, the detective asserted, for there had been a shower in the night, and he found on the carpet distinct marks of muddy shoes. The instruments they had used on the safe were of the newest kind, and it seemed a mystery why they had not succeeded in opening it.

Having discovered the parchment with the seven signatures, they most naturally searched for the other documents found on board the derelict. Fortunately, however, the book penned by the noble Bartholomew remained in its place of security.

Of course this desperate attempt to gain possession of it removed all doubt that there was some one else besides myself endeavouring to solve the secret. But who could it be? Who could possibly know what was written upon those dry old parchments save Job Seal, Mr. Staffurth and myself? Seal was an honest man, quite content with the share of the spoil already in his hands, while it was to the interest of the old palæographist to solve the mystery in conjunction with myself.

Did the hoard of the sea-rover still exist?

Hundreds of times I put to myself that question. For answer I could only reflect that there was some one else, an unknown rival, who believed that it did, and who was sparing no effort to obtain the secret of its hiding-place.

Of course, it was quite possible that when the place of concealment was discovered it might be empty. Over three hundred years had passed, and in that time accident might have led to its discovery. There had certainly not been any betrayal of the secret, for while one cryptic document had been in the hands of the Knuttons, the key to it had been afloat, or submerged beneath the sea.

I took Mr. Staffurth aside, and we agreed to tell the police as little as possible, lest the facts should leak out to the newspapers. Therefore the old expert explained that the parchment books in his possession were precious ones, and most probably the thieves desired to obtain possession of them on behalf of some other person. So the detective, with an assistant, made copious notes, examined the marks of chisels and jemmies, and after a great show of investigation left the house.

"Ah, doctor," exclaimed the old man with a sigh of relief, after they had gone; "I had no idea that our rivals were so close upon us. I think you had better deposit that book in your bank for greater security. The scoundrels, whoever they were, may pay me another visit."

I expressed regret that he should thus have suffered on my account, but the poor old gentleman only laughed, saying, "My dear doctor, how could you help it? They want to get hold of the key to their cipher. Possibly, in their document, it is stated that there is a key to it in existence."

"But how could they be aware that it is in your possession?"

"Because you are undoubtedly watched," he said. "I shouldn't wonder but what every movement of yours is known to your rivals."

"Well," I laughed, "fortune-hunting seems an exciting game."

"Mind that it doesn't grow dangerous," was the old man's ominous warning.

"But you don't anticipate any personal violence, do you?"

"I think it is wise to be very careful," he said. "You have a secret rival in these investigations of yours, and where a fortune is concerned some people are not over-scrupulous. We have here an illustration of their desperate efforts—the employment of professional burglars."

"But if even we found the Italian's hoard, would it not belong to the Wollertons?"

"I suppose it would. But," smiled the man, "if we could not discover any Wollerton, and held the property for ourselves, I think our position would practically be impregnable."

"The Government might claim it."

"No. It would not be treasure-trove. We have all the facts concerning it in our possession. It would not be a hoard accidentally discovered and without owner. One-third of it, remember, has to go to a Knutton."

"Yes, to that drunken fool down at Rockingham. He deserves, at any rate, to lose his portion," I said.

WILLIAM LE QUEUX

Mr. Staffurth brought forth the old parchment-book from the safe, and opening it at a place marked with a slip of paper, re-examined the straight row of cipher letters with their equivalents, while I rose and looked over his shoulder.

"The writer was a careful and methodical man, even though he might have been a fierce and blood-thirsty sea-rover, and a terror to the slave-raiders. He certainly took the very best precaution possible so that the secret of the whereabouts of his hoard should not be discovered, for, as you see, the document left in the hands of the Knuttons was useless without this book, and the book useless without the document. It was evidently his intention to return to England and deposit the book in some place of safety, but before he did so disaster befell the *Seahorse*, and she went down."

Together we packed the book in brown paper, tied it with string, and securely sealed it, using the seal upon my watch guard, and that same afternoon I deposited it with the bank manager, receiving a receipt for it.

But before leaving old Mr. Staffurth I assisted him to put his books in order, and we chatted together the while.

It was his opinion that if I went to Rockingham again I might obtain some news of the movements of the man Purvis. Indeed, he was in favour of my making a short visit there in order, if possible, to ascertain the identity of any person making inquiries.

"You see," he said, "we are working quite in the dark. Our rivals know us, but we do not know them. That places us at a distinct disadvantage. If we knew them we might outwit them."

I saw the force of his argument. He was a man of sound common sense, and never gave an opinion without careful consideration. It certainly seemed quite feasible that our rivals might be down at Rockingham or Caldecott.

"Do you think it worth while to rent the Manor House from the Kenways?" I suggested. "They are only too anxious to get out."

"Is the rent high?"

"About fifty pounds a year."

"Well, doctor," responded the old gentleman, "I certainly think that the affair is worth spending fifty pounds upon. You see, you've bought Captain Seal out of it, and the matter is now practically your own affair. Besides, if you rented the Manor you would keep out your rivals. Yes. Most decidedly; go down and take the place for a year."

"Not a very desirable place of residence," I laughed.

"I know. But be careful these other people don't again forestall you. Go down there to-morrow and make the bargain at once. The old place may contain the treasure, or it may not. In any case, no harm will be done by your being the tenant for a year."

Thus it was that in the blaze of the noontide sun I next day passed up the little main street of Caldecott, traversed the somewhat odorous farm-yard, and entered the silent, moss-grown court of the Manor House.

A fair-haired slip of a girl came to the door in response to my ring, and after a little while Mrs. Kenway, who had gone to put herself tidy to receive visitors, entered the dining-room—that room which contained my pet abomination, furniture covered with brown American cloth.

The good woman seemed quite pleased to see me again. Her husband was out on his round, she said, but nevertheless she offered me the simple hospitality of a glass of milk.

"Well, Mrs. Kenway," I commenced, after I had grown a little cool, "I've come on an errand which I dare say will give you some gratification. When I was here some time ago you told me you wished to sub-let your house. I have spoken to my friend about it, and he has sent me to take it on his behalf. I forget exactly the rent you named."

"Well, sir," responded the woman, "funnily enough I'm in treaty with a gentleman who wants to take the place. I promised to make no arrangement until I heard from him."

"Who is he?" I asked, quickly. "What is his name?"

"I forget, sir, but I have it written on an envelope upstairs. I'll go and get it." And she left the room.

I determined to take the place at all hazards. I was by no means a rich man, but even if I had to pay a hundred pounds to secure the ramshackle old house it must be done.

She returned with a crumpled envelope in her hand, upon which was scribbled in pencil: "George Purvis, 7, Calthorpe Street, Gray's Inn Road, London."

My heart gave a bound. Here was the actual address of the man of whom I had been for weeks in search, the purchaser of the key to the hidden wealth! I endeavoured to betray no surprise, but to conceal my jubilant feeling was certainly difficult. If I had a clue to my rivals, I had also a clue to the employers of those burglars who had so terribly upset poor old Mr. Staffurth's study.

"How long ago is it since this gentleman came to see you?" I inquired, scribbling the address on my shirt-cuff and handing back the envelope.

"His first visit was two or three days after you came," the woman said. "He seemed very much taken with that coat o' arms on the wall outside, and asked me if I knew anything of the history of the place. Of course I don't. I only know that somebody named Walshe lived here about a hundred years ago, for their graves are in the churchyard. The gentleman stayed at the Sonde Arms at Rockingham for a day or two, but before he went back to London he told me that he might possibly take the house off my hands. He came again, about a week ago, had another look round, and then made me promise not to let it until I heard from him."

"What rent did you ask?"

"Fifty pounds a year."

"And he thought it too much?"

"Well, he seemed to hesitate. Perhaps he thinks he can get it cheaper, but he won't."

I wondered whether this hesitation was due to want of funds. More probably, however, it was because of the uncertainty of the whereabouts of the hidden loot.

"The house would just suit my friend, who wants quiet for his studies," I said, "and if you will let it, I'm prepared to pay you a year's rent down, at this minute."

She shook her head.

I had misjudged her, believing that ready money would tempt her to a bargain. But she was a woman of her word, it seemed, for her answer was:—

"No, sir. I'm very sorry, but you see I gave a promise to the gentleman, and I can't break it."

"But you didn't give your promise in writing, did you? You did not give him an option of the property?"

"I wrote nothing. I merely told him that I wouldn't let it before he had given me a decided answer."

"He may be a year deciding, or even more!" I pointed out. "Are you prepared to wait all that time?"

"No. I can write to him."

Such a course would not suit me. If she wrote saying that she had another prospective tenant, then he would clinch his bargain at once.

No; my object was to oust him in this. He had outwitted me once, but I was determined he should not get the better of me on a second occasion.

My next thought was to offer a higher rent than that asked, so as to give her a margin of profit on the transaction, but suddenly a thought occurred to me that it was her husband, not herself, who held the lease, and perhaps I might not find him so scrupulous about keeping promises if there was a ten-pound note to be got out of the bargain.

So I expressed regret and all that sort of thing, and said that I would like to see Mr. Kenway on his return.

"He went to Stamford by train this morning," she replied. "I'm expecting him every minute."

So I went out and wandered through the neglected wilderness that had once been a garden. Everywhere were signs of a long departed glory, broken statuary, ivy-grown balustrades, and a fine old sculptured sundial, now, alas, entirely hidden by creepers and ivy.

Mrs. Kenway's husband returned in about half an hour—a thin-faced, dark-bearded, thick-set little man with a pair of sharp black eyes, which told me the instant I was introduced to him that he was a good business man and ready for a bargain.

Seated with him on an American cloth-covered chair in that inartistic dining-room, I commenced to chat about insurance matters, and learnt that business was not very good about those parts. Then, in his wife's presence, I approached the proposal for taking the house off his hands, explaining what Mrs. Kenway had told me on a previous visit regarding its unsuitability for the reception of paying guests.

"Well," he said, in a gruff voice, "things do happen strangely. You're the second gentleman we've had after the house within a week or two. We'd be pleased enough to let it, only my wife has promised somebody else in London."

"She has told me that," I said. "Of course, if you refuse to let the place, well and good. But not only am I ready to sign an agreement with you this afternoon and pay you the whole year's rent in advance to-day, but in order to secure the place for my friend I'm ready to make a bargain with you."

"What's that?"

"I'll give an extra ten-pound note over and above what you've asked this other gentleman."

Husband and wife exchanged glances. I saw, as I had expected, that ten pounds and release from the burden of the house, which was far too large for people in their circumstances, was a temptation.

"Well, my dear?" he asked. "What do you say? Shall we let the place and clear out?"

"I've given you my offer," I interposed, with a careless air. "My friend commissioned me to find him a quiet place at once, and I am prepared to pay more than its worth because of my own family associations with the place."

"Well, we have the other gentleman, you know," insisted the woman.

"It's not at all certain if he'll take it," I said. "And if he does, he won't pay so much as I offer."

The man was ready to clinch the bargain, but the woman was one of those scrupulously honest bodies who hesitated to break her word.

They talked together for a few moments out in the hall, while I awaited their decision.

It was in my favour, and within half an hour the necessary preliminaries were executed, agreements were written out and signed, and Mr. Kenway had in his pocket my cheque for sixty pounds, in exchange for which I held his lease and his agreement handing the place over to my care, subject, of course, to the landlord's approval.

In one instance, at least, I had got the better of Mr. Purvis, and, what was more to the point, I had obtained his address.

# XVI

## Mrs. Graham's Visitor

When I returned to town that same evening and told Staffurth he became wildly excited.

"Really, doctor," he said, "the matter increases in interest daily."

"When I take possession of the Manor, I think we ought to make a search," I replied. "We must not allow burglars to enter there, or they may forestall us after all."

"Of course, of course. The treasure may be hidden in the house for aught we know. It is important that we should be the first to make a thorough examination of the place."

"But what is most important of all is that we've gained the address of this man Purvis."

"Calthorpe Street is not the most respectable neighbourhood in London," he observed. "Do you know it?"

I confessed to ignorance, but next morning went to Gray's Inn Road and found the dingy street running off to the right, opposite the end of Guilford Street. No. 7 was, I discovered, a grimy, smoke-blackened private house, like most of the others, set back behind iron railings, with a deep basement. The windows sadly required cleaning, and at them hung limp and sooty lace curtains which had once been white.

Walking on the opposite side of the pavement I passed and repassed it several times, noting its exterior well. The windows of the first floor were better kept than those of the dining-room, and on a small round table I noticed a doll. From those facts I gathered that the place was let out in apartments, and that the occupants of the first floor were a man with his wife and little daughter. It was not yet eight o'clock, and the newspaper man passing left a paper beneath the knocker—a *Sporting Life*, which further showed the racing proclivities of at least one of the inmates. Presently, as I watched, the postman came along, and, slipping several letters into the slit in the front door, passed on without knocking.

I hurried along the street into the King's Cross Road, and, when he turned the corner, accosted him.

At first he was inclined to be uncommunicative, as a good servant of the Post Office should be, but by the application of a small refresher his tongue was unloosened, and he told me that the occupants of No. 7 were racing people.

"They're bookmakers, I fancy," he added. "They have lots of letters by every post, and post-cards about tips and things."

"Do you know the name of George Purvis?"

"Yes. It's some one who has, I think, come to live there lately."

"Do you know him?"

"Not at all. Never seen him."

"How long ago did you deliver the first letter addressed to Purvis?"

"About three weeks, I think. But if you want to know more, why don't you ask the servant? She's doing the steps now. I daresay she'd tell you all about him."

I took the man's advice, and returning to the house found a dirty, ill-dressed girl in canvas apron slopping water over the front steps and rubbing hearthstone upon them.

With some caution I addressed her, and, having slipped half a crown into her hand, told her to say nothing of my inquiries, but to respond to my questions.

"Do you know a gentleman named Mr. George Purvis who lives here?" I asked.

"I know Mr. Purvis, sir, but 'e don't live 'ere. 'E only calls for his letters sometimes, and missus gives them to him."

"What's your mistress's name?"

"Mrs. Graham."

"And who are the people who live upstairs?"

"They're the Johnsons. Mr. Johnson is on the turf, they say. 'E goes to race-meetin's in a white hat and a bag slung over his shoulder."

"But where does Mr. Purvis live?"

"I don't know, sir. He comes sometimes to see Mrs. Graham."

"Does he receive many letters?"

"Oh, two or three a week, perhaps."

"Well," I said, "if you want to earn a sovereign you can do so very easily. Find out for me where Mr. Purvis lives, and I'll give you a sovereign."

The girl, although of true Cockney type, dirty and slatternly, was nevertheless intelligent.

She seemed somewhat dubious, replying:—

"I'm very much afraid, sir, that I won't be able to do it. But I'll try, if you like."

"Yes, try," I said eagerly. "I shall pass by now and again about this same hour in the morning, and when you've been successful, tell me. By the way, what kind of man is Mr. Purvis?"

"Well, sir, 'e's very thin, rather tall, with a pale face and sandy hair. But I must get on; Mrs. Graham's coming down."

"Recollect what I've told you, and if you say nothing to anybody I'll make it thirty shillings. You understand?"

"All right, sir," answered the girl, bending again to her work, and I passed along the street and out again to the Gray's Inn Road.

I was once more disappointed, for I believed that I had tracked my rival to his home. But it seemed that the fellow was far too wary. He received his correspondence through the hands of this woman, Mrs. Graham, thus showing that he wished to conceal his place of abode. When a woman is the receiver of a man's letters, it is always looked upon by the police as a bad sign.

Having a description of this man Purvis, I resolved to lay in wait for him to visit Mrs. Graham, and then to follow him home. Therefore, through that day and several days following I kept such a watchful eye upon all that went on in Calthorpe Street that I saw the policeman on the beat suspected me of loitering for the purpose of committing a felony. I therefore called him aside, gave him a card, and told him that I was keeping observation for the arrival of a tall, fair, thin gentleman, who would call at No. 7, and that if he assisted me I would make it worth his while.

We were not long in making the compact, and the fact that he could watch while I went into a saloon bar in the Gray's Inn Road to snatch my hasty meals made the observation much more certain and easy.

A whole week I spent in those squalid, smoky streets, sometimes lounging at one end of Calthorpe Street and sometimes at the other, relieved now and then by the constable, who came and stood at the opposite corner as signal that I was allowed half an hour's repose.

Try yourself a day at the corner of a London street awaiting the arrival of a person you have never seen, but whose description has been given to you, and you will at once discover how wearisome a task it is. Hundreds of men nearly answering the description will pass you, and your hopes are raised as every one approaches.

Still, I intended to outwit this clever adventurer, whoever he was. He, or his accomplices, had obtained possession of at least one object that was my property, the document with the seven signatures, and I

WILLIAM LE QUEUX

intended that he should be hoist by his own petard even though I had to wait for him a year.

The servant girl was entirely in my confidence. Each morning as she "did" the steps I passed the time of day with her, and she informed me that Mr. Purvis had not called, although her mistress was expecting him, as letters were awaiting him.

Now, it seemed to me probable that if Mrs. Graham knew the man's address, and he did not fetch his letters, she would either send him a line or re-address the correspondence. Therefore, I gave instructions to the girl to be on the lookout for the address on any letter she might be sent to post, and make a note of it for me.

One afternoon about five o'clock, while I was hastily taking a cup of tea in a shop in King's Cross Road, my friend the constable put his head inside and beckoned me out.

"The cove you're waiting for has just gone into No. 7, sir," he said; "tall, fair moustache, freckled face, and wearin' a straw hat."

In an instant I was on the alert and, full of excitement, walked back with him to the corner of Calthorpe Street.

"You're going to follow him, I suppose?"

"Certainly. I want to discover where he lives."

"Does he know you?"

"Probably he does."

"Then you'll have to be wary if you're going to follow him."

"Trust me," I replied confidently. "I shall take every precaution."

We separated, and impatiently I awaited the appearance of the man who was my rival.

Already Mr. Kenway had written to the landlord of the Manor House, and only that morning I had received his consent. Therefore, the matter was concluded, and I held the tenancy of a lonely, weather-worn old place, without possessing a stick of furniture to make it habitable.

But I was anxious to see what manner of man was this Purvis, the smart investigator who had paid half a sovereign for that most precious of all documents. How was it possible that he could have knowledge of the affair, save, perhaps, from the local legend that the Knutton family were entitled to a fortune? The gossip in Rockingham and elsewhere might possibly have aroused his curiosity, but if so he must also have been aware that I held the key to the cipher. Thereby hung a mystery.

Once it occurred to me that Job Seal might be working against me, but on full reflection I saw that such suspicion was unfounded. Seal had foregone his claim in return for half of the gold, and had sailed for the Mediterranean perfectly satisfied.

No. The affair had, I saw, grown into a desperate one; a fortune was awaiting one or other of us—the man who was clever enough to outwit the other.

For an hour I waited at the street corner, my eyes ever upon that flight of steps which led to the dark green sun-blistered door, until I was weary and exhausted. Purvis was undoubtedly having tea and gossiping with the widow.

I saw my friend the servant girl come to the dining-room window, pull the yellow lace curtains aside, and, putting her head out, look up and down the street. She caught sight of me, and with the knowledge that I was on guard, quickly withdrew.

Was it a signal that he was about to come forth?

I waited. Seven o'clock struck, then eight, but still no sign of him. He was surely making a long visit. As darkness closed in I moved nearer the house, in order that he might not be able to slip away unobserved.

Suddenly, a little after nine, the girl opened the door and a visitor emerged. But I was disappointed. A woman in deep black descended the steps and turned to walk in my direction. The instant I saw this I hurried on, crossed the road, and then slackened pace in order that she should overtake me.

She was not long in doing so, and as she passed I turned and looked her full in the face.

Judge my surprise when I recognized her to be none other than the girl who had taken me on that mysterious journey to Blackheath!

# XVII

## The Seller of the Secret

"W hy, Miss Bristowe!" I cried. "Perhaps you don't recollect me?"

She started quickly, and drew back for a moment, her countenance blanching; then looking into my face, she said, with a timid laugh: "Why, of course, doctor! But have you forgiven me for taking you on that fool's errand?"

"Yes, long ago," I laughed. "But our meeting this evening is certainly unexpected. Have you friends in this neighbourhood?"

She replied in the affirmative, but without giving me any explanation.

"And your brother?" I asked, recollecting Whitworth's declaration that he had never heard of her. "Is he any better?"

"Oh, a great deal, thanks," was her reply. "He took a turn for the better that night I came to you, and has improved ever since."

She looked, I think, prettier than on that night when we had driven together to Blackheath. But she had deceived me in regard to her statement concerning Dr. Whitworth, so I supposed she was deceiving me now.

She was in a hurry to get home, she told me, and my first impulse was to follow her secretly, but when I recollected that the man for whom I had been so long in wait was actually inside No. 7, I decided to keep watch upon him rather than upon her.

The fact that she had come from that house was in itself curious, and made me suspect that her visit to me on that night in Walworth had some secret connection with the scheme of this man Purvis.

The manner in which she was hurrying when I stopped her made it plain that she was late for some appointment.

There were two courses open to me, namely: to follow her, or else to remain and await Purvis. The discovery that she was friendly with some person at No. 7 had suddenly aroused within me a desire to know her place of abode in order to make secret inquiries concerning her. Yet, after all, my chief business was with Purvis, so I decided to remain on watch for him.

With her consent, therefore, I saw her into an omnibus for Ludgate Hill, whence she told me she would take train home, and when I parted from her I expressed a fervent hope that we might meet again before very long.

"Good-night," she said, as we shook hands. "Yes, I hope we shall meet again—in more fortunate circumstances than to-night." And she mounted into the omnibus and left me.

What could she mean by more fortunate circumstances? I was puzzled at her words, but at last their truth became apparent.

Through many hours, till far into the night, I waited in that vicinity for the man who was my rival. But he never came out, neither that day nor the next.

The reason, I afterwards found, was simple enough. The servant had played me false and told him everything; therefore he had waited until darkness set in, and then climbed over several garden walls into Wells Street, a short thoroughfare running parallel at the back, and quietly emerged into Gray's Inn Road.

So while I had waited patiently in front he had ingeniously escaped at the back, aided most probably by the mysterious Miss Bristowe and Mrs. Graham, whose character, of course, I had no means of ascertaining. According, however, to my friend the constable, some shifty individuals lived in that neighbourhood.

In any case I had the dissatisfaction of knowing that all my vigilance had been naught, and that the man Purvis would never again run the gauntlet of Calthorpe Street. He would no doubt arrange for another address, and if so I might obtain it by means of the Kenways, providing, of course, that they had not yet told him the house was let.

I took counsel with Mr. Staffurth, as I did very frequently nowadays.

I blamed myself that on that night I was alone. Had I an assistant with me he might have followed the young lady home. Staffurth being of the same opinion, suggested that I should accept the services of his nephew, a young bank clerk who had been compelled to leave his occupation in the City temporarily on account of ill-health. This young fellow, whom I had met once or twice at Clapham, was named Philip Reilly. Smart, well dressed, and well educated, he had been an athlete before his illness, and had carried off many prizes at Lillie Bridge and other places.

He was just the sort of young man to be useful, and when that evening he sat in his uncle's study and the full facts of the case were related to him in confidence, he became highly excited over it, and announced his eagerness to act under my directions.

"We have a formidable enemy to contend with, Philip," the old gentleman pointed out. "And recollect that whatever may happen you must act with due caution so as not to play into the hands of our rivals."

"Trust me for that," he said. "The affair sounds exciting, at all events."

"Yes," I remarked, "and matters will grow more exciting before long, I anticipate."

"But this Miss Bristowe," he exclaimed. "Have we no means of rediscovering her?"

"At present, I am sorry to say, we haven't," I responded. "We may possibly get hold of Purvis's new postal address, and if we do so it may lead us back to Miss Bristowe, who seems to me somehow associated with him. How, of course, I can't tell."

Reilly sat with folded arms, his clean-shaven face bearing a deep, thoughtful look as he puffed his pipe. It is not given to every one to be engaged on a treasure hunt, and from the first moment when he was told about it its interest overwhelmed him and he was eager to make a commencement.

After a long consultation it was arranged that we should both go down to Caldecott and endeavour to find out Purvis's new address. It was also agreed that before we took another step we ought to be acquainted with the personal appearance of our rival.

To work in the dark any longer might, we foresaw, prove fatal to our object; therefore, on the following day, I introduced Reilly to the Kenways as the new tenant of the Manor House.

Fortunately they had not communicated with Purvis. Hence I took them somewhat into my confidence, and induced Mr. Kenway to write a letter to Calthorpe Street, asking whether he intended to take the house, and requesting the favour of a reply.

This he did at my dictation, and I had the satisfaction of putting the letter in the post-box at Rockingham. By that ruse I hoped to gain knowledge of Purvis's new address. As had already been proved, he was what is vulgarly known as "a slippery customer," but both Reilly and myself determined that if we once knew his postal address we would very quickly come up with him.

We had taken up our quarters at the Sonde Arms, at Rockingham, and very comfortable and rustic they were after the dust and heat of London. My long and unavailing vigil in that stifling side street had rather pulled me down. Day after day I had waited there, often hungry and thirsty, and at all times dusty and uncomfortable, compelled to eat as I could, and to hobnob with all and sundry, until my very heart seemed stifled by the dust of the throbbing city.

But in old-world Rockingham, even on the most sultry day, were soft zephyrs that fanned our cheeks. We ate in a room at the back, and to us, through the open window, came the sweet scent of the climbing roses and honeysuckle, and the mingled perfume of the old-fashioned cottage garden behind. The fare was plain and wholesome, the ale home-brewed and of the best, and we also had an opportunity to gossip with the drink-sodden old simpleton Ben Knutton.

The Kenways were looking for other quarters, therefore we could not yet take possession of the Manor House. Reilly had given forth that he was a student, a man of means, and something of an invalid, therefore he had hired the house for the purposes of being quiet and able to study without such distractions as there were in London.

He was full of ingenuity, which I quickly recognized after he had associated himself with me. He made a minute inspection of the house I had taken for him, and afterwards became possessed of the fixed idea that the treasure was secreted behind the panelling of the centre upstairs room. Why, I know not. But no argument of mine would remove the idea, and he was frantically anxious to obtain possession of the premises in order to secure the old Italian's hoard.

We were, however, compelled to exercise considerable patience. We could not hurry the outgoing tenants, neither dare we betray any undue anxiety regarding the place. We could only await a response from Purvis.

It came at last after nearly a week of idle waiting. Mr. Kenway handed it to me, saying:—

"It seems as though he wants to take the place after all."

"He's too late," I laughed, and eagerly read the letter, which was to the effect that he had not yet decided, but would write giving a definite answer in a couple of days. The letter was headed, "14, Sterndale Road, Hammersmith, London," and to that address Mr. Kenway was asked to write.

Our ruse had worked satisfactorily. We were again cognizant of the address—the postal address—of our mysterious rival.

Reilly was eager to return to London in search of him, but we remained at Rockingham yet another day, making inquiries and getting on good terms with most of the people with whom we came into contact.

Ben Knutton was, of course, closely questioned, and in reply to my inquiry whether he had since met the gentleman who purchased the bit of parchment from him, he said:—

"Yes. 'E came about a fortni't ago and asked me if I had anything else to sell, and I told him that I hadn't."

"He called on you at your cottage?"

"Yes. One night after I came 'ome from work. He made me let him look through all the things I had. I told him that I'd heard that the parchment I sold him was worth a lot o' money, and he asked who told me. I explained that a gentleman from London had been asking about it after he had bought it, and he laughed, saying: 'I know the man; 'e's a fool, 'e is.'"

"Meaning me, eh?"

"I suppose so, sir, of course, beggin' your pardon."

"Well, Mr. Knutton, I don't think I'm much of a fool," I laughed. "That man swindled you, that's all."

"Then do you really think, sir, that the parchment had something to do with our property?" he asked in surprise.

"Possibly it may have," was my response. "Of course I've never seen it, so can't say."

"Well, sir," the old labourer burst forth, "I don't like that man at all. 'E ain't no gentleman, that I'm sure."

He had, I supposed, failed to "stand" the necessary quantity of beer which, in Knutton's eyes, stamped the gentleman.

"Why not?" I inquired.

"Because he made a lot of unkind remarks about you, sir," was his answer. "He told me that you were trying to swindle me out of the money we ought to have, and a long yarn showing you up to be one of the worst o' blackguards."

"Very kind of him, I'm sure," I laughed. "One day, however, we shall see who's the scoundrel and adventurer. In the meantime, Knutton, just beware of any future dealings with him."

"I will, sir," was the man's reply. "I'm very sorry I ever sold that parchment. I only wish I'd showed it to you. You're a gentleman as would perhaps have been able to read it."

"Ah, Knutton, I only wish you had kept it for me," I responded, with a heartfelt sigh. "But it's useless to cry over spilt milk, you know. We must make the best of it. All you have to do, however, is to keep a still tongue in your head and beware of any other gentleman from London."

"Oh, I will, sir, now. You can rely on me—that you can." And the old fellow raised his great mug of beer and emptied it at a single gulp.

His capacity for ale, like that of many farm labourers, was simply astounding.

# XVIII

## The Silent Man's Warning

P hilip Reilly, whose energy seemed indefatigable, although he was
yet half an invalid, left me next morning and returned to town.

In council, in my airy little bedroom with the attic window
embowered by creeping roses, we arrived at the conclusion that he
would have more chance of success in gaining information than myself,
therefore I dispatched him to London in order to keep an observant eye
upon the address in Sterndale Road.

For several reasons I remained in the neighbourhood of Caldecott. First,
I was apprehensive lest Purvis and his associates—for I felt convinced that
he was not acting alone—might make a forcible attempt to investigate the
Manor House. It was quite evident they suspected that the treasure might
be hidden therein, otherwise they would not have been in treaty for a lease
of the place. When they knew that I had forestalled them their chagrin
would, I anticipated, know no bounds. Hence I felt constrained to remain
on guard, as it were, until I could take possession of the place.

Those warm autumn days were charming. I had brought with me a
camera, and, as excuse for remaining in that rural neighbourhood, took
photographs. I found many picturesque pastoral scenes in the vicinity,
and wandered hither and thither almost every day. The Countess of
Cardigan kindly permitted me to photograph on her estate, and I
took many pictures of the beautiful old hall at Deene, one of the most
imposing and historic homes of Northamptonshire, the Park, and the
picturesque lake, which was once the fishpond of the monks, when
Deene was an abbey and carp the weekly fare on Fridays. To Laxton
Hall, to Fineshade Abbey, to Blatherwycke Park, to Apethorpe Hall,
the noble Jacobean seat of the Westmorland family, and to Milton, the
fine Elizabethan house of the Fitzwilliams, I went, taking pictures for
amusement, and endeavouring to make the villagers of Rockingham
and Caldecott believe that I was a photographic enthusiast. Truth to
tell, I was not. I entertain a righteous horror of the man with a camera,
and if I were Chancellor of the Exchequer I would put a tax on cameras
as upon dogs. The man who takes snap-shots can surely afford to pay
seven-and-sixpence a year towards the expenses of his country.

Letters from Reilly showed that although he was keeping a careful observation upon 14, Sterndale Road—which had turned out to be the shop of a small newsvendor—he had not been able to meet the gaunt, fair-moustached individual whom we knew as George Purvis.

The days passed, for me long, idle days, when time hung heavily on my hands. Nothing occurred to disturb the quiet tenor of my life in that rural spot, until late one evening while I was walking along the high road from Caldecott back to Rockingham.

There had been a garden *fête* given by the Vicar, and in order to kill time I had attended it, returning home later than I had anticipated, because I had met Mr. Kenway and we had gossiped. He had found another house, and was to move a week later.

The Sonde Arms at Rockingham is by no means a gay hostelry. It is quiet, old-fashioned, and eminently respectable. Roysterers and hard drinkers like Ben Knutton were relegated to a "tap" at the rear of the premises, and were never encouraged by the innkeeper.

It was past eleven o'clock, a dark, overcast night, and as I trudged along the road to Rockingham, lonely at that hour, I was wondering what success Reilly had had in London. For some days I had received no word from him, and had become somewhat anxious, for it had been arranged between us that he should either write or wire every alternate day, so that we should always be in touch with each other.

I had traversed nearly half the distance between the two villages, and had entered the part of the road which, passing through a spinney, was lined on either side by oaks, which entirely shut out every ray of faint light, so that I was compelled to walk with my stick held forward to feel the way. The complete darkness did not extend for more than a hundred yards or so, but as there were, I knew, deep ditches at each side of the road I guided myself with caution.

Suddenly, without warning, I heard a stealthy movement behind me, and ere I could turn felt myself seized by the coat-collar in such a manner that I was unable to turn and face my assailant, while almost at the same instant I felt other hands going over me in front. My wrists were held while my money was carefully extracted from my pocket, and my wallet—probably because it was believed to contain bank-notes—was also taken from me. I shouted, but no one came to my assistance. I was too far from either village.

So dark it was that I could not distinguish the thieves, but I believed there were three of them. The hands that held my wrists were soft, as though unused to manual labour, but the muscles seemed like iron. I was utterly powerless, and even though I shouted again and again no single word was uttered by the robbers. They made short work of my pockets, save that they did not think to feel inside my waistcoat where, in a secret pocket I generally have there, I carried a serviceable Colt. I, however, had no opportunity for self-defence, because when they had finished I was run backwards, struck violently on the head, and tripped up into the ditch at the wayside, while they made good their escape. Fortunately, I fell upon my hands, and managed to save myself from going into the water.

In an instant I was on my feet, revolver in hand, standing on guard.

But as I stood with ears strained to the wind I heard the sound of footsteps hurrying in the distance, and from afar off there came to me a low, ominous whistle. The fellows were probably tramps, but I knew quite well that they were a desperate party, for in the struggle I had grasped a formidable life preserver which one of them was carrying. It was a pity that the darkness was too complete to allow me to see their faces. No doubt the final blow on the head had been delivered with the life preserver and was meant to stun me, but fortunately it did not.

The attack had been so sudden and complete that for a moment I remained stock still. Then, angered that I should have fallen so completely into their power, I walked on to Rockingham. I prized my watch and chain as a gift from my mother, long since dead. They were not valuable; indeed, no pawn-broker would have given three pounds for the lot, therefore the haul of the thieves had not been a great one so far as value was concerned.

Having reached the Sonde Arms and related my unpleasant experience, the village constable was called, and I gave him a description of the property stolen from me.

"I expect they were tramps, sir," he said; "just lately I've noticed several suspicious-looking characters loitering in the neighbourhood and sleeping under haystacks. They mostly come from London. I made some inquiries a couple of days ago at an inn in Lyddington, where three of them had been drinking, and learnt that by his companions one of the men is called Bennett."

"Bennett!" I repeated, wondering for the moment in what connexion that name had been impressed upon me. Then I recollected the scribbled warning of the Mysterious Man:—

"Beware of Black Bennett!"

"What you tell me is very interesting," I exclaimed to the constable. "I think that in all probability this man Bennett had some connexion with the theft. If found, I hope the police will question and search him. I may be mistaken, but I believe that individual is well known by the appellation of Black Bennett."

I gave the constable the description of my watch for circulation, and then, after a long chat with my host, the innkeeper, went to bed.

The days went by, but no word came from Philip Reilly. I wired to his father's house at Upper Tooting, but received a reply expressing surprise, and stating that Philip had not been seen for ten days. A telegram to Mr. Staffurth brought no more satisfactory reply; therefore, as the Kenways were to give up possession of the Manor in a couple of days and my presence there would be essential to guard against any interlopers, I resolved to run up to London.

My anxiety for Reilly's welfare increased when all my inquiries regarding his whereabouts were futile.

According to Mr. Staffurth, the young man came there in a great state of excitement about nine o'clock one evening. He was dressed in his oldest suit, wore a golf cap and carried a stout stick. He said that he had made certain inquiries regarding Purvis, had seen him and talked with him. But that night he intended to make a bold bid to get at the secret of our enemies and, if possible, to obtain possession of the all-important document that had been sold by the drunken Knutton.

He had taken some whisky and water with his uncle, and left about ten, without saying in what direction he was going or explaining all that he had found out.

He told his uncle, however, to inform me to be forewarned of a man named Bennett, and had explained his silence by saying that at present it was not wise for him either to wire or write to Rockingham, as there was some one there acting the spy.

This, then, accounted for his silence. But after his departure from his uncle's house that night nothing had been seen or heard of him.

I called at my own rooms in Chelsea, where my landlady met me in great excitement. Not knowing my address she had been unable to write to me, but it appeared that one evening, three days before, some one had quietly entered the house with my latchkey, ascended to my rooms, and ransacked everything.

Now, my keys had been attached to one end of my watch-chain, and had, therefore, been stolen with the watch. The entry had been made on the night following the robbery from me, and although my roll-top writing-table had been opened and all my private papers and letters tossed about, I missed nothing.

The thieves had been in search of something; probably of that parchment-book of Bartholomew da Schorno which, fortunately, reposed in the strong-room at my bank.

All this, however, showed the ingenious and desperate character of our rivals. They would, I felt convinced, hesitate at nothing in order to obtain possession of the treasure.

The strange disappearance of Philip Reilly had now grown alarming. I made inquiries at the bank in Lombard Street, where he had been employed, but none of his friends there had seen him for weeks. His father, who was manager of a large linen warehouse in Cannon Street, was equally anxious as to his welfare.

We were playing a dangerous and exciting game, and my only fear was that, having made one or two discoveries, he had become too bold, and acted with the indiscretion of youth. He had, however, always seemed clear, level-headed, and cautious, and his father expressed a belief that he was not the kind of young man to fall into a trap.

I watched the small newsagent's in Sterndale Road, Hammersmith, having sent an envelope, with a blank sheet of paper within, addressed to Purvis. I had arranged that Mr. Kenway should remain at the Manor a few days longer, and now turned my attention to finding the man who had bought the secret. Reilly had discovered him; why should I not be equally successful?

But although I waited in that street two long, never-ending days, I saw no tall, fair man enter there.

That some serious misfortune had occurred to Philip Reilly I felt convinced, but of what character I dreaded to contemplate. Twelve days had gone by, and not a word had been received from him by any one.

The mysteries of London are many—and profound.

# XIX

## The Lady from Bayswater

On the second evening of my vigil in Sterndale Road my watchfulness was rewarded by seeing a neat and familiar figure pass up the street and enter the little newsagent's.

It needed no second glance to tell me that the visitor to the shop was the mysterious girl who called me on that memorable night, from the dispensary at Walworth—Miss Bristowe.

Fortunately she had not noticed my presence. Therefore I at once concealed myself up a side passage and waiting till she emerged with a letter in her hand—the one I had addressed to Purvis, I expect—I started to follow her. Every moment I feared lest she might look round and discover me, for in those back streets of Hammersmith there is not much traffic. But I was determined on this occasion to follow her to her home or to the hiding-place of Purvis.

Turning down Brook Green Road, she walked as far as the Hammersmith Station of the Underground Railway, where she bought a ticket for Notting Hill and entered the next train going west. On alighting she traversed hurriedly the Lancaster Road, for it had begun to rain and she was without an umbrella, and, turning at last into the Cornwall Road, ascended the front steps of one of the dark, smoke-blackened houses in that thoroughfare, not far from the corner of Portobello Road. She rang, the door was immediately opened by a servant, and she disappeared within.

Then, after a brief wait, I passed the house near enough to note that its number was 120. She went in at half-past seven, and, although I waited in the rain until half an hour before midnight, she did not come forth again. I therefore concluded that I had at last gained knowledge of her place of abode.

I wondered whether Purvis lived in that same house. She had called for his letters at Sterndale Road, and would probably hand them to him at once. Therefore, after long reflection, I came to the conclusion that he must live at that address.

It was past one when I re-entered my own rooms, and for an hour before turning in, occupied myself in re-arranging the chaos effected by the unknown intruders. The latter had certainly been disappointed with the result of their investigation, for they had not troubled themselves about two of the valuable old manuscripts I had found on board the *Seahorse*—the *Decretales Summa* of the Monk Henry and the *Book of John Trethemius*—both of which were lying upon the mantelshelf. No, it was the key of the cipher of which they had been in such active search, but which was fortunately far beyond their reach.

Early next morning I renewed my vigil at the corner of the Portobello and Cornwall Roads, hoping to meet the pretty woman who had so charmed me.

Two hours I waited, until at last she emerged, as usual neatly dressed in black. Through the maze of complicated streets she walked to Westbourne Grove. She had made some purchases, and was gazing into one of Whiteley's shop windows when I came up beside her and, raising my hat, greeted her.

She turned quickly, open-mouthed, and then, recovering from her surprise, at once gave me her hand and greeted me quite light-heartedly.

"Really, doctor," she laughed, "you seem quite ubiquitous. You are always running up against me."

"Well, it's a doctor's profession to go hither and thither quickly," I answered. "How is your brother?"

"Greatly better," was her prompt reply, although I thought I could detect duplicity in her answer. But she swiftly sought to change the subject, and as I walked beside her she chatted quite merrily. I did not, of course, let her know that I was aware of her abode, but, on the contrary, spoke of it as though it were away at Blackheath, and she did not seek to contradict me. Miss Bristowe was a clever woman in every sense of the word, but at the same time she was sweet and winning—most charming.

In her chatter was a light, irresponsible air that gave to her a *chic* seldom found in an Englishwoman, while her small hands and feet, her narrow waist, wide swinging hips, and the manner of her coiffure all savoured of the Parisienne rather than of the Londoner.

My object was to learn from her something definite regarding the man Purvis and his movements; her object was to conceal everything and to mislead me.

She seemed, however, nothing loth to allow me to accompany her into the several shops where she made small purchases. Once I referred to our meeting in Calthorpe Street, recollecting how cleverly Purvis had escaped me there, but she only laughed saying:—

"You must have thought me very rude to hurry away as I did, but I wanted to get home."

There were many matters I wished she would explain, but how could I ask her point-blank? For what reason had she taken me to Blackheath that night on a fruitless errand, and what connexion had she with the mysterious Purvis?

Again, it occurred to me that if Reilly had watched that newsagent's in Sterndale Road he had probably met her. He might even have become acquainted with her for aught I knew. I had, I remembered, given him a detailed description.

But if they were acquainted, she would be utterly unaware of the young man's association with me; hence I dare not broach the subject.

While I lingered at her side I could not help remarking, within myself, upon her affable courtesy and modest reserve towards me. A mystery surrounded her; that was certain. But in that half-hour I spent with her in Westbourne Grove I felt that she was not an adventuress, as I had half believed her to be, and that, save for the fact that she scrupulously concealed her place of abode, she was open and honest-minded, with a pleasing grace and sweet smile.

Again, just as I had noticed on the first occasion we had met, I detected that concealed within her heart was some deep-rooted sorrow, some painful memory of the past, perhaps, that she could not forget, and that now and then the sympathetic chord was struck that brought it all back to her, causing that expression of sadness which appeared at intervals in her eyes, and those half-suppressed sighs which she believed I did not notice.

Near midday she took leave of me at Queen's Road Station, for she would not allow me to remain with her longer.

"You are really mysterious, Miss Bristowe," I laughed; "I've spent a most delightful hour, and am most unwilling to end our chat."

"Ah," she said, earnestly; "you must, doctor. You've been with me already too long. Among all these people passing there may be one who knows me, and has noticed me walking with a stranger."

"Well, is it such a terrible sin?" I laughed.

"All sins are pleasant," was her quick answer; "that included. But you must really leave me now. Please do."

"When you took me to Blackheath you sent me back without satisfying my curiosity regarding your address," I said, reproachfully. "Are you going to act to-day in the same manner? Surely I may know where I can write to you in order that we may one day enjoy another of these pleasant gossips," I pleaded.

She shook her head. Yet I saw that my words had created an impression upon her, and furthermore that she was in no way averse to my companionship.

"Why do you send me away like this? Do you fear lest we should be seen together?"

She sighed that same sigh which had escaped her several times during our walk. Noticing her apprehension I attributed it to the fear of some jealous lover. A girl may flirt desperately, but she always hates to be thought false by the man who loves her.

If she had nothing to conceal from me, why did she not give me her true address in Cornwall Road? But she had much to hide from my knowledge, and with her honest woman's heart it required all her nerve and ingenuity to successfully mislead me.

"No," she faltered, at last; "we must not be seen together. You think the manner I treated you that night at Blackheath extraordinary. So it was. But it was imperative—for your sake!"

"I don't understand you, Miss Bristowe," I declared, quickly. "How was it for my sake?"

"Ah!" she cried, as though in distress. "Believe me, I acted for your own welfare! I can give you no further explanation."

"But you mystify me!" I said. "My curiosity is but natural."

"Certainly; but I'm sorry that at present I am unable to satisfy it," and her lips compressed themselves as a slight sigh again escaped them.

I was undecided whether she was wilfully deceiving me or whether it was under dire compulsion that she was concealing her motives.

"By your words you lead me to believe that you are my friend, Miss Bristowe; therefore it is surely permissible to give me an address where, in the future, I may write to you?"

"But I can't see what good can come of it," she responded, hesitatingly. "In fact, only harm can result in our acquaintanceship."

"What do you mean?"

"I mean what I have said. If we remain apart it will be better for both of us. Yet, somehow, Fate seems to throw us constantly into each other's society."

She was, of course, in ignorance of how I had traced her from Sterndale Road.

"True," I remarked, "and that seems to me all the more reason why you should name some place where I may write."

"Well," she said at last, after long hesitation and blushing slightly; "if you should, at any time, really desire to write to me, you may address your letter to Farmer's Library, Kensington High Street."

Thanking her I scribbled the address, then tried to persuade her to allow me to remain longer. But she steadily refused.

"I must go now," she said, "and although it sounds ungracious, I trust it may be a long time before we meet again."

"Why!" I asked, in surprise.

"Because such meetings place us both in peril," was her vague yet ominous answer.

"You perhaps object to my company?"

"On the contrary," she hastened to reassure me, "I find it most agreeable. But it behoves all of us, at certain times, to be circumspect."

She allowed me to shake her hand, then wishing me "Adieu!" turned back again towards Westbourne Grove, with an excuse that she had forgotten to make a purchase.

I saw through her ruse, and, by traversing the side streets, arrived at Cornwall Road before her, and standing in an entry unobserved watched her re-enter the house with a latch-key.

As far as that morning's work was concerned it was highly satisfactory. The chief fact that worried me now was the remarkable disappearance of Philip Reilly. He was smart, wary, athletic, the very last fellow to fall into any trap. Yet my apprehensions, just as those of his friends, were rendered grave by reason of his continued silence. All I knew was that he had been successful in his observations on the newsagent's shop in Sterndale Road, but in what manner he had not explained.

Like most young men who endeavour to solve a mystery, he had quickly become an enthusiast, with a fixed notion that we should discover the treasure.

Myself, I was far from sanguine, although, on the face of it, only that document sold by Ben Knutton stood between us and fortune. If we could but gain possession of that parchment for half an hour the secret of the hiding-place would be ours.

But George Purvis and his unknown but unscrupulous associates knew its value, just as we did, therefore it was far too well guarded.

WILLIAM LE QUEUX

# XX

## Philip Reilly Tells a Strange Story

During the three days that followed I kept watch in Cornwall Road, haunting the neighbouring thoroughfares of Ladbroke Grove, Silchester Road, Ledbury Road, and Powis Square, watching the movements of Miss Bristowe, and ever on the alert for the coming of that tall, fair-moustached individual, as the man Purvis had been described.

The girl whom I had found so charming went out often—once down to Catford to visit friends. Apparently she lived in apartments, and did her own shopping. She, however, had no male companion, and so close a watch did I keep upon the house that I arrived at the conclusion that Purvis did not live there after all.

Staffurth had grown very uneasy about his nephew, and although we put our wits together we could devise no plan by which the mystery of his disappearance might be solved. That the persons who were our rivals in the affair would not stick at trifles had already been proved, hence our apprehensions were of the gravest. Not being aware of the identity of these people we were heavily handicapped, for they were most probably cognizant of my every movement while I remained utterly in the dark as to theirs.

Matters were certainly growing serious. I had received a letter from Mr. Kenway telling me that he was compelled to remove his furniture from the Manor House on the morrow, therefore I would be obliged to go down to Caldecott again and do watch-dog duty. It was most important that Reilly should be with me, for I intended to commence a search throughout the house as soon as the Kenways had left. For that reason I bought a pick, shovel, and a quantity of other tools I thought might be useful, and had sent them down, packed in a case in order not to excite suspicion.

Sitting in my own room at Chelsea I pondered over the future, trying to decide upon some judicious plan of action. It was long past midnight. My green-shaded oil lamp was burning low and had already begun to splutter, but I could see no way out of the cul-de-sac. My first thoughts were, of course, for the safety of Philip, and he being still missing I did not feel myself justified in carrying the search farther before the mystery of his disappearance was cleared up.

I had found, on my return home, a letter from Seal, posted from Smyrna. It was a rather grimy note, bluff, brief, and written in that heavy hand that I knew so well in the log of the *Thrush*. The chief paragraph of the letter ran:—

"I hope you've got something out of Old Mystery by this time and also that you're full sail, with a fair wind, towards that treasure. Don't write to me, as I leave to-morrow straight for Fresh Wharf, and hope to see you within a fortnight."

The clock on my mantelshelf struck two, and I was about to put out my light and turn in, when of a sudden there came a violent ringing of the bell. It startled me at that hour, and pulling aside my curtains I looked down into the street, only to discover, to my joy, that Philip Reilly stood below, looking up anxiously at my window.

"Come down, doc, and let me in!" he cried, and in response I soon unchained the front door and was wringing his hand.

Walking before me he ascended the stairs and not until he had come into the light of my room did I notice the change wrought in him.

"Good heavens, my dear fellow! Wherever have you been?" I cried, glaring at him in surprise, for his clothes seemed half torn from his back, his face dirty with a stubbly beard, as though he had not shaved for a week, while his trousers were caked with mud and his white face bore a nasty cut only half healed. It extended almost from the eye to the chin, and with the blood still caked there, gave him a hideous and forbidding appearance.

"Ah!" he gasped, throwing himself into an arm-chair, "you may well ask. I've had a splendid time of it. Have you got a drop of brandy or anything by you? I feel faint."

He looked it, and I rushed to my cupboard and got out a bottle of Martell and a siphon of soda.

I allowed him to take a long steady drink before questioning him, in the meantime noting the terrible gash on his face. I saw also that his left hand had been cut on the inside.

"Well," I said, "we've all been most anxious about you, fearing something bad had happened. Tell me all about it."

"Anxious?" he laughed. "Not more anxious than I've been about myself, I can tell you. As for what happened, well I must collect my thoughts in order to tell you how it all began and what was the ultimate result. But before I begin I may as well give you my own opinion, and that is, I don't believe that we shall ever find that treasure."

"Why not?"

"Because the others know far more about it than we do," was his reply. "When I resolved to take a share in the investigation I never dreamed that the game could be such a desperate one as it is. By Jove! those fellows would murder both of us without the least compunction. We must go armed in future."

"But what occurred to you?" I asked, all anxiety to learn the reason of his long silence.

"Well," he said, finishing his brandy at one gulp; "it happened like this. When I left you I came up to town and started to keep observation on that newsagent's in Sterndale Road. The job was a terrible wearying one, but I was rewarded on the third evening by seeing the man you described—tall, fair, and freckled—call for a letter. Unobserved by him. I followed him home to St. Peter's Square, Hammersmith. Then I resolved to exercise a strict vigil over that house in order to find out all about its inmates. During the following day I discovered that Purvis was a bachelor of means and was very often in the habit of receiving visits from men of rather shady character. By constant watchfulness I came to know by sight all these men, five in number, including one named Bennett."

"Bennett?" I interrupted. "I wonder if he's Black Bennett?"

"Don't know," was my friend's rejoinder. "I can only tell you that they are as fine specimens of rascally adventurers as can be found at this moment in London. Purvis, being a good billiard player, often spends his evenings at the Crown, in Hammersmith Broadway, playing sometimes with Bennett and sometimes with one or other of his companions. Having obtained this piece of knowledge from observation, I took a bedroom at the Crown, in order that I might be able to saunter into the billiard-room at odd hours. As you know, I can play a fair game, and my object was to get into touch with Purvis by playing with him.

"I had not long to wait, for one evening he was there alone, and having made some casual remarks he invited me to play. From the first he seemed somewhat surprised to find that my form was slightly better than his, and before long I saw from his play that he was used to the ruses of sharks and thieves. He seemed to me to be rather well educated, the kind of man whose exterior was that of a gentleman, but who lives by his wits. He offered to bet me a sovereign on the game, and, in order to content him, I agreed. Very quickly the game was entirely in my hands, but so that he might become friendly I allowed him to win and paid him the sovereign.

"Bennett came in hurriedly just than and whispered something in an undertone, whereupon Purvis excused himself from playing further, put on his coat, and followed his friend out. That mysterious message aroused my curiosity; therefore as soon as the door was closed I threw on my coat and slipped out just in time to see the pair enter a hansom. They drove away and I drove after them, at a respectable distance, in order that they should not detect my vigilance.

"We drove for more than half an hour through Shepherd's Bush and Kensal Green, until we entered the Edgware Road, near Kilburn Station, and, crossing it, Purvis and Bennett alighted before a house in a dark side-street. When they had disappeared inside I dismissed my own cab and took a good look at the exterior of the place. It was a semi-detached house of rather neglected appearance, approached by a small strip of garden lying behind the iron railings. The place was in total darkness, however—not even a light over the front door. They had entered so quickly that I believe they must have used a latch-key.

"Half-a-dozen times I passed and repassed the dark silent place, wondering what was the object of their journey there, until, the blinds being up and the front rooms all being unlit, it occurred to me that whatever was taking place was at the rear of the premises. So, resolving to try and ascertain for myself the reason of the hurried visit, I entered the little garden and crept silently round to the back, where in a room on the first floor was a light, and even from where I stood I could hear men's voices. I saw that the yellow holland blind, having been pulled down violently, had given way from the roller, and a piece hung down. This would afford me a view of the room if only I could climb high enough. Now, beneath the window in question was a lean-to conservatory, built out from what was, I supposed, the drawing-room, but upon the roof of such a fragile structure I dared not venture. I noticed some iron piping going straight up, and, aided by the wooden lattice on the wall, it occurred to me that I might safely accomplish the feat. As you know, I am rather fond of climbing; therefore I quickly took off my boots and commenced to work my way up towards the coign of vantage.

"To reach a level high enough, however, was a task much more difficult than I had at first anticipated, especially as the creeper-covered lattice work, being old and rotten, gave way almost each time I grasped it. At last, however, swinging myself over, I succeeded in clutching what seemed like a safe piece of trellis close to the spot that afforded a view into the room. Just at that very moment, when my eyes came to the window where hung the corner of the blind untacked from its roller, a loud scream issued forth—the agonized cry of a woman.

"Clinging with hands and feet to the insecure woodwork I craned my neck until I could get a view of the interior of the room. The sight that greeted me was one that I was certainly unprepared for. The apartment was a back parlour, fairly well furnished. Within stood Purvis, Bennett, and two other men whom I recognized as constant visitors to St. Peter's Square. The door was open, and one of the men stood holding by the arm a young, well-dressed woman. She had evidently been dragged in there against her will, for she had covered her pale face with her hand to shut out from her eyes the terrible object she had been brought there to see—the corpse of a young man."

"What!" I cried, starting up; "have they actually committed murder?"

"I suppose so," was Reilly's reply. "I merely tell you what I saw with my own eyes. The dead man was in evening dress, and was lying on his back on the carpet, his limbs slightly drawn up. There was on his shirt-front a large ugly stain of blood, while his face was as white as paper. The unfeeling brutes actually compelled the poor girl to touch the dead man's face, and she drew her fingers away from its cold contact as though she had been stung. Then Bennett, addressing her with biting sarcasm, said: 'You didn't believe us, miss, but you'll believe now, I think, and recollect that if you do not act exactly as we order you'll be served in the same way. You know me well enough to be aware that I never repeat a threat—I carry it out!'

"'You are cruel—inhuman!' she cried, facing the four men, with an angry passion suddenly lighting up her face. 'He had done no harm, and you killed him!—killed him because you are cowards!' 'Enough girl!' cried Bennett, and raising his fist he struck her on the mouth, cutting her lip, while the other blackguards stood there, not attempting to interfere. Purvis gave the body of the dead man a contemptuous kick, and then bending down took the watch and chain from the poor fellow's pocket and, handing it to the man who stood in the doorway, said, 'Here's a souvenir of to-night's work. Like to have it?' The bearded ruffian grinned and slipped the dead man's property into his pocket. 'You shall pay for this!' the girl cried, defiantly, staunching the blood with her handkerchief. 'Oh!' cried Bennett, 'you dare to say a word and the rats will make a meal off you pretty quick—remember that! There!' he exclaimed to the man who had pocketed the watch and who still held her arm, 'take the wench away! She'll know her manners before long.' She was dragged out, and I heard her and her captor descending the stairs. Then, from my perilous position, I could overhear the other three discussing what should be done with the body, whereupon it was decided to convey it in a travelling-trunk to the cloak-room of one of the termini—which of them was not stated. I watched the trunk brought in—one of those large ones, of compressed cane—and saw them first mutilate the face of the corpse beyond all recognition.

"Then they packed the body in, locking the trunk and securing it with cord. This done, a careful examination was made of the room. One or two blood-stains were removed by Purvis with water and a sponge, and then all three carried the trunk down to the hall to await a four-wheeled cab. Purvis and Bennett returned again to the room where the light burned, and I heard the latter say: 'That's one the less—and without much trouble either. He might have proved a nuisance.' Whereupon Purvis remarked: 'The girl was, I believe, in love with him.' 'Love be hanged!' Bennett returned, roughly. 'That's the very reason why I had her brought here—to show her that his death was due to her association with him. She'll blame herself for the tragedy now, and be our servant more then ever; don't you see?'

"Then a few minutes later, the man who had gone to the nearest cab-rank returned, and all four went out, after extinguishing the lamp. I heard the cab drive away, when it suddenly occurred to me that I ought to attempt to follow it and ascertain where they deposited the evidence of their crime. In my haste I made a false move and felt the woodwork suddenly break from my hands. I tried to steady myself but could not, and, overbalancing backwards, fell with a crash through the conservatory roof, alighting upon the concrete floor.

"I know no more, save that when I came to I was lying in bed in an hospital with a policeman sitting by my side—under arrest for attempted burglary, they said. In two days I was sufficiently well to be taken to the police-court, where, having refused to give any account of myself, I was sent to prison for fourteen days as a rogue and vagabond. I saw it was useless to recount what I had witnessed in that house, as the marks of the crime had already been carefully obliterated; hence I did my fourteen days, which expired this morning."

"But the woman?" I exclaimed, utterly dumfounded by his startling story. "Had you seen her before?"

"Yes, once, while I was waiting outside the newsagent's in Sterndale Road. She had called there on two occasions."

"Was it Miss Bristowe?" I asked, describing her.

"Exactly as you say; dark, pretty, with a rather pointed chin; dressed in black," he answered.

Then a strange thought took possession of me. I wondered if by her refusal to conduct me to her brother's bedside at Blackheath on that memorable night I had escaped a similar fate to that dead unknown.

The veil of mystery was certainly growing more than ever impenetrable.

# XXI

## We Make a Discovery in the Manor House

Reilly's story was a strange one. Although he had suffered imprisonment as a rogue—no burglarious instruments being found upon him—I could do nothing else than congratulate him upon his firm determination not to expose his hand. But the incident was no good augury for the future.

We were, of course, in possession of a fact that might prove of greatest use to us. He had seen the murdered man with his own eyes, although the identity of the victim was at present a mystery. Miss Bristowe knew him, too, and from her I hoped one day to obtain information as to who he really was.

Although Philip had passed through an exciting time, it had been by no means a futile one, for he had witnessed certain events which gave us true and adequate knowledge of what manner of persons we had to deal with. It was my friend's belief that Miss Bristowe and the man who had conducted her to that house had left before the accident had occurred to him, and further, that the other three men, having left in a cab with the travelling trunk and its gruesome contents, remained in ignorance of his discovery by the neighbours, who were awakened by the crash.

We could, of course, fix the house wherein the assassination had taken place from the report in the police books regarding the discovery of Reilly, but, as he most wisely pointed out, the story of the murder would never be believed, and if he gave information—first, no traces would be found, and secondly, we should only prematurely betray our knowledge to our enemies.

So we resolved to remain, for the present, silent. I saw now quite well the reason of the tragic vein in the character of the sweet girl who had so charmed me. I alone knew the secret of how the man, who was probably her lover, had been murdered in cold blood by those scoundrels, who had carried their fiendishness so far as to compel her to touch the corpse.

I dressed the cut on Reilly's face, for it appeared that on coming out of prison that morning he had taken off the bandage, although the doctor had forbidden him to do so. Believing that I must still be on guard at Caldecott, he had paid visits to several other people before coming to me. On hearing that the Kenways were leaving the Manor on the morrow, he was instantly keen on travelling down there and taking possession of the place.

He slept on the couch in my sitting-room, and next morning, at ten o'clock, we left London for Rockingham, having previously laid in a stock of various necessaries, including lamps, cord, candles, and matches, which we did not wish to purchase in the village.

At one o'clock we were back in our pleasant rustic quarters in the Sonde Arms, where we lunched off cold beef, bread, and ale, and then walked over to Caldecott, arriving there just before the van containing the household goods of the Kenways was driven away. The insurance agent and his wife were anxious to depart, therefore, after a hurried conversation, they gave me over the keys, and we watched the van lumber noisily out upon the highway over the moss-grown cobbles.

So we were left in possession of a rather dirty house minus a scrap of furniture. Indeed, it was only then that we were awakened to the fact that it would be necessary to obtain at least a table, a couple of camp bedsteads, and a couple of chairs, if we intended to inhabit the place.

Leaving Reilly in possession I hired a trap at the Plough, drove to Uppingham, and there purchased the necessary equipment of a cheap and temporary character, not forgetting a couple of drinking glasses, of course.

All were delivered by seven o'clock that night, and working in our shirt sleeves we cleaned out one of the big upstairs rooms and set up the narrow little beds, one in each corner. At first we thought of taking separate rooms, but decided that if any midnight attack were made upon us it would be best if we were in company.

We made a big wood fire in the room to air the mattresses and blankets, and filled two pails with water from the pump wherewith to perform our matutinal ablutions. Imagine how excited we were, possessors of a house wherein a great and valuable treasure awaited our discovery.

In order to avert village gossip we explained at the Plough that Mr. Reilly's furniture was coming from Southampton, and what we had purchased was for temporary accommodation. But poor Reilly's face, I still remember, was an ugly picture with the deep red scar where the glass roof had cut him. We made arrangements at the Plough to take our meals there, except tea, which we could brew ourselves, and it was nearly midnight when, sitting out in the garden yawning, we knocked out our pipes and went up to bed. Hours before we had been round to examine the catches and locks of doors and windows, and to fasten them; therefore we retired with a certain feeling that all was secure.

Beyond the thumping and squealing of rats beneath the boards, nothing disturbed our peace and we rose early, prepared to make our first tour of inspection. Therefore, after a wash and shave, we each took hammer and chisel from the box I had sent on in advance, and together had a superficial look round.

By tapping the panelling and walls we discovered dozens of hollow places, but a fact we had hitherto overlooked very soon occurred to us, that if we commenced to break down the walls we should injure the property to the tune of some hundreds of pounds, and be compelled to put it in order again; not a very bright out-look, especially as we had one of the chosen race as landlord.

One object we had to keep constantly in view was the satisfaction of the curiosity of the villagers. Two men cannot take an empty house and live in it, almost devoid of furniture, without exciting some comments; hence our story of the furniture in transit from the South of England.

The whole of the first day we devoted to a careful survey of the upstairs rooms as being the most likely spot where the treasure was concealed. In one of them—the one Reilly had suspected—the central room over the main entrance hall, the leopard rampant of da Schorno was sculptured in marble over the big open fireplace, executed evidently by an Italian hand. Probably, when old Bartholomew built the place or altered it according to his liking, he had with him one or two of his compatriots. To me it seemed as though one had been a sculptor, for on the stone balustrade of the stairs and around other fireplaces, wherein modern grates had since been placed, were fine specimens of sixteenth-century ornament.

On the following morning, after we had brewed our tea and boiled some eggs, we commenced investigations in that upstairs centre room, which had probably been at one time the best bedroom. The wall on the left, parting it from the next room, had attracted our attention, owing to its abnormal thickness, and when we sounded it with a hammer it seemed at one point to emit a hollow sound. This hollowness only extended for about two feet square, starting from the skirting-board.

We were neither carpenters nor plasterers, therefore we could not ourselves repair any damage that we might cause. But after some consultation we arrived at the conclusion that the only way was to make a thorough search, irrespective of consequences. Therefore, with hammer and chisel, I started to break into what I hoped would be a secret cavity. As soon as I commenced I saw that the wall was plastered at that point, and not of stone as in other parts. This encouraged me, and aided by Reilly we forced out the skirting-board, and had very soon made a considerable hole. The plaster was, however, fully six inches thick, and having penetrated it my chisel suddenly struck wood.

The dull sound caused the hearts of both of us to leap in expectation.

Another blow and a great piece of plaster came away.

"Why, there's a door here!" I cried; "a small oak door that's been fastened and plastered up."

I stopped working while Philip examined it. He agreed that it was a hard panel of oak, but whether of a door it was impossible to say.

Again I resumed work, and within a quarter of an hour had laid bare the square strong door of a cupboard.

Reilly, by this time, was literally dancing with excitement. What, we wondered, could be contained therein?

It certainly had not been opened for centuries. Indeed, although the small door had long iron hinges stretching nearly right across it, there seemed no sign of lock or bolt.

"The way it's closed is a secret, depend upon it, doctor," my companion cried. "I really believe the treasure's in here. Fancy digging out this at the first trial!"

But, myself, I was not so sanguine. I preferred to work steadily without undue excitement, for I saw that in such an investigation quietness and method were essential to success.

I don't, of course, deny that I was actually on the tiptoe of expectation, for I, like Mr. Staffurth and Philip, had arrived at the firm conclusion that if the old Italian's treasure still existed it was hidden somewhere in that house.

Therefore, at any blow of the hammer, the secret, so well guarded through three hundred years, might become revealed to us.

The clouds of white dust that I had raised rendered it thirsty work; therefore Philip, on going downstairs for the pickaxe, also brought up a bottle of ale, which we drank with avidity—from the bottle. That closed door proved a more formidable barrier than we had anticipated. Of well-seasoned oak, it was studded with rusty nails, and resisted all our efforts to prise it open. There was no lock, so far as we could see, nor any bolt; only the two long rusty hinges. Again and again we tried to insert a crowbar between the lintel and the door, but although both of us toiled through the greater part of the morning the door would not budge.

Reilly, with his long, athletic arms, attacked it with the pick, but the noise he made sounded through the empty house like the explosion of bombshells, and the dust raised was suffocating. All these efforts being futile, we resolved to cut the door out bodily, and with that object I commenced with centre-bit at a spot where the lock would, in ordinary circumstances, be situated. I drilled and drilled, slowly cutting a circular hole in the wood, and had penetrated to a depth of fully four inches when a harsh grating sound told us the unwelcome truth.

The back of the door was covered by an iron plate.

"We can't cut it; that's very certain!" I declared, withdrawing the drill. On examining the hole by aid of a candle I could see where the drill had cut a scratch on the face of the plate. I sounded the iron with a small crowbar and noted that it seemed of considerable thickness. Moreover, it was probably bolted to the woodwork by the nails which studded the side of the door towards us.

"There must be something inside," Reilly declared. "No one would have taken such precaution if there was nothing of value within. Let's persevere!"

"Of course," I agreed, "but we must proceed scientifically; it's useless working in the dark. Now, my own idea is that we might perhaps cut away the wall on the side where the door is fastened and thus get a hole for leverage. I believe that's the only way."

Reilly was of similar opinion, therefore we both set to work with a will, I holding the chisel and my companion swinging the heavy hammer. The plaster was, of course, soon cut out, but when we came to the rough stone of the wall our hard work commenced. By dint of constant labour, with pick and crowbar, we gradually loosened one of the larger stones, and in half an hour had levered it out upon the floor of the room.

It carried us but little farther, for the stone wall was far thicker than we anticipated. It had been built in a day long before contract jobs and jerry builders were known, and by men who constructed houses intended to last through centuries. There was no single brick in the whole place, only stone, of that kind known as Barnack rag.

The loosening of the first stone was hardest of all, and it being near one o'clock, our luncheon hour at the Plough, we washed, tidied ourselves, and sauntered along to the inn, smoking cigarettes, as though nothing had occurred. Our hands itched to be back at work again, but, having to act with circumspection in order not to betray the nature of our operations, we were compelled to eat our meal leisurely.

Soon after two we went eagerly back again, and stone after stone we succeeded in removing, until we obtained sufficient space between the stone and the door to allow of leverage.

Then, inserting our strongest crowbar, which was about four feet long and had a curved end, we both bore all our weight against it to break the door from its unseen fastenings. Time after time, yo-hoing like sailors and springing our full weight upon the bar, we endeavoured to force the stout old door, but alas! to no avail.

It then occurred to us that it opened into the room wherein we stood, but on examination of the wall, now broken through to the size of half a man's hand, we discovered that it opened either way.

Suddenly another idea struck the ingenious Reilly. We had a screw-jack, and perhaps by its use might be able to force the door inwards.

A long time elapsed before we could fix it sufficiently securely to bear the enormous strain, but presently we got it adjusted, and began turning it. Then very soon the groaning of the old oak told its tremendous resistance and we steadily screwed on, until the creaking and splitting of the wood showed the enormous pressure it was still bearing.

Of a sudden, however, without warning, there was a loud report like the explosion of a cannon, as the bolts were broken off in their sockets, and before us was open a dark hole from which a cloud of suffocating dust belched forth into the room.

# XXII

## Black Bennett

On the previous night we had trimmed the hurricane lamp that I had purchased in London as part of our equipment, therefore we soon had it alight and eagerly entered the doorway to explore.

Reilly went first, bending low, lamp in one hand and a short crowbar in the other, while I followed with an axe as one of the most useful of implements.

The door had been forced from its fastenings and had gone far back upon its hinges, almost uninjured, save that it was split in places and badly twisted. Within we found a rough-walled, close-smelling chamber, about 4 ft. across and about 9 ft. long, low, dark as pitch, and, to our abject disappointment, absolutely empty.

One object alone we found within—an old leather drinking mug, hard, dry and cracked, that lay in one corner long forgotten.

Reilly's idea was that the place was a "priests' hole," one of the secret hiding-places of the Roman Catholic priests after the Reformation, so often found in old houses, and in this I was inclined to agree with him. Still, after a whole day's work, and a hard one, too, our raised hopes had only been dashed by a negative discovery. The wreck we had made of the wall was appalling, and if we proceeded for long in that manner I dreaded to think what might be the amount claimed for dilapidations.

My young friend was, however, enthusiastic and nothing daunted. He lit a cigarette and, puffing at it vigorously, silently regarded the yawning hole in the wall.

"No doubt it was a place of concealment for those unfortunate Johnnies who were so badly badgered after Henry VIII's decree," he remarked. "Old Bartholomew was a staunch Catholic and, of course, in his house any priest found shelter and concealment who asked for it. That accounts for the mug being there. The last man who occupied the place before it was closed up and plastered over probably drank his ale out of it."

"Well," I said, disappointedly, "we've made a pretty mess, and we'd best start to clear it up tidily before we do anything more. Method is everything in a complete search like this."

"Of course," was my young friend's remark; "only I wish we could get a sight of that parchment which that drunken sot sold for half a sovereign. If we could, we shouldn't go on working in the dark like this."

"Ah, Philip," I said, with a sigh, "we shall never get sight of that, I fear. Purvis and his friends keep it too safely guarded."

"I wonder if they know that we are tenants of this place?"

"Probably. Kenway wrote to him two days ago."

"Then, knowing the kind of men they are, I feel rather apprehensive that they may endeavour to turn us out, or do something desperate."

"Let them try!" I laughed. "We've both got revolvers, and neither of us would be afraid to use them if the worst came."

"We must mind they don't take us unawares. Men like that never fight square. Bennett has the ingenuity of the Evil One himself."

I reflected for a moment, then said:—

"If we only knew the identity of the victim of the tragedy and could establish his death we might have the whole crowd under arrest."

"Yes. But how can we establish his identity?" Reilly queried. "They were smart enough to dispose of the body successfully."

"But if the police made inquiries they might discover the cabman who was called, and by that means find out what had been done with the trunk."

"No," replied the young bank clerk. "That girl Bristowe could tell us a lot if she wished. You know her—why not try to pump her? I don't think it would be difficult to discover something from her, for she was horror-struck when they revealed to her the poor fellow's fate."

His suggestion seemed an excellent one, but not at present practicable. We were at that moment in possession of a house which our enemies were straining every nerve to search, like ourselves. Surely it was not policy to leave it at that juncture, empty and at their mercy. Reilly did not care to remain alone in charge, and certainly I was by no means anxious to live in that awful, depressing place without a companion.

A careful review of the position impressed upon us the necessity of continuing our search. We possessed certain documentary evidence which showed, first, that a treasure had been stored away; secondly, that it had been stored in a place of safety, with the Knuttons as guardians; thirdly, that the Knuttons had been installed by Bartholomew himself in the Manor Farm, the old house in close proximity. Therefore we could arrive at but one conclusion, namely, that the treasure was stored upon the premises now in our possession. If not, why had the

Knuttons been established there? Richard Knutton, of the Port of Sandwich, who was Bartholomew's trusted lieutenant, would surely be placed on guard in the vicinity of the secret hiding-place. Sea-dogs they all were, and clever ones too. Probably few had seen more hand-to-hand fighting and more fierce bloodshed than the seven signatories, and their prize money had undoubtedly amounted to a handsome sum.

Reilly was impatient and rather headstrong. He made lots of wild suggestions. If Purvis and his friends had hired burglars to search his uncle's study, why should we not, by similar means, try and possess ourselves of that all-important document which the drunken Knutton had sold to our enemies? Which argument was, of course, logical, but it did not appeal to me. My own opinion was that if we acted firmly, with caution and patience, we should one day satisfactorily clear up the mystery. Still, our position was irksome, for we dared not to leave the place for long together, fearing that our enemies might be working against us in secret.

Through several days we continued our search, taking up the worm-eaten floor boards, but exposing nothing more interesting than rat runs; wrenching out the old oak panelling, and searching for any hollow-sounding places in the walls. Our investigation was certainly thorough, for we took room by room, methodically measuring, sounding, and making openings everywhere.

One morning the rural postman brought me a letter from Seal, explaining that the *Thrush* had at last gone into dry dock, where she would remain for three weeks at least to be scraped and patched, therefore he was coming down next day to help us. This was good news, for with three of us on guard we could each be allowed more liberty. So I went over to Uppingham again and purchased another camp bed and some cheap furniture, sufficient to make us up a sitting-room. That same night it arrived, and we then turned one of the smaller rooms on the ground floor into a smoking-room, with three cane chairs, a table, and a window-blind.

I met Seal at Rockingham Station on the following day.

"What ho, sonny!" the burly skipper cried, rolling his huge carcass from the train and slapping his great hand into mine. "My kit's in the van there. Thought you hadn't got a bed for me, so I brought my own and a few other things," and at the same moment I saw, pitched out upon the platform, a sailor's hold-all lashed with rope.

WILLIAM LE QUEUX

"Well, captain," I said, after giving instructions to the railway porter to wheel the skipper's luggage up to the Manor House, "and how are you?"

"Fit as a fiddle, doctor," and his bronzed face broadened and beamed; "you cured that rheumatism of mine." Then he halted and inhaled the air deeply. "Christmas!" he exclaimed; "this does a chap good, after too much sea. I can smell them flowers," and he glanced at some growing in the station-master's garden. "I never see flowers, you know, doctor."

Together we crossed the bridge and entered the village. The bluff old fellow was dressed, as usual, in blue serge, with a big silver watch-chain, of cable pattern, across his waistcoat, and his nautical cap stuck slightly askew, ridiculously small for his enormous head.

"Seen anything more of them other swabs?" he asked, as he rolled along at my side.

"We've heard plenty about them," I answered, "but have seen nothing."

"They'd better not show their ugly mugs while I'm here," he retorted, meaningly.

I laughed. Seal's roar of anger would in itself be sufficient to frighten away the whole of Purvis and Company.

When I took him into the grass-grown yard of the old house he looked the place up and down, and remarked:—

"A bit dilapidated, ain't it? I should reckon we might overhaul a ghost or two inside if we had a mind to."

"Ah, you're superstitious, captain," I said. "Mr. Reilly doesn't believe in ghosts any more than I do. Come along and be introduced to him."

We found Philip smoking a cigarette and reading a newspaper under a tree in the tangled old garden. Then, when I had made the introduction, Seal said:—

"Glad to make your acquaintance, sir. Toughish job this, ain't it? You don't seem to have much luck up to the present. At every port I touched I expected to hear that you had found the stuff and bagged it."

"You are best off, I think, captain," I remarked.

"Up to now, yes. I sold my lot the day before yesterday to a dealer in Piccadilly for eight hundred and forty-six quid, and I've put that money safe in the bank," he said, with evident satisfaction. "I'd rather have modern money than a collection of old coins. But I'd like to see you get your whack out of it, doctor. You deserve it—you do."

"Well," I said, "we're having a good try to find where it is hidden." And then we took him inside and showed him how we were pulling the old place to pieces.

"Jehoshaphat!" he exclaimed, with a whistle. "You're making a pretty fine mess, and no gammon! The landlord's hair will stand on end when he sees it."

"I expect so," I laughed. "But now we've started we must go through with it—and you must help us."

"Help yer? Why, of course. Shiver me, we'll pull the whole crazy house down, if you like."

The porter had delivered the skipper's sack, so we carried it up to the room we had prepared for him adjoining ours.

"Wait, you chaps, till I've unlashed my kit," he said, addressing us, and bending over the white canvas sack he quickly uncorded it and began to unpack.

It was filled with a collection of articles that surprised us. Not only had he brought his bed, but also his big yellow oilskin, "in case the weather was dirty," he informed us. Three fine melons, from Algiers, rolled across the floor; a box of cigars was handed to each of us, as a present, and then, from careful wrappings, he produced two wicker-covered bottles of Black Head rum.

"Now, mates!" he cried, "get three glasses, and we'll drink success to this outcome o' Noah's Ark."

Rum was not our habitual beverage before one o'clock in the day, but in order to show our appreciation of his goodwill we each tossed down a little of the neat spirit after he had chinked his glass with ours, saying:—

"'Ere's luck to all three of us, and a thousand of Old Nick's best brand o' curses on them swabs."

Having locked up the place securely, as we always did during our temporary absences, we took Seal round to the Plough, where we sat together in the little back parlour and, amid boisterous laughter, lunched off cold roast beef and mashed potatoes, our usual fare, for the menu of that rural hostelry was not very extensive.

The skipper, whose normal state was one of hunger, ate with an enormous appetite, smacking his lips and declaring that after food afloat a bit of real English beef was very toothsome. And so it was. I recollected well the culinary arrangements of the *Thrush*, and the greasy, gritty, unappetizing dishes that sometimes came from the galley for our approval.

The home-brewed ale was a change, too, after his eternal "noggins," and a thirst being upon him he swallowed several glasses with great gusto.

Then, when we smoked and his big bronzed face beamed through the suffocating cloud, he told us that we were certainly giving him a good time.

We had been laughing at some quaint remark of the skipper's, and as the peal of merriment had subsided the innkeeper's sister who waited upon us entered to clear off the plates. As she did so the sound of a man's gruff voice, in conversation, reached us from the bar outside.

Seal's jaw dropped in an instant. The merriment died out of his face. He listened for a moment as though to make certain, then springing from his chair he passed through the doorway, in order, I suppose, to get sight of the stranger.

I had watched the skipper's countenance and had noticed the puzzled expression on it.

Next instant he was back with us, returning on tiptoe. The young woman had gone out, and he closed the door quietly behind her. Then, turning to us, he said, in a low, hoarse voice of alarm, his countenance entirely changed:—

"Look here, lads! This is a blessed sight more than I bargained for when I offered to come down and give yer a hand. Why, Black Bennett's here! Black Bennett!" he added, looking at our puzzled faces. "Black Bennett! Don't you understand?"

# XXIII

## Job Seal Relates His Adventures

W e admitted that we did not understand.

"I've heard of this Black Bennett," I said in surprise, "but who is he? Tell us."

"Who is he?" growled Seal, knitting his shaggy brows darkly. "Who is he? Why, he's about the worst swab I've ever met—and that's saying a good deal!"

"But what is there against him?" I demanded anxiously.

"Almost everything short of murder. Christmas! I didn't know that he was mixed up in this affair. You will have to be cute, doctor, for if Black Bennett's one of 'em you can bet your boots that the crowd ain't particular good company."

"Well," I said, "I'd like to get a glance at this very interesting person." And, rising, I opened the door and passed through into the bar on the pretext of obtaining some matches.

The man, who was seated on the edge of the beery table smoking a briar and drinking a tankard of ale, gave me the impression of an idle lounger. He was above the average height, with a round, red face, grey hair and beard, and dressed in what appeared to me to be a ready-made suit of dark tweed. His straw hat was browned by the sun and much the worse for wear. As I entered he glanced at me quickly with his keen dark eyes; then, turning as though he did not recognize me, he lifted his glass and took a deep drink.

In the fellow's appearance there was certainly little to recommend him. I did not like his eyes. His round, ruddy face would have passed as that of an easy-going, contented man, had it not been for the hard, cruel expression when he had glanced at me. I noticed his hands. One held his pipe and the other rested upon the edge of the table. He carried it three parts doubled up, with the nails pointing in towards the palm, while on his knuckles were old scars. These signs told me at once that he was a sailor, although there was nothing nautical about his dress. The drawn-up hand betrayed constant rope-hauling, and the scars were those of old salt cracks which the water had made on his hands in his early days at sea.

Having obtained the matches I rejoined my companions, whereupon Reilly slipped out through the stable yard and was absent only a minute or two. When he returned he said to us in a low voice, "Yes; that's the man who struck Miss Bristowe. I'd recognize him among a million." And at that moment we heard the man wish the landlady "good-day" and depart.

Then, at my suggestion, Reilly related to Seal all that he had witnessed on that memorable night at Kilburn.

"You think that Bennett killed the poor fellow?" the skipper said, between long reflective puffs at his cigar.

"I certainly believe he is the murderer," was the other's reply. "But at present we can charge them with nothing. We have no tangible evidence of a crime."

"The girl—what's her name—could tell you sufficient to gaol the lot of 'em," was Job Seal's rejoinder. "She knows all about it. The dead man was her lover without a doubt."

"I could recognize the victim if I saw his photograph," Reilly declared. "I'll never forget that ghastly white face till my dying day."

"I wonder where they disposed of the body?" I queried. "We must keep our eyes on the papers for any discovery. If they left it at a cloak-room it must be found sooner or later."

What Reilly had related gave the skipper of the *Thrush* evident satisfaction.

"You've got the best side o' them swabs, Mr. Reilly, if you're only careful. They're in ignorance of what you've seen. Excellent! All you do now is to wait; but in the meantime be very careful that these men don't get the better of you."

"I can't imagine how the Mysterious Man could have given us that warning," I remarked, afterwards explaining to Seal the words that the madman had written: "Beware of Black Bennett!"

"Ah!" exclaimed the skipper, "there's no tellin' what Old Mister Mystery knows. He's a son of Davy Jones himself, I really believe."

"You hold the old fellow in superstitious dread, captain," I laughed.

"Well," responded the skipper bluntly, "the old fire-eater with his rusty sword may be a couple of hundred years old, for all we know."

"But what can he possibly know about this man Bennett?"

"What can he know? Why, what other people know—what I know. I sailed with him once, and it was a lively trip, I can tell you," growled the old skipper, sucking his teeth, a habit of his when any recollection of the past was unpleasant.

"I'm anxious to know all about him," I said. "Tell us the story, captain."

"Well, it's nigh twenty years ago now since I first made the acquaintance of Black Bennett. I was sailing in the brig *Maria Martin*, of Liverpool, in those days, and one night while we were lying at Naples an English sailor was shipped, while drunk, as a forecastle hand. He turned out to be Bennett. We were bound for the Cape of Good Hope, but long before we reached Gib. our new hand had turned the craft topsy-turvy. He wouldn't work, notwithstanding the strong language of the first mate—and he could swear a brick wall down—and for days and days he only lay in his bunk smoking like a philosopher. I was sent to clear him out, and he sprang at me like a tiger. There was a tussle, and—well, I needn't describe the rounds we had, except to say that my reach proved a bit too long for him, and he lay insensible for an hour. That was the beginning of bad blood between us; he never liked me afterwards. When he came to he called a meeting of the men, and in an hour the whole bloomin' crew were in mutiny. The skipper, chief mate, and myself armed ourselves, and expected some shooting, for they were about six to one, so the struggle wasn't very fair. This continued until we were off the West Coast of Africa, when Bennett, as leader of the mutineers, proved himself a perfect fiend.

"His first move was to send one of the apprentices secretly to the skipper's cabin for the ship's papers, and having obtained them he weighted them with a lump of iron and, after exhibiting them to the captain, calmly pitched the lot overboard. Our skipper almost went mad. He danced with rage like a bear at a show, all the hands laughing at him. Well, after that the mutineers took possession of the craft, clapped us all three in our cabins, and then broached the rum and other spirits we had aboard. Sails were reefed, and we lay to for nearly a week while the whole crew were roaring drunk. Then a little bad weather sobered them, and they ran in shore. Within sight of land a boat was lowered, into which they placed us, tossing some of our belongings after us, and then sent us adrift. Fortunately they had given us a pair of oars, and we rowed ashore. It was a tropical country, we found, and as we beached the boat we saw that the brig had altered her course, and was steering straight out across the Atlantic. The natives proved friendly, and after some wanderings in the forests we were guided by a black boy to the English settlement of Cape Coast Castle. Before the Governor we related our experiences, and after some weeks were sent home to London.

"That was my first acquaintance with Black Bennett, the most brutal of all skippers."

"And what became of the *Maria Martin*?"

"She was found about three years afterwards aground and abandoned a few miles south of Rio. According to the report to the Board of Trade there were evidences that Black Bennett and his men had run her as a pirate, making havoc with the Brazilian coasting trade, but as nothing was seen of him in England the authorities were powerless. Next he was heard of in New York, where he shipped under an assumed name on a German steamer bound for Sydney. The German skipper was pleased at shipping a whole crowd of tough English sailors, but before he had got half-way across the Atlantic he had a very rude awakening. The new hands were none other than Black Bennett and his men, and they made fine sport of that Hamburg steamer. There was some powder-play that time, and more than one on both sides went to Davy Jones. But in the end Bennett took command, set the Germans adrift near Mauritius, and then, steering back to Buenos Ayres, they unshipped the cargo and eventually sold it. Afterwards Bennett and his crew steamed away to Australia, and there became engaged in the Kanaka labour trade—a kind of genteel slave-trade. Five years ago, when my owners made Leghorn a final port of discharge on account of the cheapness of Italian hands and the fact that they don't get drunk, Bennett tried to ship with me, intending, no doubt, to play his tricks with the *Thrush*. Fortunately I recognized him, told Mr. Carmichael, the British Consul, and the result was that he made himself scarce out of Leghorn pretty quickly. Oh, yes," added Seal, "Black Bennett is an ingenious rogue, I can tell you."

"But I thought piracy was dead in these days," I remarked.

"So it is. But it wasn't fifteen years ago. They didn't wear cutlasses and overhaul ships, but they knew a trick worth two of that. They seized the ship on which they sailed, repainted her, altered her appearance, gave her a new name and port, and eventually sold her to some foreigner. They, however, sailed under the black flag all the same."

"But what do you think Bennett's game is now?" asked Reilly.

"To get the better of you in this search. He's evidently aware of the existence of the Italian's treasure, and intends to have it. All I warn you of is that he's a treacherous friend and a formidable enemy."

"But if you assist us, captain, we need have no fear," I remarked.

"There's bad blood between us, doctor," he answered dubiously. "If we met, something might happen," he added meaningly.

"But haven't we sufficient evidence to place before the police?" I suggested.

"How can you prove it?" he asked, settling himself seriously. "I could, of course, prove the seizing of the *Maria Martin* twenty years ago, but even then the case might fall through. Besides, we have no time to lose just now in the work we've undertaken. Again," he added, "if we were arrested, he would most certainly declare that you were searching after treasure, and the Jew who owns the Manor House would at once put a stop to your little game, while the Treasury would keep a pretty watchful eye on you for treasure-trove. No, doctor, we must hold our tongues for the present, and pretend to know absolutely nothing."

"But Purvis? Have you ever heard his name?"

"No. I expect, however, he's one of the gang. Perhaps Old Mister Mystery has had something to do with the piratical crew at one time or another. That would account for his mind wandering back to Black Bennett."

This theory seemed a sound one. It was evident that the old-man-of-the-sea entertained no very good feeling towards the man of whom he had warned us. The mystery was, however, how Purvis, Bennett, and the rest had obtained knowledge of the Italian's hoard.

The only way I could account for it was the deep and curious interest which that rather superior seaman, Harding, had taken in the documents before he had left the *Thrush*. I had not forgotten the apparently easy manner in which he had read off the old documents, nor his insolence towards me when I remonstrated with him.

I saw, too, that Seal, the intrepid skipper, the deep-voiced man whom nothing daunted, had been seized by a curious and incomprehensible anxiety now that he recognized who was our rival in this exciting search.

I felt sure that he had not told us all he knew concerning the red-faced man who was watching our movements so closely.

Why was he concealing the truth from us?

# XXIV

## The Mystery of Margaret Knutton

We returned to the Manor, and Seal, refreshed by his lunch, seized a crowbar and wielding it with his great strength announced himself ready to assist us.

Like ourselves, he felt certain that, the treasure being hidden somewhere in that house, diligent search would have its reward. So he started on his own account tapping walls and investigating loose boards and hollow wainscotting.

We had seen no more of Bennett. He had come to the Plough probably with the object of ascertaining who we were, and had departed as quietly as he had come. Indeed, we should have been in ignorance of his visit had it not been that the skipper had recognized his voice. Job Seal had a very quick ear. He had told me long ago on board the *Thrush* that if he heard a man's voice once he could recognize it again years afterwards. Sometimes partial blindness goes with that faculty, but not so in Seal's case. No man had quicker eye or ear.

After half an hour's search the skipper hit upon a likely spot which we had overlooked. At one end of the corridor, which upstairs ran the whole length of the house, was a small diamond-paned window, while at the other was a blank wall. The latter, when tapped, gave forth a hollow sound. There was a second spot of which we had also suspicion, namely, at the side of the fireplace in the modernized dining-room below.

Upon the latter we commenced first, all three of us working with a will. The afternoon was hot, therefore Seal threw off his coat and vest, rolled up his sleeves, and, blowing like a walrus, wielded the hammer necessary to drive the chisel into the wall.

Before long we had broken into the hollow, but again only disappointment awaited us. It was merely one of those little long cupboards which are so often seen beside the fireplaces in old houses. Upon the shelf within was plenty of dust, but only one object, a well-preserved halfpenny bearing the effigy of King Charles II.

"That's for luck!" Seal cried humorously. "Let's try upstairs, lads."

So up we went, all three of us, and attacked the hollow place in that outer wall. The task was not so easy as that we had just concluded, for it seemed that only a small portion of the wall had been filled with plaster, the rest being very hard concrete, which we had to chip out laboriously with hammer and chisel.

The skipper was, however, enthusiastic in his new sphere. From navigating the *Thrush* he had turned housebreaker, and the fact that the treasure might be there concealed added a keen zest to the work of investigation. He worked, puffing and blowing, until the perspiration rolled off his great furrowed face. The part he had attacked was a particularly hard piece of concrete, which he was painfully chipping out. The plaster we had already removed disclosed a sheet of rusty iron, probably placed over a door, and its discovery had excited the skipper greatly. He expressed himself confident that we were on the verge of a discovery. And so we were.

The dust we raised was suffocating, while the chips of concrete flying in all directions proved a source of considerable danger to one's eyes. A piece went into Reilly's left eye, but we quickly dislodged it, and we continued to work on, eager to ascertain what was concealed behind that iron-cased door.

The previous door we had opened had been a labour in vain, but the iron upon this one had raised our hopes, and we all worked with a will, cutting out of the wall a piece nearly four feet square.

Seal with our long crowbar attacked the iron itself. When he struck it the hollow sound was like an explosion.

"There's a room in here, I'm sure!" cried the skipper.

Then, while we continued, he set to work with the measuring tape, taking the distance from the door of the room to the wall we were attacking, and afterwards measuring inside the room from the door to the end wall. He found a considerable difference in the measurements, by which his excitement was increased.

We worked on without breathing space, for the eager anticipation was contagious. Yet we were compelled to progress by slow degrees and to chip away bit by bit of that hard concrete which they knew how to make so well centuries ago. It was almost as durable as stone itself.

At last we had cut it all away, and the dark iron-cased door stood revealed to us, looking like a modern fire-proof safe, only that it was not green and had no brass handle.

"Je-rusalem!" exclaimed the skipper, "I really believe this is the actual place! Look how carefully it's been concealed! And the iron door, too. Let's have it open, lads, if we have to pull down the bloomin' house to get at it. We'll get the best of Bennett and those murderous swabs yet!"

Again with his long crowbar he attacked the door, but it was unyielding. Gradually, however, Reilly, working more slowly and carefully, was enabled to wedge his chisel between the iron and the stonework. Then, after some difficulty, the skipper's long bar was wedged in the place, and all three of us bore heavily upon it.

Once, twice, thrice we bore down, Seal giving us a sailor's ahoy, and all bearing together.

At last and of a sudden with a terrific wrench the bolts gave way, and the door flew back with a crash and a cloud of dust, disclosing a small room which had been walled up for centuries. The old house, indeed, seemed full of secret chambers.

Reilly lit the hurricane lamp and handed it to me, for I was the first to enter.

The moment I crossed the threshold into the dark little place, no bigger than a good-sized cupboard, I drew back in horror.

On the floor in the thick dust lay a human skeleton!

"What's the matter, doctor?" inquired the captain, entering quickly after me.

"Look!" I cried. "Somebody has been walled up here! Look at those bones."

Seal glanced down to the corner I indicated, and the truth was at once revealed to him. Instead of treasure concealed there, we saw evidence of what was probably some long-forgotten crime.

Reilly was beside me in an instant, but there was hardly room for three of us in the narrow place. I bent down and turned over the bones to examine them more closely. The skeleton was doubled up, as though death had taken place from hunger rather than from want of air.

As I held the light something sparkled, and bending I saw that upon the finger-bones stretched in the dust there still remained three splendid rings. These and the size of the skull and certain of the other bones quickly told me that the person immured there had been a woman.

The three rings I took in my hand and examined them out in the daylight. They were dull and tarnished, but the diamonds in two of them were extremely fine ones, while the third was a signet, upon which was graven the leopard rampant of Da Schorno. With the skeleton was a quantity of silk rags, the remains of the rich brocade dress worn by the victim at the time she was imprisoned there.

The discovery made a deep impression upon the superstitious skipper. Nevertheless, he assisted us to make a close and thorough search of the place. From what we found it was evident that the unfortunate woman had been entrapped there and shut up to die. From the remains of the ragged and brown garments we came to the conclusion that the tragedy had occurred back in the old Elizabethan days, for there were the distinct remains of a ruffle, while scattered about were pearls from a broken string. So long ago, indeed, had the unfortunate woman been placed there to linger until death released her that now, open to the air, the bones were crumbling. The hair on the scalp was still long and almost black, while entangled in it was a small but beautiful rope of pearls of a kind that was the fashion for women to wear in the later days of Queen Bess.

"I suppose it's her ghost that haunts the place," laughed Reilly, as he assisted me to turn over the gruesome remains.

"What?" asked Seal seriously. "Is this house haunted?"

"Oh, the villagers say so," was the reply; "but we've never seen anything, and are not likely to."

"Well, whoever placed the woman there took very good care to conceal her whereabouts," Seal remarked.

"Yes," I said. "Without doubt the poor woman was entrapped and then walled up."

"The same as I've heard certain nuns were treated in the old days before the Reformation," Reilly said. "I've read of remains of women being found walled up in convents."

"Well, in this case death was certainly not voluntary. You see there is no crucifix or image of any saint," and, re-entering, I raised the lantern and examined the rough plastered walls. Suddenly my eyes caught a faint inscription scratched with some sharp instrument on the wall. It told me two things: first, that the woman before her death had a light there; and, second, it gave the name of the victim—

"Margaret Knutton."

The writing was in that upright Elizabethan character, and below was an elaborate flourish. There was no date, only the name, scratched probably with one of the pieces of sharp stone that lay upon the rough floor.

My companions examined it with interest, and were of my opinion that it had been traced by the hand of the woman before she sank and died. Probably she had been held prisoner there for some time before her death, because high up I discovered a small hole in the wall that seemed to run through to the exterior and had once admitted air, but was now

WILLIAM LE QUEUX

blocked up. My examination, too, showed that the woman had had her right arm broken in her youth, and that it had been set unskilfully.

The discovery was not only a complete surprise but also a bitter disappointment, and when we all three had completed our examination of that long-walled-up chamber we closed the door and regarded the great hole in the wall with considerable regret.

We were playing sad havoc with the house, for scarcely a room did not bear the marks of our chisels and crowbars.

Evening fell, and having washed at the pump we went across to the Plough for supper. The day's work had been unsatisfactory, and Seal was silent and thoughtful, as was his habit when things went badly.

We had revealed one gruesome secret of the Manor House if nothing else.

We sat out in the tangled garden for an hour after our return. The sunny place seemed to have lost its charm. The trail of decay and desolation seemed more apparent than usual as my eyes travelled from the broken sundial to the straggling flowers. On going indoors we smoked, the skipper insisting that we should drink rum and hot water. The conversation was mostly a discussion upon likely spots to be opened on the morrow, for, although the captain had been bitterly disappointed, in discovering bones instead of gold, he was still undaunted.

"The treasure is here, I feel sure," he exclaimed a dozen times, in his deep voice. "We'll find it, as sure as my name's Job Seal."

The existence of those secret chambers had certainly raised our hopes, yet we only longed for sight of that cipher plan which the drunken Knutton had sold to our enemies. The only consolation we had was that the plan in question was just as useless to them as it was to us.

That night, after several tots of the spirit which the skipper had brought us, we retired to bed. The night was a perfect one, bright moonlight without a leaf stirring, one of those calm nights when it seems a pity to turn in.

I sleep heavily as a rule, and I must have been in bed three hours or so when a touch on the shoulder suddenly awakened me, and I saw in the moonlight the skipper, in his shirt and trousers, standing by me. A revolver shone in his right hand.

"Wake up, doctor," he whispered. "There's something going on in this house."

He had already awakened Reilly, who was noiselessly slipping on his clothes.

I started up and stared at him, as yet only half awake.

"Don't kick up a row," Seal urged, in a deep whisper. "Listen, do you hear anything?"

A curious noise fell on my ear like slow sawing.

"It's rats," I declared. "This place is worse than the *Thrush* for them."

"No, doctor, it ain't. I know rats well enough. Where's your pistol? You may want it."

I nipped out of bed, and in a couple of minutes stood ready, revolver in hand. Awakened suddenly out of my sleep I moved mechanically, convinced that the finding of the bones and the superstition of the skipper were responsible for it all. But he was deadly in earnest, I saw, and I think that aroused me to a true sense of the situation.

To move about without noise in an empty house is a rather difficult matter, but we all three crept out into the corridor and listened.

The noise seemed to proceed from the centre room—the one wherein we had first discovered a hidden chamber. We opened the door and entered noiselessly.

Yes, the sound came distinctly from the secret hiding-place. Carefully we pushed open the thick oak door and stepped inside.

The sawing stopped, but below where we stood we heard men's voices speaking in gruff undertones.

Our enemies were undermining the house!

WILLIAM LE QUEUX

# XXV

## Reveals the Death-Trap

We strained our ears to distinguish the words spoken by the men beneath us, but without avail.

They seemed to be at work apparently in the thickness of the ponderous wall some few feet below where we stood. Was it possible that they had ascertained from their plan the place where the gold was hidden?

Sometimes it seemed as though they were working upwards towards us, for we could hear a pick upon the stones; and so we waited there, as terriers wait for rats.

Through the remainder of the night we kept a watchful vigil, but about four o'clock in the morning the sounds ceased, and we concluded that they had completed their work—at least for the present. We waited an hour, and hearing no further sound resolved to open the flooring of the place wherein we stood and investigate.

This did not take us long, for as soon as we had cut through the cement we discovered, to our surprise, a wooden trap-door, and on pulling it up there was disclosed a narrow winding-stair in the thickness of the wall, leading down into the foundations of the house. The place smelt damp and musty, and the up-draught blew out the naked candle which the skipper held.

With Reilly holding his hurricane lamp, I descended the rough-hewn stairs, revolver in hand, prepared for any attack. At the bottom, which I judged to be on a level with the cellars, was a stout door that had been recently sawn through, for the sawdust was fresh, and there lay near by several candle-heads. The door had succumbed to the attack of our enemies, and the latter, having opened a way into the house, had evidently retired until the following night.

I chuckled to myself that we were forearmed against any secret attack, and then went forward, finding myself in a dark and narrow tunnel built round with rough stone and sloping downwards. In places the stonework had given way, and it was with difficulty that I squeezed past the fallen earth. Behind me came Reilly with the swinging lantern, the skipper following us close in the rear.

Scarcely a word was uttered by either of us. We were in a long, tortuous burrow that ran deep into the bowels of the earth. I had often read of subterranean passages made in ancient days to provide secret means of egress, but to traverse one was an entirely new and exciting experience.

Bennett and his accomplices had left some of their tools near the scene of their operations, thus showing that they intended to return. But the passage seemed never-ending, now ascending, and again descending sharply. In places water percolated through the roof and fell in cold showers upon us as we passed, while beneath our feet it ran in a small channel onward before us.

On we went, determined to trace the burrow to its end, when, having gone fully a quarter of a mile, I suddenly stumbled, lost my breath, and found myself falling through space into a Stygian darkness. A moment later I struck water, and with my hands frantically clutched at some slimy stones around.

Where I was I had no idea, for the darkness there was impenetrable. I only felt my body in water that was icy cold, and my hands slipping in the thick slime. I cried out loudly for help, and heard the skipper's answering shout.

"Are you hurt, doctor?" I heard him inquire, and looking up I saw the light shining like a star far above me, and the form of my two companions peering down.

Then I knew the truth. I had fallen into a well which, dug right across the path, served as a man-trap to any traversing the tunnel with hostile purpose.

I shouted back to them to return to the house and get ropes.

"Can you hold on?" Reilly inquired.

"Not for long," I answered, for the cold was already cramping my limbs, and in that blackness I dared not move, lest my grip should slip and I should sink. Near me water trickled; beyond that there was no other sound. The air, too, was bad, although, fortunately, it was not poisonous, as is so often the case in wells. The tunnel above was well ventilated, for in places the draught was quite strong, showing that at the end it was open to the air.

Above, my companions held consultation. There was but one lamp, and whoever went back would be compelled to take it. Reilly, being fleet of foot, sped away, leaving the skipper lying full length with his head peering over the edge of the abyss.

He tried to cheer me and keep up my spirits, but I knew from the tremor in his voice how anxious he was.

"Them swabs bridged this place over with planks," he informed me. "But when they retired they drew back the boards after them. Keep up your pecker, doctor, Mr. Reilly will be back in a moment and we'll soon haul you out."

"I'm cold," I said wearily.

"Don't think of it," came his cheery voice through the darkness. "You're going to have a drop o' grog hot when you come up. We can't see you from up here. How far are you down?"

I guessed at about seventy feet, and told him so. But, of course, distances are very deceptive in the dark.

The minutes seemed hours, and a dozen times I felt that my strength must fail before the return of Reilly. But at last I saw a welcome glimmer of light above, and gradually it approached me, let down by a string.

Then I realized my desperate position. Half submerged in the black water, I had only been saved by a jutting piece of stone to which I was clinging. Save for this one piece, all else was smooth and covered with a thick grey slime, while from the light blind newts and strange creeping things scuttled away into their holes in the stones.

Very quickly a rope was dangling near me, and after some effort, my limbs being so cramped, I succeeded in securing it round my waist.

Then, having given the signal, my two friends hauled me out of the death-trap.

Across the abyss there lay two planks that had been used by Bennett and his men, but, not being able to reach them, we all three returned to the house, where I changed my clothes and took a nip of brandy to steady my nerves. My revolver I had lost at the bottom of the well.

Eager to explore the tunnel to its end, my companions obtained two stout planks from the out-house and presently we retraced our steps in slow procession until we came to the death-trap. This we succeeded in bridging successfully, and then continued onward, stumbling over mounds of fallen earth and squeezing through places where the tunnel had collapsed.

Certainly, whoever built the Manor House, whether old Bartholomew or some one before him, had taken precaution to provide a secret mode of egress. For nearly a mile the burrow ran, and although we held the lantern close to the ground, we discovered no other trap for the unwary. Suddenly the narrow way began to ascend, slowly at first, then abruptly. A strange noise caused us to halt and listen. Horses' hoofs and wheels sounded above us. We were beneath a highway.

At last we came to a flight of rough-hewn stone steps leading straight up, with a closed door. We only spoke in whispers, and I, walking first, ascended and tried the latch. It yielded.

Slowly I opened the door, but it creaked upon its hinges, and to our dazzled eyes shone the light of day. Then I slipped through, followed by the others, and we found ourselves beneath a large barn.

This did not take us many minutes to explore, for peering out at the open door we found ourselves in a small farmyard, amid unfamiliar surroundings. The farmhouse, a long, low, thatched place half hidden by roses, lay a little distance off, and as we watched in secret we saw before the house a young girl with cotton sun-bonnet feeding a flock of cackling geese.

We were undecided how to act. It was clear that this was the starting-point of our enemies. Beyond the house lay a small village surrounding a church, therefore it was agreed that while Reilly went into the place to make inquiry as to the occupants of the farm, I should conceal myself with the skipper somewhere in the immediate vicinity.

Therefore, one by one we slipped from beneath the barn, and crossed unnoticed to a small spinney in the rear. From a point of vantage we were afforded a good view of the farm premises, and while I waited with Seal, Reilly took a roundabout route to the village.

We lit our pipes, and, concealed amid the undergrowth, waited and watched. The house seemed a pleasant, old-fashioned one, but, with the exception of an aged labourer in a smock and the goose-girl, there seemed no sign of life. It was just after nine o'clock, a beautiful bright morning, and in the small garden there was a wealth of cottage flowers, the fresh scent of which reached us even in our hiding-place.

The barn beneath which the subterranean passage ended was very old, with patched roof and blackened gables, dating from the same period as the farmhouse, with its mullioned windows and small green diamond panes. Some of the windows had, however, been blocked up in order to avoid the window tax of long ago.

Nearly an hour had passed, and Seal had been yawning, as was his wont, when of a sudden a neat female figure in dark blue appeared in the garden, stooping to gather flowers. She wore a large straw hat which flopped over her face, but as I looked she raised her head in my direction, and I uttered a cry of surprise.

WILLIAM LE QUEUX

The figure was none other than that of Miss Bristowe.

"Look!" I cried, to Seal. "Look at that girl in the garden. That's Miss Bristowe."

The old skipper shaded his eyes with his hands, then exclaimed:—

"Je-hoshaphat! She's a stunning fine woman, that she is! Then it's her lover who's missing?"

"Yes."

"I wonder what she's doing here?"

"Ah, that's the mystery!" I said, watching her gathering the old-fashioned flowers into a great posy.

"You'll need to have a chat with her, doctor. If she likes she can tell us a lot, that's certain."

"But she won't," was my response.

"She may, now that the rascals have made away with the man she loves."

"But don't you recollect what Reilly overheard?" I said. "It seems that, in obedience to the orders of the gang, she deceived him and enticed him, so that he fell into their hands. By that they managed to make her an accessory in the crime, and so ensure her secrecy."

"That's a bit of Black Bennett's cunning ingenuity. He's always artful enough to fix the blame on other people, which accounts for his hair-breadth escapes from the police."

The girl, having gathered sufficient flowers, halted and, leaning her arms upon a small gate, looked wistfully away across the fields. I was near enough to see how wan and pale was her face, and how haggard and worn she seemed. A great change had been wrought in her since our first meeting in that dingy little consulting-room at Walworth.

She had been my friend then. Was she still? I had never ceased to think of her even in the wild excitement of that search after fortune. That pale, beautiful face was ever before me. Those dark, wistful eyes, that told of a dread secret hidden within her heart, seemed everywhere to gaze into mine, just as they had gazed on the last occasion we had met.

I confess to you, my reader, that I loved her—yet she was unapproachable.

# XXVI

## IN WHICH BEN KNUTTON GROWS CONFIDENTIAL

R eilly returned shortly afterwards with a budget of information. When we had traversed the little wood and were out on the highway he told us certain facts that were interesting.

The village was called Bringhurst, distant a mile and a quarter from Caldecott. The place where we had emerged was called the Glebe Farm, and was occupied by an old man called Page, who had as lodgers a gentleman named Purvis and his niece. They often had visitors, two gentlemen who came over from Kettering, and from their description one was Bennett. Purvis had lived there on and off for three weeks, but the young lady had only recently come.

Reilly had learned all this at the little beerhouse at Bringhurst. And he had learned something more, namely, that there was some village gossip regarding the young lady.

"Gossip!" I demanded. "What is it?"

"Well," answered Reilly, "the old innkeeper says that she's been seen out walking late at night with that drunken scamp who sold Purvis the parchment."

"What!" I cried. "With old Ben Knutton, of Rockingham?"

"That's so."

"Then he knows her," I exclaimed, quickly. "He'll be able to tell me something. I must see him to-day. A pot or two of beer will make him talk."

According to Reilly the villagers of Bringhurst had no suspicion of the reason Purvis lived at the Glebe Farm, nor were they aware of the existence of the secret communication between the two villages. It was certain, however, that Purvis and Bennett knew of it, and for that reason the former had taken up his quarters there. The man Page was probably unaware of the tunnel, for it led from beneath his barn with the entry well concealed. One fact, however, I had not overlooked. At the bottom of the steps which led up to the surface a wall had been recently broken down, showing that the tunnel had been closed up for years and had only recently been opened.

The men who had worked so assiduously during the night were probably within the farmhouse. At any rate, on our walk back to Caldecott along the white highway through the village of Great Easton we saw nothing of them.

When we returned to the Manor a ridiculous position presented itself. We were locked out! All windows and doors we had barred on the inside; therefore Reilly, an adept at scaling walls, clambered up a rain-spout and effected an entrance by one of the upper windows.

We took counsel together and arrived at two conclusions, namely, that our rivals had by some means obtained possession of the secret of the underground passage, and, secondly, that they, like ourselves, were convinced that the treasure lay hidden upon the premises we occupied.

This caused our excitement to increase rather than diminish; but after lunch at the Plough I strolled down to Rockingham, while my companions returned to resume their investigations.

I found that Ben Knutton was at work. He was cleaning out a ditch on the edge of Thoroughsale Wood, and I was directed to the spot, about a mile away. I discovered the old fellow without much difficulty, and my appearance there was something of a surprise to him.

At my request he put down his spade and came to the stile whereon I seated myself.

"Well, Knutton," I said, "I've come to have another little chat with you—a confidential chat, you understand. Now look here, before we begin I've one thing to say, and that is if you answer all my questions truthfully there's half a sovereign for you."

"Thankee, sir," responded the bibulous old rascal, touching his hat. "What did you want to know, sir?"

"Listen," I said. "There's a young lady staying over at Mr. Page's at Bringhurst. You know her?"

"Yes, sir, I knows 'er. I've knowed 'er since she were a little girl."

"Then tell me all about her," I said.

"Well, there ain't very much to tell," responded the old man. "I don't know who was 'er father. She came to my sister-in-law as a nurse-child from London when she was about two years old. They say 'er father and mother were rich people. But Fanny Stanion, my sister-in-law, who lived over at Deenethorpe, brought her up, and got paid for it by a lawyer in Oundle. You don't know Deenethorpe. It's about five miles from here."

"Near Deene?" I suggested, for I had been photographing in Lady Cardigan's beautiful park.

"Yes, close by," was the labourer's reply. "Fanny had 'er with 'er nigh on twelve years and was like a mother to 'er, and often brought 'er over to Rockingham to see us. Then, when Fanny died, she was sent back to London, an' some lady, I believe, took charge of 'er and sent her to boardin' school somewhere in Devonshire. I ain't seen little Dolly these seven years till the other day when she came to my cottage. My! Ain't she grown to be a fine young 'ooman? I didn't know 'er ag'in," and the old man leaned upon the rail and laughed. Men who work in the fields at all hours and in hot and cold weather age very early; the furrows grow deep on their faces and the skin is crossed and recrossed with multitudinous lines like a spider's web, the spine gets bent from the long hours of stooping over the earth, and the heat and the damp and the frost all turn by turn enter into the bones, and stiffen and cramp them before old age is due.

"Is nothing known regarding her parentage?" I asked. "Have you never heard any story about her?"

"No, nothing. The lawyer in Oundle who used to pay Fanny monthly probably knew all about it, but he's dead now. Fanny had the child brought to her through answerin' an advertisement in the *Stamford Mercury*. My poor wife used to be particular fond o' little Dolly."

"And why did she call to see you? Had she an object in doing so?"

"I suppose she wanted to visit the cottage ag'in," was the old man's answer. "But she's growed such a fine London lady that I was quite taken aback when she told me she was Dolly Drummond."

"Drummond! Why, that's not her name," I cried. "I mean Miss Bristowe."

"You said the young lady who lives at Mr. Page's, eh?"

"Certainly. A tall, dark young lady."

"That's Dolly Drummond. There's only one lady livin' there. She's with her uncle, Mr. Purvis."

"Do you know anything about him?"

"Only that he's 'er uncle—'er guardian, too, I fancy. She didn't tell me much about him, and I haven't seen him myself."

"Well," I said; "you may be surprised to know that he's the man to whom you sold that piece of parchment."

"What!" cried the old man, glaring at me. "Is he 'er uncle? Why, then, that accounts for the questions she put to me."

"What about?"

"About the old secret way from the Glebe Farm into the Manor House at Caldecott. My father knew about it, and told me of it, but nobody's been able to find it yet."

"And the young lady came to you for information?"

"She's heard me mention it when she were a girl, so I suppose her curiosity was aroused and that was why she came to me for information."

"More likely that the man Purvis sent her. Perhaps they've discovered what was written on that parchment, and are now making use of it. But I hear you've met her at night."

"Who told you so?" he asked, starting at my words.

"It is common gossip in Bringhurst."

The old fellow laughed heartily, and in his broad dialect said:—

"They'll be saying next that I'm the young lady's father, and that I want it kept secret."

"Why did you meet her at such late hours?"

"Because she wanted to talk to me about her youth. She seems very anxious to find out who were her parents, and for that reason I believe she's down here."

"Isn't it rather remarkable that Purvis should be with her?"

"It is. I don't like that man. I'm very sorry I didn't show you the parchment afore I sold it to him, sir."

With that latter sentiment I heartily coincided. Had I not been forestalled, the treasure would have undoubtedly been ours long ago.

"But tell me more about Miss Drummond," I urged.

"What is there to tell? When she was old enough Fanny sent 'er to the national school at Deenethorpe. But she wasn't at all like the village children. She was always the lady, even when quite young."

"Your sister-in-law was well paid, I suppose?"

"Yes. She was a widow, and only had the money from the lawyer to live upon. Her husband was a wood-cutter, and was killed by a tree falling on him over in Carlton Purlieus. One time Fanny fell ill, and we had little Dolly with us at Rockingham for nigh on a year."

Little wonder was it that she should have sought out the good-for-nothing old labourer who had in his younger and more sober days been as guardian to her.

"But I can't understand why she should wish to meet you late at night," I remarked.

"She didn't wish her uncle to know of our meetin', she said. Besides, she had a lot to ask me about her earlier days, and a lot to tell me of how she had fared since she had left these parts."

"Did she make any mention of that story about the fortune of the Knuttons?"

"Well, sir, she did," responded the old fellow, rather puzzled at what I had divined. "She told me how she remembered me telling her all about it when a girl, and how her Aunt Fanny, as she called her, used to prophesy that one day we should be very rich."

"And what else?"

"She made me point out the route which I believed was taken by the old subterranean passage. That's why we walked through the fields and were seen together."

"Well," I said at last, "I want you to do something for me, Knutton, and if you carry it through successfully I'll give you a sovereign instead of half a sovereign. I want you to go over to the Glebe Farm this afternoon and take a letter to her. It must be given to her in secret, remember. Ask for a reply, merely yes or no. You understand?"

"Oh, I'll take the letter, sir, an' be glad to do it," the old labourer cried eagerly.

"Very well, we'll go back together to your cottage and I'll write it. Then you take it, and I'll wait at the Sonde Arms until you return with the reply. You must be careful, however, that this man Purvis doesn't see you, or you may make it awkward for Miss Drummond in a variety of ways."

"Trust me, sir," was his response. "I knows my way about the Glebe Farm. I worked there on and off for three years."

"Then you know the big barn. Underneath it is a door leading to some steps. Do you know them?"

"Know them, why, o' course I do. The steps lead nowhere. There was once a well at the bottom, they say, but it's been bricked up because it used to over-flow up to the barn door."

It was evident that the entrance had been unsuspected, and that the subterranean communication had only very recently been opened.

The old fellow shouldered his spade and with bent back walked beside me into Rockingham, where, upon a leaf from my note-book, I wrote an urgent line to the woman whose great beauty and sweet grace had enchanted me. I prayed of her to do me a favour and give me an appointment at a spot on the high road between Great Easton and Caldecott which I had noticed that morning—a place where, according to the sign-post, the road to Market Harborough joined that to Wellingborough. I sealed the note and, having watched the old fellow down the road, turned into the Sonde Arms to smoke and kill time until his return.

What he had told me added a further touch of romance to that pale-faced, troubled woman who had so strangely entered my life. Impatient and fidgety I lounged in the inn, smoking and trying to read the newspaper, until at last Ben, after an absence of an hour and a half, returned.

"I managed to send a message in to her by old Sam Lucas, the shepherd, and she came out and met me behind the barn. She read your letter, sir, and turned a little red. She seemed to hesitate like, and then asked me if I knowed you. When I told her I did, she said I was to say she'd meet you at eight o'clock to-night at the place you mentioned."

My heart leaped for joy.

I slipped the coin agreed upon into the old fellow's horny palm, and with injunctions to secrecy left the place and hurried along the road, over the level crossing, into Caldecott, where I told my companions of my tryst.

During my absence they had taken up the flooring of one of the downstairs rooms, but the search had been in vain, and they were now working in their shirt-sleeves replacing the boards.

"We shall have another visit from them swabs to-night, doctor," Seal said, as he mopped the perspiration from his sea-bronzed face. "There'll be some fun in this house before morning, that's my firm belief."

By "fun," the skipper meant fighting, for if he met Black Bennett we knew there would be blows—and hard ones too.

Punctually at eight o'clock I halted beneath the weather-worn sign-post. The crimson after-glow had faded and the still evening was far advanced. Away in the west the red glow still showed from behind the hills, but in the east crept up the dark night-clouds. The hour struck from the church towers of several villages, and away in the far distance the curfew commenced to toll solemnly, just as it has ever done since the far-back Norman days.

With eyes and ears on the alert, I stood awaiting her coming.

She was late—as a woman always is—but at last I saw the flutter of a light dress approaching in the twilight, and went eagerly forward to meet her.

In the fading light I saw her face. To me it looked more beautiful than before, because the cheeks were slightly flushed as I raised my hat to greet her.

I took her hand, and it trembled in my grasp. She looked for a single instant into my face, then dropped her eyes without uttering a word. By that sign I felt convinced that the satisfaction of our clandestine meeting was mutual.

Ah! how deeply I loved her! So deeply, indeed, that in the first moments of our meeting I was tongue-tied.

Surely ours was a strange wooing; but, as will be seen, its dénouement was far stranger.

# XXVII

## Dorothy Drummond Prefers Secrecy

Dorothy looked more worn and anxious than on that morning when I had walked with her in Westbourne Grove. But the air of mystery enveloped her still, and to even the casual observer her face was interesting as that of a woman with some tragic history.

"Miss Drummond," I said, "it is a real pleasure to me that we meet again."

She started at the mention of her name, but made no comment, except to say, in her sweet, well-modulated voice:—

"The pleasure is mutual, I assure you, Dr. Pickering." Then she asked: "How did you know I was staying in this neighbourhood?"

I explained how I had seen her emerge from the farmhouse and gather the flowers, and what old Ben Knutton had told me of her youth.

"I had no idea that you knew this district," I added.

"Yes," she responded, looking around her, "I've known it all my life. Every house, every field, every tree is familiar to me, for here I spent my happiest days," and a slight sigh escaped her as her memory ran back.

We were walking together slowly along a path beside the winding Welland. She knew the way, and had led me through a gate and across a small strip of pasture down to the river. We were safer from observation there than upon the open highway, she said.

After we had been chatting some time she suddenly grew serious, and said:—

"Do you know, Doctor Pickering, why I've come to you to-night?"

"No, but I hoped it was to resume our pleasant companionship," I said.

"It was to warn you."

"Of what?"

"Of your enemies."

"You mean those men Bennett and Purvis," I said, hoping to learn something from her. "Purvis is your uncle, is he not?"

She glanced at me quickly, and responded in the affirmative.

"Tell me, Miss Drummond," I urged, "are you aware of the reason I am staying here?"

"I know it all," she replied, in a strained voice. "I am well aware that you are searching for the hidden gold, which you cannot find. I am aware, too, that you hold the key to the plan, and that by aid of that key the place of concealment could be at once ascertained."

"Mr. Purvis bought the plan from old Knutton," I remarked.

"Yes; the drunken old idiot sold it, even though it had been in possession of his family for centuries. The treasure would be partly his if it could be discovered."

"But does Mr. Purvis know anything definite regarding the place where it is hidden?"

"He believes it to be in the Manor House, and for that reason they have reopened the old subway from the Glebe to the Manor. He has with him the man Bennett, said to be one of the worst characters outside the walls of a gaol."

"I know; they call him Black Bennett," I said.

"Beware of them," she urged. "They will hesitate at nothing to possess themselves of the treasure. They would kill you."

The recollection of what Reilly had witnessed in London flashed through my mind. It was on the tip of my tongue to mention it, yet I feared to do so, not knowing what effect it might have upon her highly strung temperament.

"What Knutton has told me regarding your romantic life has aroused my interest, Miss Drummond," I said presently. "Did you never know your parents?"

"Alas! no. They died when I was quite young. All I know about them is that they lived somewhere in Norfolk, and that my father was ruined by speculation just before his death. I was fourteen when the good woman who brought me up died, and my Aunt Lewis sent me to school. Then on her death, quite recently, Mr. Purvis became my guardian."

"But who and what is this man Purvis?" I asked. "I know you are unhappy. Confide in me everything. I give you my bond of secrecy," I said earnestly.

"I knew nothing of his existence until a few weeks ago, when Aunt Lewis died and Mr. Purvis came forward and promised to look after me. I had taken up typewriting and obtained a clerkship in a City office, which I held until I resigned a fortnight ago to come down here."

"At Purvis's suggestion?"

"Yes, because I am acquainted with the district."

"Then you lived alone in Bayswater?" I suggested.

"Yes. I have never lived under the same roof with Purvis, except here at Page's, because I—I hate him."

"Why?"

Her pale, quivering lips compressed, but no word escaped them.

I knew the truth. The man was implicated in the assassination of her lover, if not the actual murderer. Therefore she held him in loathing.

"Well," I said at length, as we strolled along beside the dark, silent stream, "tell me the story of the treasure as my enemies know it. We are friends, Miss Drummond, and our enemies are mutual. Cannot we unite forces and combat them?"

"Oh!" she sighed, "I only wish we could. I fear, however, that it is impossible." There was a pathos in her voice which showed that the words came direct from a heart overburdened with grief.

"What do these men know about me?" I inquired.

"Everything. They have watched you vigilantly day and night, and are aware of every movement on your part. They know the whole story of how you discovered the derelict, and what you found on board. They even know the contents of certain of the parchments you recovered— one, I think, had a number of signatures upon it."

"The one stolen from Mr. Staffurth's?" I cried.

"Yes. But they had a copy of that long before. From what I've heard, there was on board your steamer a man named Harding, who had sailed as seaman, but who was a professor of Latin who had come down in the world. It was he who made the copy and translation and sold it to some one, who afterwards sold it to Purvis. The latter lost no time in coming here and buying the parchment from Knutton, thus forestalling you."

"Was Harding previously acquainted with Purvis?"

"I think so. The copy and information were not, however, sold direct, but through a third person."

"Are they sanguine of success?"

"Oh, yes," she answered. "By some means they've discovered evidence that the gold is concealed in the Manor House."

"In what part?"

"Ah! That is not known. They intend to make a search. To-night they will probably break through—four of them. Therefore be on the alert."

I explained how we had been aroused on the previous night by the cutting of the door, and how we had explored the passage as far as the Glebe Farm. Then, laying her hand upon my arm, she said earnestly—

"Oh, Dr. Pickering, do be careful! I fear that you may come to harm at the hands of these unscrupulous men."

"But why have you associated yourself with them?" I asked, taking her hand and speaking very seriously.

She was silent. Then at last she answered:—

"Because I am unfortunately compelled."

"But the fact that this man Purvis is your guardian is no reason why you should participate in his scheme. He seems an adventurer, just as Bennett is known to be one."

"Ah! doctor," she cried, turning to me suddenly, her whole form trembling, "do not argue thus! You do not know; you cannot know all."

But I knew, and regarded her with pity born of love.

Those men held her to them by threats of exposure. She had enticed that unknown man to his death, and was therefore an accessory. The hideous truth was plain. She was the puppet and decoy of these scoundrels. She had decoyed me on that night when she had taken me to Blackheath, but at the last moment her better nature had rebelled and she had sent me back without any explanation more than a lame excuse.

I saw how utterly helpless she was in the hands of that pair of assassins. When I questioned her I found that the sum Purvis allowed her was very small, and that long before the death of her Aunt Lewis she had earned her own living as a typewriter.

By dint of careful questioning I endeavoured to obtain from her some facts regarding Purvis' private life, but she appeared to know but little of it. He now lived at Hammersmith, she said, but she never visited his house unless at his orders, and then the motive was generally in connexion with their scheme to gain possession of the treasure.

It is always advantageous to have a friend in the camp of the enemy, and in this case what Dorothy Drummond told me ultimately proved of the greatest service to us.

I longed to explain the knowledge I possessed regarding the murder at Kilburn, yet how could I? If she suspected that I knew the truth she would, in her present agitated state of mind, flee from me in terror lest I should betray her.

"Cannot you sever yourself entirely from these men?" I suggested. "Indeed, Miss Drummond, I hate to think of you participating in the desperate schemes of such adventurers. Suppose they should fall into the hands of the police, you also may be implicated!"

She burst into a torrent of tears at my words and, halting, covered her face with her hands. Tenderly I strove to console her, and placing my hand upon her shoulder, there in the darkness, I bent to her ear and in hot, fervent words told her my secret—that I loved her.

She heard me in silence, sobbing till the end. Then, in a hoarse, broken voice, she answered:—

"No. It is impossible! You must not tell me this—you must not entertain any affection for me."

"Why not, Dorothy?" I asked, calling her for the first time by her Christian name. "Have I not confessed to you how I love you with all the passion of which a man is capable? For weeks and weeks you have been my all in all. Waking or sleeping, your face has been ever before me, and I feel by a mysterious intuition that our lives in future are bound to one another."

"Ah, spare me!" she cried, through her tears. "Spare me! I cannot bear to hear your words. Would that I might return your love, but I dare not. No, I dare not—for your sake, as well as for mine."

Was she thinking of her dead lover, and of the traitorous part she had been compelled to play? Yes. She hated herself, and at the same time held me in fear.

"But you love me, Dorothy?" I whispered. "Tell me, truthfully and honestly."

"No, no," she urged. "Do not seek to wring the truth from me. Let us part. We must never meet again after to-night. I—I saved you once from death, that night when I took you to Blackheath," she went on breathlessly. "It suddenly dawned upon me that they meant to kill you and secure all the documents which you had found on board the derelict. They awaited you in a house they had taken for the purpose, and compelled me to come to you with a fictitious story regarding my brother, and to induce you to walk into the trap. Held in bondage, I dared not disobey, and came to you. But at the last moment I compelled you to return and went back to face their anger. Why did I act as I did? Cannot you guess?"

"Perhaps, Dorothy, it was because you entertained a spark of affection for me?"

A silence fell between us for some moments. Then she answered in a low voice, only just audible:—

"You have guessed aright. It was."

I leant towards her and kissed her cold, hard-set lips. She made no remonstrance, only she shuddered in my grasp, and a second later returned my caress and then burst again into tears.

"Ah, you must not care for me," she declared. "I am unworthy. You don't know everything, or you would hate me rather than love me."

"But I love you with the whole strength of my being, Dorothy!" I declared, in deep earnestness. "That is enough. Now that you reciprocate my affection I am satisfied. I want for no more. You are mine, darling, and I am yours—for ever."

"But I fear that you may bitterly repent this—I fear that when you know all my past your love will turn to hatred and your admiration to loathing."

"The past does not concern us, dearest," I answered tenderly, with my arm about her slim waist. "It is for the future we must live, and to that end assist one another." And again I pressed my lips to hers fondly in all the ecstasy of my new-found happiness.

What further description can I give of those moments of bliss? You, my reader, know well the sweet idyllic peace that comes in the stillness of night when two hearts beat in unison. Wisely or unwisely, you have loved with all the ardour of your nature, just as I loved. You remember well the passion of those first caresses, the music of those fervent words of devotion, and the opening vista of happiness unalloyed.

Pause for a moment and reflect upon first your own love, and you will know something of my tender feelings toward the poor hapless woman whose pure and loving heart was frozen by the terror of exposure.

WILLIAM LE QUEUX

# XXVIII

## We Receive Midnight Visitors

I took leave of my love reluctantly at ten o'clock, just outside Bringhurst village. She was anxious to be back at the farm before the return of Purvis, who had gone that morning to London on some secret errand, and was returning by the last train.

She had entirely enchanted me. The more I saw of her, the more graceful, the more charming, she seemed. There was nothing loud or masculine about her; she was a sweet, modest woman, yearning for love, sympathy, and protection.

The manner in which she was bound to this clever gang of rogues was still a mystery. In me she had confided many things during those two calm hours of our new-born love, but from me she still concealed the real reason why her interests were bound up in those of Purvis, Bennett, and their two accomplices. I guessed, and believed that I guessed aright. The tragedy at Kilburn held her to them irrevocably. She was entirely and helplessly in their hands, to fetch and carry, to do their bidding; indeed, to act unlawfully at their command.

If that were so, surely no woman could be in a more horrible position—compelled to be the accomplice of assassins.

I thought it all over as, in the darkness, I walked back to Caldecott.

True, I had gained her affection that night. Yet, together with the perfect bliss that comes in the first hour of true love, there had also come to me the hideous truth of her bondage.

The last train from Rugby having rushed past, sparks flying from the engine and awakening the echoes of the night, stopped for a moment at Rockingham Station and then continued its journey eastward. And presently, as I walked onward in the darkness, I encountered a man whose face I could not see, for we passed each other beneath the shadow of some trees. I saw he was tall and thin, and wore a long light overcoat. He was whistling to himself, as a lonely man sometimes whistles to keep himself company.

His silhouette stood out distinctly in the gloom, and although I saw not his countenance I knew well that it was my enemy Purvis—the man who held my love in bondage.

Back at the Manor I found everything prepared for siege. Seal was not a man to stand idle if there was any chance of a scrimmage. Like all giants in strength, he loved fighting. His hesitation to face Black Bennett had now entirely disappeared, and over his rum that night he expressed a most fervent hope that the "white-livered swabs," as he termed them, would appear in the secret passage.

On the table between us lay three revolvers, and as we took counsel together each of us smoked furiously. I told them something of what Dorothy Drummond had related to me, how our enemies meant to raid us, and of their firm belief that the treasure was concealed there. But I said nothing of my tender passion, nor did I allow them to suspect the real object of our clandestine meeting.

"Ah!" remarked Reilly. "If you could only get Miss Drummond, or Bristowe, or whatever is her real name, to secure that parchment of old Knutton's, then the game would be entirely in our own hands."

"That's unfortunately impossible," I answered. "The man Purvis has it securely put away. I have already mentioned it to her, and she tells me that she has no idea where it is."

"Well," remarked the skipper, "Black Bennett and his men are just as much in the dark as we are. Let 'em come. They'll get a warm reception. How many of 'em are there?"

"Four. Bennett and the other two are lodging in Kettering."

"The only reason of the secret attack upon us, as far as I can see, is in order to gag and secure us while they make a thorough search of the premises. They surely wouldn't dare to kill the whole three of us in our beds!" said Reilly.

"They won't kill Job Seal, you can bet your sea-boots on that," remarked the skipper with a grin upon his great furrowed face.

But my mind was running upon the tragedy at Kilburn, and I was trying to devise some means by which we might denounce the whole gang, and hand them over to the police.

There was, alas! one fact which would ever prevent us taking such an action. If we boldly charged them with murder, Dorothy must be implicated. To arrest them would mean arrest for her. She had acted as decoy, and could not deny it!

So I was compelled to abandon all hope in that direction. By sheer force we would be compelled to combat this quartette of unscrupulous adventurers, and to that end we awaited their coming.

So thoroughly and carefully had we examined every hole and corner

WILLIAM LE QUEUX

of the house that all three of us were beginning to despair of ever discovering the hidden hoard. In an old-fashioned mansion of that character there were a thousand and one places where gold might be stored. In chimneys, under stairs, beneath the flags of the big, vaulted cellars, behind the large, open fireplaces—some of which still had their quaint iron dogs of ancient days—all these places we had investigated in vain. Not a single room was there but bore traces of our chisels, picks and crowbars. The result of our search consisted in two or three copper coins, an old letter dated in 1796, a skeleton with rings upon the fingers, an old leathern mug, and two or three articles not worth enumeration.

We were sorely disappointed. We could not conceal from ourselves the bare fact that at any rate in the Manor House the treasure of Bartholomew da Schorno was non-existent, and, furthermore, we feared that some one in generations past had been before us and secured it in secret.

Nevertheless, the careful and ingenious actions of our enemies in order to gain entry into the place puzzled us. From what my love had told me, they were evidently in possession of some information of which we were in ignorance—information which made it plain that, after all, the treasure was actually there.

They meant mischief; we had no doubt about that. But, being forewarned, we calmly awaited their coming, Seal chuckling to himself at the reception they would receive.

The church clock struck midnight. We had moved into the room from which the secret way opened, and, Reilly having produced a pack of cards, we played nap in under-tones, our weapons lying at hand in case of need.

Now and then—indeed, after every game—one or other of us rose and listened within the secret chamber for the approach of the invaders. One o'clock passed, two o'clock, yet no sound save the familiar thumping and squealing of the rats and the dismal howling of the wind in the wide, old-fashioned chimney.

Seal had lost five shillings, and had therefore become engrossed in the game, when of a sudden we heard a low grating noise. In an instant we were on our feet, revolver in hand, and according to our pre-arranged plan our light was at once extinguished.

It was our object to watch and take the intruders by surprise.

Without a sound we all three moved across the room and out into the corridor, concealing ourselves in a big cupboard upon which Reilly had placed an inside fastening. Our bedrooms we had locked and had the keys in our pockets, intending that our enemies should believe us to be asleep. In the cupboard door Reilly had bored holes that enabled us to see without being seen, while beside us were lamps ready to be lit in case of emergency.

Boxed up there, we waited, scarce daring to breathe lest we should betray our presence. We could hear low, gruff whispers and expressions of surprise as the invaders crept out of the secret chamber into the room. From their muffled tread we knew they had stockings pulled over their boots, and from our spy-holes we saw Bennett, lantern in hand, emerge into the corridor and look up and down to see that all was clear. Then he crept out, followed by three others, one of whom, I saw, was tall and gaunt, with fair moustache—the man who held my love beneath his thrall.

Creeping along quietly, they passed us in procession, carrying chisels and picks, and taking every precaution against surprise. Having traversed the corridor, they descended the wide oaken stairs to the ground floor, where the uncertain light of the lanterns was quickly lost to view.

As soon as they had passed out of hearing, Reilly took up the hurricane lamp and opening the cupboard let us out, whispering:—

"Watch them, doctor. See where they try, but don't give the alarm until I return." Then he left us, and we heard nothing more of him. His quick disappearance was a surprise to both of us, for he had previously told us nothing of his intentions, and had apparently acted on the spur of the moment.

At first Seal had been inclined to meet them at their entrance and drive them back, but to me such a proceeding seemed useless. My idea was to watch and ascertain where they went. Their own actions would betray the spot where they believed the gold was concealed. Our council had been a long one, but my suggestion had been adopted. Hence our retirement into the cupboard.

Job Seal had no love for Black Bennett, and as we crept along the corridor after them he gave vent to a strong nautical imprecation between his teeth. At the top of the staircase we listened, but could hear no sound. Therefore we crept down, fearing every moment the creaking oak might betray us, for the thin-worn old stairs were loose in places and gave forth sounds that in the night awakened the echoes of the empty place.

We arrived safely in the stone hall and halted, our ears strained to catch the slightest sound. We, however, heard nothing. All was silent as the grave. Indeed, the invaders with their swinging lanterns had passed by us silently in single file and seemed to have disappeared.

"They must have gone down to the cellars," I whispered to Seal. Therefore we passed through the big stone kitchen into a small scullery beyond, from which a flight of stone steps led into the deep vaulted basement. The stout door was closed, but listening at it we heard voices quite distinctly. Our enemies were below, apparently divided in opinion as to the exact spot to open.

We heard one authoritative voice, which the skipper at once recognized as Bennett's, saying:—

"I tell you that it's here, in this side wall. Don't you remember that the old fortune-teller said three times three from the bottom of the steps. Look!" and we heard him count one, two, three—to nine, as he measured the paces. "It's in this wall, here. Come, let's get to work, and don't make any noise, either. Is the door above closed?"

Somebody gave an affirmative response, and soon afterwards we heard the sound of chisels upon the stones. They worked with very little noise, so little, indeed, that had we been asleep the sound would not have reached us.

With Seal standing beside me, his fingers itching to come in contact with Bennett, I think I must have stood there nearly half an hour. The work went on unceasingly, silently, hardly a word being spoken. Reilly's absence surprised me, but soon we heard a low whisper inquiring where the intruders were, and our companion stood beside us listening.

"They evidently know something of the right spot," I whispered to him. "They're taking down part of the foundations. Hark!"

A man was speaking—probably Purvis.

"Now we're here, we ought to see whether they've made any investigations. Come, Harding, let's go up and have a look round while they're getting those stones out. We'll only be ten minutes or so. Have you got the torch?"

"All right," responded the other, and I knew by the name and the voice that it was the seaman of the *Thrush* who had read those documents and who had been insolent at my remonstrance.

The instant, however, we heard their intention we sprang out of the kitchen and upstairs to our previous hiding-place. The cupboard was not in the least suspicious—one of those generally built in old houses for the storage of linen. If they found it locked they would not risk awakening us by forcing the door.

Up came the two men a few minutes later, passing from one open room to the other, taking a general look at the place with an electric torch, and expressing whispered surprise at the havoc we had played with the walls. Finding the doors of our two bedrooms locked, they did not touch them for fear of disturbing us.

Seal was impatient to make an attack upon them, but I considered that discretion was best, and that to watch was more politic than to show fight. So we waited in silence, until the grey dawn shone through the long corridor. Then at last we heard a slight movement, and the men re-passed in procession as noiselessly as they had come, and disappeared into the room.

Reilly opened the cupboard and listened. We heard a bang as the door in the flooring was shut down after they had descended to the underground burrow; then in a moment he was all excitement.

"Come, help me quickly!" he cried, rushing forward into the secret chamber. "Quick! pile up these stones so that they cannot re-open the flap! They will return very soon. Quick!" And he began frantically heaping upon the trap-door the stones that we had taken from the wall, a work in which Seal and I assisted with a will.

When at last we had secured it by wedging two crowbars across the heap of stones so that it could not possibly be opened from below, Reilly burst into loud laughter and danced with delight, saying:—

"We've trapped them, doctor! Trapped them all like vermin! When I left you I rushed down the passage to the well and found it bridged. I drew the boards away and tossed them down into the water. They can't get across by any means. Come! Let's close the door!" And he pulled back into its place the stout, iron-studded oak with the supreme satisfaction of knowing that he had entombed the invaders in that damp, dismal burrow which they themselves had discovered.

WILLIAM LE QUEUX

# XXIX

## Dorothy Makes a Confession

"Trapped the swabs!" cried Job Seal, rubbing his big hands with undisguised delight, although he seemed disappointed that we had not allowed him to come face to face with Bennett. From the skipper's determined attitude I knew that murder would be done if the two men met, therefore I took to myself some credit for having kept them apart, even though they had passed within a yard of one another.

"Trapped the whole four of 'em!" he exclaimed, his great face lit by a grin as he placed his hands to his sides. "Mr. Reilly," he added, "I've respect for you, sir. You've checkmated 'em entirely."

"I'd thought it all over," was the younger man's reply. "And if any of them fall down the well it isn't our look-out. They had no right to intrude here."

"But can they get across by any means?" I queried, knowing well the characters of the quartette.

"Impossible—absolutely impossible," Reilly replied. "I can jump as far as most men, but I couldn't jump that. They have no ropes, or any means by which to bridge the death-trap."

I glanced at my watch. It was then a quarter past four. Morning broke, bright and sunny, with a slight mist rising from the river, but still we waited in that upstairs room for signs of the invaders returning.

Half an hour went by, and suddenly we heard noises below.

They were trying to raise the trap-door down which they had passed, but we knew that all efforts to do so were useless, for, besides the stones upon it, we had so wedged the crowbars across and into holes in the wall that to push up the flap was utterly impossible.

From where we stood we could hear their voices mingled with the groans of their united efforts.

"Stay there, you unutterable sons of dogs!" growled Job Seal, and although those were not exactly the words he used, they were synonymous.

I stood listening, and could hear the low curses of the men whom we had captured like rats in a run.

Together we went downstairs and out into the early sunshine. The bright air refreshed us, although our thoughts were with those four men consigned to a living tomb.

Presently we re-entered the house and descended to the cellar where they had been at work. By the light of a candle which the skipper carried we were surprised to see what an enormous hole they had made through the foundations into the earth beyond. Indeed, they had taken out a great piece of the wall, and through the rough arch had driven a tunnel two yards high and some three yards long. It was there they had evidently expected to discover the treasure, but, like ourselves, they had worked in vain.

The strong-smelling earth excavated lay piled in the cellar up to the roof, and the manner in which the work had been performed showed that at least one of the party was used to such operations. But there was nothing else there, save a few candle-ends.

It struck us all three as very remarkable why the intruders should have gone straight to that spot and commenced their investigation there. Evidently they were in possession of certain precise information of which we were in utter ignorance, yet, holding them entrapped in that long, subterranean passage without exit, we should now be enabled to pursue further investigations in the direction they themselves had indicated.

Seal, without coat or vest, spent an hour in tapping every part of the wall, but was compelled to admit that he discovered no hollow place. Therefore, recollecting the mention of the paces from the bottom of the steps, we measured them in an opposite direction and began to attack the wall.

Through the whole morning we all three worked in the semi-darkness, but having cut out a great circular piece from the huge wall we only found the soft, chalky earth beyond, and no sign whatever of the presence of gold.

All was disappointing—utterly disheartening.

At noon we made ourselves presentable, and went over to the Plough for lunch. While we were still seated at table the inn-keeper's sister entered and told me that Ben Knutton wished to speak with me, a request to which I responded with alacrity.

Outside I found the bent old fellow awaiting me. The very fact that he would not enter the inn told me that what he wished to say was in secrecy.

WILLIAM LE QUEUX

"Mornin', sir," he exclaimed, in a low voice, touching his battered hat respectfully. "Dolly's sent me, sir, with a message to you." And fumbling in his trousers pocket he placed in my hand a crumpled letter.

We were standing behind a blank wall, with none to watch our movements; therefore I tore open the missive eagerly and read the few hastily-scribbled lines therein.

"Dear Paul," *she wrote,* "I am returning to London at once.
If you write, do not address the letter to the library at
Kensington, but to me at 120, Cornwall Road, Bayswater.
Recollect the warning I gave you yesterday. Mr. P. went out
last night, but he has not returned.

Yours,
D. D.

"Has Miss Drummond left Bringhurst?" I asked the old labourer.

"Yes, sir. I saw her off by the train for London. She's not coming back, she said."

This surprised me. What, I wondered, could have occurred to take her away so suddenly, especially after our exchange of vows on the previous night? Re-reading the letter I found it cold and rather reserved, scarcely the communication of a woman filled with passionate love, as I believed her to be. She gave no reason for her sudden flight, although she warned me again of impending danger. Evidently she did not know that the four malefactors were entombed.

I returned to my companions, and became filled with a longing to go up to London.

I think Job Seal had had almost enough of the Manor House. That skeleton troubled his superstitious mind, therefore he was the first to hail my suggestion with approval. He had to see his owners, he said, and wanted to run down and see how the *Thrush* was progressing in dry dock. Reilly, however, seemed rather loth to leave the place before he had ascertained the fate of the invaders. He prided himself upon his ingenuity, and he certainly was a smart fellow, and never at a loss to wriggle out of a difficulty.

We locked up the place carefully, and although neither Reilly nor myself took any luggage, the skipper insisted upon taking his bed. He could sleep on no other, he declared. That night I slept in my own rooms at Chelsea, and next morning about eleven I met Reilly by appointment at Notting Hill Gate Station and took him with me to Cornwall Road, in order to introduce him to my well-beloved. I really don't know what induced me to do this, save that I felt that the interests of all three of us were in common, and a man is always eager and proud to introduce to his friends the woman he loves.

When we were ushered by the maid into Dorothy's small, neatly-arranged sitting-room on the second floor, she rose from a little writing-table to greet us with a cry of surprise. She wore a black skirt and clean cotton blouse, which gave her countenance a bright, fresh appearance. As her eyes met mine her cheeks flushed with pleasure, but at Reilly she glanced inquiringly, as though she considered him an intruder.

At once I introduced him, and they were instantly friends.

The arrangement of the room betrayed the hand of a refined and tasteful woman. The furniture was of the type found in every Bayswater lodging-house, but by the judicious addition of a few art covers, Liberty cushions, and knick-knacks, the general aspect was changed into one of good taste and perfect harmony.

"Really, Dr. Pickering, this is indeed a pleasant surprise! I had no idea you were coming to town," she exclaimed, placing chairs for both of us.

I briefly explained that, finding our search in the Manor House fruitless, we had relinquished our investigations for a few days. I also told her that my companion was my assistant, and that we had been at work together.

"But I've heard that you had another friend with you—a man called Seal, I think, a sea-captain," she remarked.

"True. But who told you?"

"I heard Mr. Purvis talking of him with his friends. Mr. Bennett seems especially antagonistic towards him."

"And well he may be," I answered. Then in a few brief words I told her the story which the skipper had related to us. My words did not surprise her in the least. She evidently knew Black Bennett too well.

Upon the mantelshelf in a heavy silver frame was a half-length cabinet photograph of a clean-shaven and rather good-looking young man. My eyes fell upon it once or twice, and I wondered who was the original. Perhaps it was my natural jealousy which caused that sudden interest.

Presently, while we were talking, a rap came at the door, and the servant called my love outside to hand her something from a tradesman.

The moment she had disappeared behind the screen placed across the door Reilly bent to me and, in a quick whisper, said:—

"See that photo? That's the man who was murdered at Kilburn! Ask her about him. I'll make an excuse to go."

I looked again at the picture. He was not more than twenty, with well-cut, refined features, a pair of merry eyes, and a well-formed mouth that in some way bore a slight resemblance to hers.

When she re-entered Reilly rose and stretched out his hand, expressing regret that he had an appointment in the City.

"I won't take Dr. Pickering away from you, Miss Drummond," he laughed mischievously. "You are one of our rivals in this treasure-hunt, but perhaps you both can arrange to combine forces—eh?"

She laughed in chorus, and although she pressed him to remain I saw that at heart she was glad when he had taken leave of us. Every woman likes to be alone with her lover.

"Well, Dorothy," I said, as she came back again, smiling, to my side, and allowed me to kiss her sweet lips, "and why have you fled from Bringhurst like this? Tell me the whole truth."

"By Mr. Purvis' orders. After leaving you I returned to the farm, half an hour before he got back. Then he told me I was to pack and return to London by the morning train. I have not seen him since."

"You are unaware of the reason he wished you to leave Bringhurst?"

"Quite. After I had gone to bed I heard Bennett's voice, but they went out together late, and I heard no more of them."

"Bennett is not your friend?" I suggested, watching her the while.

Her eyes lit up in an instant.

"My friend!" she cried. "Bennett my friend! No, Paul, he is my worst and most bitter enemy."

"Tell me, Dorothy," I asked, after a brief pause, during which I held her soft, slim hand in mine, "who is that young man there—the photograph in the silver frame?" And I pointed to it.

For a moment she did not reply. "That—that!" she gasped, her face blanching as she caught her breath quickly, her lips trembling, her eyes fixed upon me in abject fear. "A friend," she laughed, falteringly. "Only a friend—no one that you know."

And her breast rose and fell quickly as she strove to conceal the storm of conflicting emotions that arose within her.

"But I really think you ought to tell me who it is, dearest," I said. "Now that we are lovers, I surely have a right to know!"

"He is dead," she cried. "Dead!"

And with trembling fingers she took up the frame and turned it with reverence face towards the wall.

"It is the picture of a dead friend, Paul," she added. "Need I tell you more than that?" she asked, with an effort.

"What was his name?" I demanded in a low, serious voice.

"His name!" she cried in blank dismay. "No. Paul! I cannot tell you that. I love you—I love you with every fibre of my being, but in this," she cried, clinging to me with trembling hands, "in this one small matter I beg of you to let me keep my secret. Be generous, and if you really love me let the dead rest."

"He was your lover." I blurted forth.

"Ah! no!" she cried. "You misjudge me! He was never my lover, although I confess to you that I—I loved him."

And she buried her face upon my shoulder, and sobbed as though her overburdened heart would break.

# XXX

## The Silent Man's Story

On the following morning I entered Dr. Macfarlane's consulting-room in response to a letter from him.

"Your foundling is a lot better, Pickering," exclaimed the great lunacy specialist, rising and giving me his hand. "I've got him round at last. Not only is he quite rational, but he has found his voice, or as much of it as he will ever have. Brand, the surgeon, has discovered that he has an injury to the tongue which prevents him properly articulating."

"Is he quite in his right mind?" I asked, eagerly.

"As right as you are, my dear fellow. I thought from the first it was only temporary," he answered. "He has told me his story, and, by Jove! it's a remarkable one."

"What account does he give of himself?"

"Oh, you'd better come with me down to Ealing, and hear it from his own lips. I'm going to High Elms in half an hour."

When the Mysterious Man entered the doctor's private room at the asylum I saw at once what a change had been wrought in him. Neatly dressed in blue serge, his grey hair was well-trimmed, and he no longer wore that long Rip Van Winkle beard of which the hands of the *Thrush* had made such fun. He was now shaven, with a well-twisted white moustache, smart, fresh-looking, and no longer decrepit. He walked with springy step, and seemed at least twenty years younger. Only when he spoke one realized his infirmity, although he seemed an educated man. His mouth emitted a strange, hollow sound, and several letters he could not pronounce intelligibly.

"I have, I believe, to thank you, doctor," he said, politely, as he came in. "You were one of those who rescued me."

"Yes," I answered. "I found you on board the old ship, the *Seahorse*, and we took you with us to the steamer."

"Ah!" he sighed. "I had a narrow escape, doctor—a very narrow escape. I've been mad, they say. It's true, I suppose, otherwise I should not be here, in an asylum. But I assure you I recollect very little after I boarded that coffin-ship."

I watched his dark eyes. They were no longer shifty, but calm and steady. He was quite sane now, and had at Macfarlane's invitation seated himself between us.

"We are all very much interested in you," I said. "Will you tell me the whole story?"

"Well, I can't talk very plainly, you know, but I'll try and explain everything," he said. Then with a renewed effort he went on:—

"It is no sailor's yarn, but the truth, even though it may sound a remarkable story. You see, it was like this. I'd been at sea all my life, and in Liverpool Bob Usher, first mate of the *City of Chester*, was well known twelve years ago. Like a good many other men I got sick of my work, and in a fit of anger with the skipper I deserted in Sydney. After the *City of Chester* had sailed for home I joined another steamer, the *Goldfinch*, bound for Shanghai, but instead of putting in there we ran up the Chinese coast, and when a couple of cannon were produced and the forecastle hands armed themselves with rifles and cutlasses, the truth dawned upon me. It was not long before we painted our name on the bows, and commenced doing a bit of piracy among the junks. Our quick-firing guns, manned by old naval men, played havoc among the Chinese boats, and before a fortnight we had quite a cargo of loot—silks, ivories, tea, opium, and such things—all of which we ran to Adelaide, where the skipper disposed of them to one of those agents who asked no questions.

"At first I had thoughts of leaving the ship, for I had no desire to be overhauled by a British cruiser, nor to be sunk as a pirate. Still, the life was full of excitement, and the hands were as adventurous and as light-hearted a crew as ever sailed the Pacific. Although the gunboats were constantly on the lookout for us, we had wonderful good luck. In the China seas there is still a lot of piracy, mostly by the Chinese themselves, but sometimes by European steamers. We always gave the British squadron a very wide berth, constantly changing our name and altering the colour of our funnel. This went on for nearly a year, when at last the chase after us grew a bit too hot, and we sailed out of Perth for Liverpool. We had rounded the Cape and were steaming up the West Coast of Africa, when one day a Danish seaman named Jansen made a trifling mistake in executing one of the captain's orders. The skipper swore, the Dane answered him back, whereupon the captain shot the poor fellow like a dog, and with the aid of the second mate pitched him to the sharks before he was dead. This was a bit too much for me.

I remonstrated at such cold-blooded murder, but scarcely had the words left my mouth when the captain, Bennett by name, fired point-blank at me."

"Bennett!" I exclaimed, interrupting. "Do you mean Black Bennett?"

"Yes. The same man," he answered. "Do you know the brute?"

"I do. Go on. I'll tell you something when you have finished."

"Well, the skipper fired at me. He was the worst of bad characters. They said he'd secured a big fortune after a few years, and that it was locked up in Consols in England. All I know, however, is that he was the most cold-blooded, heartless blackguard that I've ever met. Of course Chinese don't count for much, but I'd be afraid to estimate how many he'd sent to kingdom come during our exciting cruises in Chinese waters. But that's neither here nor there. We quarrelled, he and I. Having missed me, he at once decided on another plan of getting rid of me. We were just then hugging a long, broken, and unexplored coast line, therefore he stopped the vessel and ordered the crew to lower a boat and put me ashore, knowing too well the fate of a single unarmed man among the barbarous Moors. It was a fiendish revenge to maroon me, but I was helpless. That was the last time I saw Bennett—nearly ten years ago now."

The man Usher paused for a few moments, the effort of such a long narrative having been too much for him.

"Well," he continued, "I was put ashore without food or water on a sandy, desolate spot. The surf was so strong that we narrowly escaped being upset, but getting to land at last I discovered the mouth of a river, and pushed my way beside it for a good many miles. The river, I afterwards found, was called the Tensift, and I had landed in South Morocco. I need not describe all the adventures that happened to me, save that I was seized a week after landing and carried as a slave to Morocco city, where I was sold to a powerful sheik, who probably considered that it increased his social status to possess an English slave. I was taken across the deserts and over the Atlas to a place called Aksabi, and for several years was kindly treated although held in bondage. After some time, however, my master was ordered by the Sultan to raise an army against the Riff tribes on the Mediterranean coast, and I was, of course, enrolled as a man who knew something of war. Our expedition travelled first to Fez, where we were reviewed by the Sultan himself, and then we penetrated into the fertile mountain country held by the revolutionary Riffs. But disaster after disaster befell us in that unknown country, falling into ambushes almost every day, until with others I was taken prisoner, and passed from hand to hand until I became slave to one of the powerful Riff chiefs. All my companions had been massacred in cold blood, but being a European my life had been spared, probably because my captors expected they might hold me for ransom. As slave of a tyrannical barbarian, mine was a dog's life. On any day or at any hour I knew not whether my capricious master might not order me to be put to the torture, bastinadoed, or shot, while the work in the broiling sun under a harsh negro taskmaster was so hard that it sapped my manhood. The Sheik Taiba, whose slave I was, defied the Sultan and lived in a mountain stronghold a few miles from the blue Mediterranean. Day after day I could see the open sea stretching away beyond. Ah! how I longed to be free to return to England. On one or two occasions I had been sent with other slaves (all negroes) to obtain stones from the seashore. On one occasion, at the mouth of the small river that flowed down the valley to the sea opposite the island of Alhucemas, there had been pointed out to me by one of my hapless companions, a decrepit old negro, the submerged hull of a ship lying about a quarter of a mile up from the sea, and only just covered by the clear, swift-flowing stream. It lay like this," and taking a pencil and paper he drew a plan of its position.

"It was the *Seahorse*!" I said, quickly.

"Yes. It had been there for ages, a ship the like of which I had never before seen, but by standing upon the projecting rock above I could look down upon it. Many times I visited it, for the mystery of it attracted me. Among both Moors and negroes there was a strange legend that evil spirits were contained within, hence it was held in superstitious awe. When it rose to the surface there would, it was believed, emerge from it a terrible pestilence that would sweep the whole of the Riff tribes from the face of the earth. I, however, had no such fear. Many times I dived off the rock and examined the black old hull, finding that the projecting stern had become wedged beneath the overhanging ledge, and that this apparently kept it in its place. Through the windows I could see that the water had not entered, hence it occurred to me that some buoyancy might be left in it. For two whole years I held this theory, and it was strengthened by the fact that instead of lying heavily on the sandy bottom, the bows were raised a foot or two. I could see that it was a very ancient vessel, which in some remote period had drifted over the bar into the estuary, and had stranded there when the river was low. Then when the winter snows of the Atlas had melted, the flood had risen rapidly, the projecting rock had held down the stern of the old craft, and the waters had closed over her. The one thought that possessed me was that if that overhanging rock could be removed the hull might float again. With this object I waited in patience. From the traders at Tetuan the Riffs frequently purchased explosives which they used in their periodical fights against the forces of the Kaid Maclean and the Sultan. Hence, about two years afterwards, I found in the possession of the Sheik Taiba some strange-looking substance which, although the Moors were unaware of its potency, I knew to be dynamite. I managed to secure some of it, and a week later placed it in the great rift in the rock and in the middle of the night blew it up. The quantity I used must have been much more than necessary, for the rock was split, and the ledge, blown right off, fell into the water ten yards away from the vessel, while to my great delight the craft came up to the surface, the strangest-looking object I had ever seen afloat. I swam to it, and having broken out one of its windows crept into the cabin, the current carrying me slowly out to sea.

"The explosion had alarmed the Riffs, who poured down to the spot in hundreds, only to see the strange craft which they held in such dread actually floating down the stream. The sight of it filled them with terror, and they fled, attributing the explosion to a supernatural cause. My object, of course, was to escape from slavery, and in order not to attract the attention of my enemies, the Riffs, should they board me, I threw off my slave's clothing, and finding in the cabin a pair of old Elizabethan breeches and a doublet, I donned them. The door communicating with the other part of the ship was secured so firmly that very soon I realized my position.

"Days passed, how many I cannot tell. I only knew that want of food and water—of which I had none—told upon me, as well as the punishment that had been inflicted upon me a month before my escape. For a trifling offence the Sheik Taiba had ordered my tongue to be cut out, a cruel mutilation common among the Moors. This had not actually been done, but so severely was my tongue injured by my inhuman captors that I was now unable to articulate a single word. What more can I tell you? Alone on that strange craft, hunger and thirst consumed me, my mind wandered, I grew worse, and eventually went stark mad and oblivious to everything. All I recollect is that I was placed in charge of Ben Harding, the man who acted as Bennett's second mate on the

*Goldfinch*—a broken-down gentleman who knew little about the sea, and whose previous career included a long term of imprisonment at Brisbane for being implicated in the murder of a mail-driver. But you said that you know Black Bennett," he added, with anger flashing in his eyes. "He marooned me because he feared that I should tell the truth of poor Jansen's murder when we got to Liverpool. Where is he to be found?"

# XXXI

## The House at Kilburn

R obert Usher returned with me to Chelsea and again took up his abode in Keppel Street.

To him I explained the whole of the curious circumstances, our exciting search after the hidden loot, and our utter failure—a narrative which interested him greatly, and caused him to become enthusiastic in his desire to render us assistance. I introduced him to Seal, Reilly, and old Staffurth, and we all closely analyzed his story, which at first seemed so extraordinary to us as to be beyond credence. Seal, however, as a practical seaman, examined the plan which Usher drew, and gave it as his opinion that the *Seahorse* had been preserved in the manner described by Usher. His theory was that the antique vessel had been battened down for a storm, and that the rudder being carried away the men on board were helpless. The gale also carried away the masts and blew the wreck over the bar into the river, where she became wedged by the rocky ledge, as Usher described. Then a sudden flood of the river caused the waters to rise so rapidly that before the crew could open the hatches and escape the vessel became submerged.

I suggested that the reason the crew stayed below was that being storm-driven to the land of their enemies, the Corsairs, they feared attack, therefore remained within their stronghold, hoping to float away when the gale abated, but were unfortunately overwhelmed so suddenly that escape became impossible. Death had no doubt come upon them quickly, for we recollected that the interior showed no sign of recent fighting, and that asphyxiation was evidently the cause of death.

The fate of Bennett and his men in that underground burrow caused us considerable apprehension. We had, up to the present, successfully combated the efforts of the gang to secure the treasure, but so ingenious and ubiquitous were our enemies that we knew not when or where they would turn up again. Reilly was of opinion that they were entombed, but my own idea was that with Black Bennett as leader they would certainly escape in some ingenious manner or other. I had a kind of intuition that we had not yet seen the last of that interesting quartette.

So far as we were concerned we had given up all hope of discovering the gold at Caldecott Manor. It was surely tantalizing to read that long list of the treasure in English, covering eighteen pages in the vellum book—plates and dishes of gold, jewels in profusion, collars of pearls, jewelled swords, packets of uncut gems, golden cups, and "seven chests of yron each fylled wyth monie," a list of objects which, if sold, meant an ample fortune.

Accompanied by Reilly, I visited the house at Kilburn wherein the secret tragedy had been enacted. We had but little difficulty in finding it, a good-sized semi-detached place lying back behind some dark green railings. A board showed that it was to let, and having obtained the key at a house-agent's in Edgware Road, we went over it as prospective tenants. The furniture had been removed, but on the floor-boards of the upstairs room in which the helpless man had been so foully done to death we found a small dark stain, the size of a man's palm—the stain of blood. It was, according to Reilly, the exact spot where the poor young fellow lay, his life-blood having soaked through the carpet.

We looked outside the window, and there saw the great hole in the conservatory roof through which my companion had fallen, while a piece of broken lattice-work hung away from the wall. The autumn sunshine fell full upon that dark stain on the floor, but the attention of the observer would not have been attracted thereby; it was brown, like other stains one so often sees upon deal flooring, and none would ever dream that it was evidence of a foul and cowardly crime.

On the following day I called upon Dorothy at Cornwall Road, and almost her first words were to convey to me a piece of news from Rockingham—namely, that old Ben Knutton had met with a fatal accident. While in a state of intoxication two nights before he had attempted to cross the river by the foot-bridge that leads to Great Easton, had missed his footing, fallen in, and been drowned. There was no suspicion of foul play, as a young labourer named Thoms had been with him, and had been unable to save him. The inquest had been held on the previous day at the Sonde Arms, and a verdict of "Accidental Death" returned.

The old fellow was a sad inebriate, it was true, but in common with Dorothy, I felt a certain amount of regret at his tragic end. Had it not been for the presence of a witness I should certainly have suspected foul play.

"Have you heard anything of your friends Bennett or Purvis?" I asked her as we sat together.

"Mr. Purvis was here last night," she answered. "He has told me how you entrapped them in that subterranean passage."

"Then they have escaped!" I cried. "Tell me how they managed it!"

"It appears that on leaving the Manor, and descending into the secret way, they found that you had removed the planks that bridged the well. They returned to the Manor only to discover that you had also closed down the exit securely."

"What did they do then?"

"Well, for a time there seemed no solution of the problem until Mr. Bennett, more ingenious than the rest, suggested that they should dig a hole straight upwards from the roof of the passage. This they did, and in half an hour emerged in the centre of a cornfield!"

"By Jove!" I cried, laughing. "I never thought of that! Then they are all four back in London again?"

"I think so. It seems as though they have, like you, given up all hope of making any discovery."

"Yes," I said, with a sigh, "we are, unfortunately, no nearer the truth than we were when we started." My eye fell upon the mantelshelf, and I noticed that in place of the portrait of the dead man there was now a photograph of a well-known actor. She had removed it, and had probably placed the picture among her most treasured possessions.

This thought pained me. It was on the tip of my tongue to refer to it, but I feared to give her annoyance.

I openly declare that I now thought far more of my sweet and winsome love than I did of that sordid treasure. The first-named was a living reality, the soft-voiced woman who was my all-in-all; but the latter was nothing more than a mere phantom, as fortune is so very often.

While my friends still discussed the ways and means of solving the problem I thought only of her, for I loved her with all my heart and with all my soul. How I wished she would set my troubled thoughts at rest regarding the poor fellow who had been done to death at Kilburn, yet when I recollected the reason of her secrecy I saw that she was held silent for fear of consequences. Hers was a secret—but surely not a guilty one.

Still she had admitted to me having loved him, and that had aroused the fierce fire of jealousy within me. I felt that I had a right to know who and what he was.

We sat chatting together, as lovers will, and when evening fell we went out together and dined at a restaurant. I suppose that if we had regarded conventionalities I ought not to have visited her at her lodgings, yet I found her a woman overwhelmed by a sadness; one in whose life there had been so little joy, and whose future was only a blank sea of despair. My presence, I think, cheered her, for her soft cheeks flushed, her eyes grew bright when she chatted with me, and her breast heaved and fell when I spoke of my affection.

She was so different to other women; so calm, so thoughtful, so sweet of temperament, though I knew that in her inner consciousness she was suffering all the tortures which come to the human mind when overshadowed by a crime. It was because of that I tried to take her out of herself, to give her a little pleasure beyond that dreary street in Bayswater, and to prevent her thoughts ever wandering back to that terrible night in Kilburn when those brutal men forced her to touch the cold, white face of the dead.

When dining together in the big hall of the Trocadero the crowd and the music brightened her, for evening gaiety in London is infectious, and she expressed pleasure that we had gone there. Over dinner I told her how for the present we had abandoned the search at Caldecott, and related to her Usher's remarkable story.

"And this man Bennett actually cast the poor fellow away without food or water!" she cried, when she had heard me to the end. "Why, that was as much murder as the shooting of the unfortunate Dane! I hate the man, Paul!" she added. "Truth to tell, I myself live in fear of him. He would not hesitate to kill me—that I know."

"No, no," I said reassuringly. "He dare not do that. Besides, you now have me as your protector, Dorothy." And I looked straight into her great dark eyes.

"Ah! I know," she faltered. "But—well, there are reasons why I fear he may carry out his threat."

"What!" I exclaimed. "Has he threatened you?"

She was silent for a few moments, then nodded in the affirmative.

I knew the reason. It was because she was aware of the secret at Kilburn. Perhaps he feared she might expose him, just as ten years before he had feared Robert Usher.

"If he attempts to harm you it will be the worse for him!" I cried quickly. "Remember we have in Seal and Usher witnesses who could bring him to the criminal dock. At present, however, both men are remaining silent. The whole truth is not yet revealed. There is still another crime of which certain persons have knowledge—a tragedy in London, not long ago."

Her face blanched in an instant, and next second I regretted that I had hinted at her secret.

"What is that?" she asked in a hollow voice, not daring to look me in the face.

But I managed to turn the conversation without replying to her question, and resolved that in future, although anxiety might consume me, I would refrain from further mention of the ugly affair. She would tell me nothing—indeed, how could she, implicated as she was, even though innocent?

Yet I hated to think that my love should be an associate of those malefactors, and was striving to devise a plan by which she might escape from her terrible thraldom.

After dinner I suggested the play, and we went together to see an amusing comedy. But afterwards, as I sat beside her in the cab on our return to Bayswater, she sighed, saying—

"Forgive me, Paul, but somehow I fear the future. I am too happy—and I know that this perfect contentment cannot last. I am one of those doomed from birth to disappointment and unhappiness. It has been ever so throughout my life—it is so now."

"No, no, dearest," I declared, taking her little gloved hand in mine. "You have enemies, just as I have, but if we assist each other we may successfully checkmate them. This fight for a fortune is a desperate one, it is true, but up to the present it has been a drawn game, while we hold the honours—our mutual love."

She gripped my hand in silence, but it was more expressive than any words could have been. I knew that she placed her whole trust in me.

Yes, ours was a strange wooing—brief, passionate, and complete. But I felt confident that, even though she might have entertained an affection for the man so ruthlessly assassinated at Kilburn, she loved me truly and well.

In that belief I remained perfectly content. She was mine, mine alone, and I desired no more. For me her affection was all-sufficient. I had searched for a hidden treasure, and found the greatest on earth—perfect love.

# XXXII

## What We Discovered at the Record Office

A month dragged slowly by. I saw Dorothy daily, and we were happy in each other's love. She had resumed her post of typewriter at an insurance office in Moorgate Street, and on her return home would generally spend each evening with me. Robert Usher continued to live with me in Keppel Street and proved a most entertaining companion, and Philip Reilly, bitterly disappointed, had also returned to the bank, while Job Seal had sailed from Cardiff with his usual cargo of steam coal for Malta.

Worn out with all the confusion, we had all of us given up hope of ever discovering the treasure, and my chief regret was that we had played such havoc with the interior of Caldecott Manor. What the landlord's claim for dilapidations would be I dreaded to think.

Usher was, of course, a typical adventurer. His whole life had been spent upon the sea, and yet, curiously enough, his speech was never interlarded with nautical phrases like Seal's. Some men, however long they are at sea, never become "salts," and Robert Usher was one of them. Over our pipes he often related to me his exciting adventures as slave in the interior of Morocco, and times without number gave me vivid descriptions of the old *Seahorse* as he found it held beneath the clear water by the ledge of rock. At first it had puzzled me greatly why the water had not entered the cabins when the flood closed over the vessel, but both Seal and I recollected how, after hacking away the growth of weeds and shells from the deck, the men had found the hatches covered tightly with a kind of waterproof tarpauling, which had evidently been placed there by those on board to prevent the heavy sea that washed the decks from entering the cabins. The commander and his officers had closed themselves down tightly, trusting to the one officer and his men on deck to manage the ship, but, alas! they had all perished.

At first it had seemed utterly incredible that the ship had retained its buoyancy all those years, and that the water had never entered; yet it was evident that the decomposition of the bodies of those unfortunate victims had generated gases that had increased its buoyancy, and that,

WILLIAM LE QUEUX

being held within the river bar, there were no waves to beat and break the thick, green glass of the tightly-secured windows. Had the vessel sunk in deep water, the pressure of the latter would, of course, have broken the glass at once, but resting on that soft, sandy bed, only just submerged, it had been preserved quite intact through all those years, a tribute to the stability of the stout oak and teak of which our forefathers constructed ships in Queen Elizabeth's day.

I introduced Robert Usher to the secretary of the Royal Geographical Society, and he was invited to deliver a lecture before the Fellows describing the interior of Morocco, about which so very little is known even in these days. His wanderings in the Anti-Atlas and the Jeb Grus to Figig, his captivity in Aksabi and with the warlike Riffs, and the information he gave regarding the power of the latter and the weakness of the Sultan's army were extremely interesting, and were afterwards printed in the journal of the society as a permanent record. His map of the sources of the Muluya River, on Jeb Aiahin, in the Great Atlas, was of considerable value, and was afterwards marked on the map of Morocco. It will, indeed, be found upon the revised maps of that country now published.

In the privacy of my sitting-room he related many stories regarding the man known as Black Bennett. As far as I could discover, the latter had led a curious double life for years. He possessed a small but comfortable house out at Epping, where he posed as a retired sea captain, but now and then he would disappear, sometimes for a whole year, occupying his time in depredations on the sea. The common belief in England is that piracy is dead, but it was certainly not so a dozen years ago, when Chinese waters were not watched by Japanese and European war vessels as they now are. To commit acts of piracy in the Yellow Seas would nowadays be a difficult matter.

About Harding, the man who had so cleverly copied the documents I had taken from the *Seahorse*, Usher told me a good deal. Formerly a professor at Cambridge, he had committed some fraud, and fearing arrest had, it seemed, escaped to sea. An adventurer of the same type as Bennett, the pair became inseparable, and Harding had assisted the former in many of his most daring schemes.

So the weeks went on, autumn drew to a close, and I began to glance at the *Lancet* anxiously each week to ascertain where a *locum tenens* was wanted, for, even though compelled to go to the country and leave my love alone and at the mercy of that quartette of unscrupulous scoundrels, I saw myself compelled to earn my living.

I recollected that long and tantalizing list of gold and jewels in the vellum book which I had given again into Mr. Staffurth's hands to re-examine, and sighed that they were not mine that I might marry Dorothy and give her a fitting and comfortable home.

One day I received quite an unexpected visit from Mr. Staffurth. As soon as he entered my room I saw by his flushed cheeks and excited manner that something unusual had occurred. He had even forgotten to remove his big spectacles, as he always did before he went out.

"It's briefly this," he said in reply to my eager demand. "The day before yesterday, while going through that vellum book again, there were two things that struck me for the first time. The first you will recollect, namely, that in the covers and on various folios is written in brown ink, very faded, and at a different date than when the book was first compiled, the numerical three. There are no fewer than nine huge threes in different parts of the book, but none of them have anything whatever to do with the context. The mystery of that sign puzzled me. It seemed as though it were placed there with some distinct object, for each was carefully drawn, and so boldly that it was evidently intended to arrest attention."

"I recollect quite distinctly," I said, interested. "I pointed them out to you one day, but they did not then appear to strike you as curious."

"No," answered the old man, "I was too engrossed in deciphering the manuscript at the time. But the second discovery I have made is still more curious, for I find in the back of the cover, which, as you know, is lined with vellum, there is written in the same hand as that which penned the book itself the curious entry: '3ELIZ:43.5.213.' At first I was much puzzled by it, but after a good deal of reflection I disposed of the threes at each end among those in the body of the book, and read the entry as a date, namely, the twenty-first day of May in the forty-third year of the reign of Elizabeth, or 1591. This aroused my curiosity, and I lost no time in searching at the Record Office for any documents bearing that date. I spent all yesterday there, and at last my search among the indices was rewarded, for I found an entry which indicated something of interest preserved among the Oblata Rolls. I have seen it, and I want you to come to Chancery Lane and assist me in copying it."

"When? Now?" I cried in excitement.

"Certainly. I have a cab at the door."

On our drive Staffurth told me little regarding his find, declaring that I should be allowed to inspect it in due course. You may, however, imagine my own state of mind, for I saw how highly excited the old expert was himself, although he strove not to show it.

Arrived at the new Record Office, Staffurth, who was well known there as a searcher, filled up a request form for No. 26,832 of the Oblata Rolls, and in due course an attendant handed to us at the desk, whereat we had taken seats, a small roll of rather coarse parchment, to which were attached three old red seals and a tablet bearing the catalogue number.

Staffurth unrolled it before me and exhibited the three signatures at foot. They were those of "Clement Wollerton," "John Ffreeman," and "Bartholomew da Schorno."

My eager eyes devoured it. Near the foot was sketched a strange device, very much like a plan, for in the centre of three unequal triangles was a small circle, and with them certain cabalistic signs.

"You see it is unfortunately in cipher," Staffurth pointed out. "But it no doubt has something to do with the treasure."

"But we have the key," I exclaimed. "It is written in the vellum book."

He shook his white head, saying: "No. I have already tried it. Our key is useless. This is entirely different."

"It may be a copy of the document sold by Knutton," I cried. "Possibly it has been placed among the Government records for safety, in case the Knuttons should lose the one entrusted to their care."

"Possibly," was his answer. "But our key to the cipher gives us absolutely no assistance. What I want you to do is to copy it. Take that pen and write down the letters at my dictation."

I obeyed, and with care printed in capitals as he read them off as follows—

HPSEWXOQHWHPBARLHEOWC MRS
    OWCWPASROOBK LPC AXHAHBXHO BOW RSO
BOWUAC SOP KSRSEBBNK PUA
    CJOOALAJOFCZXHO OKYSOP PORCJU O LP
BRRIPCPCO BALCJO OLPROLLPO SB OO WRCRR
    XHA CFA XH BSJSQOM
ECLSXISPBNCXCMOHOLEWXIO EHOBI OB LBS

There were some forty lines, all as utterly unintelligible as the extract given above. The parchment was yellow, and here and there were damp stains where the ink had faded until the deciphering of the capitals was a matter of some difficulty. But, with the practised eye of an expert, old Mr. Staffurth read off the rather difficult Italian hand just as easily as a newspaper.

He showed me the great difference in the English hand in Elizabeth's day to the Italian, and we concluded that it was in the autography of Bartholomew da Schorno himself. But, possessing no key to the cipher, neither of us was hopeful of reading the statement contained therein. I could not help thinking that the key in the vellum book would be of some use to us, but my friend was quite positive that it had nothing whatever to do with the present cryptic writing.

The crisp parchment was folded at the bottom, and through this fold three slits were cut, upon which pieces of parchment like broad tapes were threaded. Upon each was a seal, one of them that of Bartholomew, bearing the leopard rampant.

The curious device near the end of the document I copied as exactly as I could, and when, after Staffurth had puzzled over the yellow screed for an hour, we were about to hand it back to the attendant, the assistant-keeper approached my friend and, greeting him, asked—

"What do you find of interest in that roll, Mr. Staffurth? It has been in request by several people during the past day or two."

"Has any one else copied it?" I demanded breathlessly.

"Yes. There were two men looking at it three days ago, and they took a copy."

"Can you describe them?" asked Staffurth, dumfounded, for, like me, he feared that we had been again forestalled.

"They were fair, both of them. One was evidently well-versed in palæography. He was a thin, tall man, with a slight impediment in his speech."

Harding had been there, without a doubt!

"How did they discover it?" inquired Staffurth.

"By the unusual name—Italian, isn't it? The roll is catalogued under that. You found it in the same manner, didn't you?"

"Yes," the old expert responded. "But I suppose no one has ever discovered the key to the cipher?"

"No. Lost centuries ago, I expect."

"Unless that document of Knutton's contains it," I remarked to my friend.

"Ah!" he gasped. "I never thought of that! This may be the absolute record with the plan, and the Knutton parchment the key to the cipher."

"If so, then we've lost it! We are too late," I remarked, my heart sinking.

"Professor Campbell, of Edinburgh, was much interested in it, and tried to make it out two years ago, but utterly failed," was the assistant-keeper's remark, and a few moments later, after we had handed the roll back to the attendant, he left us, and I returned with Staffurth to his house in Clapham.

Well versed as Staffurth was in the art of cryptic writing as practised during the fifteenth and sixteenth centuries, he utterly failed to decipher what I had copied. The signatures alone were in plain script—all the rest in cipher.

I took a copy of the document for myself, and through nearly a fortnight spent my leisure in trying, with the aid of the key in the vellum book, to decipher the first line, all, however, in vain. The cryptogram was a complicated one in any case. Staffurth consulted two men he knew who were experts in such things, but both gave it up as a private cipher that could not be read without a key.

One night, however, while lying in bed reflecting, as all of us do when our minds are troubled, that oft-repeated numerical three suddenly occurred to me. Could it be possible that it was the key to the cipher? This idea became impressed upon me, so I rose and, going into my sitting-room, lit my lamp, and there and then commenced to work upon it.

After several trials in taking three as the key-number, I at last made the experiment of taking C for A, and so on, writing the third letter from the one required. The alphabet I wrote then read as follows—

ABCDEFGHIJKLMNOPQRSTUVWXYZ
CFILORUXADGJMPSVYBEHKNQTWZ

Then, with my heart beating wildly, I turned to decipher the document, but even then I found it useless. Indeed, I spent the remainder of that night in vainly trying to solve the puzzle.

That same afternoon I went to Staffurth's, told him of my inspiration, and showed him my alphabet. Adjusting his big spectacles, he regarded it for a long time in silence, but I saw that, to him, mine was a new and rather striking idea. He took a sheet of paper and tried time after time to make sense of that first long line of bewildering capitals, acting upon the supposition that three was the number.

Suddenly the old man cried excitedly, turning to me—

"I've got it! At last! See! The golden number is three. Your alphabet is the correct one, only the letters are reversed three by three. Take these first six, and then reverse them. You have SP HXWE, which by aid of your alphabet reads: 'On thys'—The Secret, whatever it is, is ours—ours!"

# XXXIII

## We Decipher the Parchment

Our excitement over the discovery was unbounded. Old Mr. Staffurth's announcement seemed hardly possible. His hand trembled as he held the paper whereon I had copied the precious document catalogued among the Oblata Rolls, while I, bending over him, stood eager but speechless.

"See!" he cried. "The cipher is cunningly reversed, in order to make it more complicated. The big threes written by the old Italian were drawn as a silent indication of the correct solution of this document. Besides, there is before and after the entry of the date of the document two threes, one at each end—meaning first the third letter, and secondly each three letters reversed."

"Let's decipher it at once—whatever it is!" I exclaimed, hastily pulling up a chair to the table beside him and taking a sheet of blank paper and pencil. Imagine for yourself the tension of my mind at that critical moment. What might not be concealed behind that bewildering array of letters? Was the secret of the whereabouts of the treasure written there, or was it, after all, only some unimportant record having no reference at all to the hidden loot?

The old man was staring at the document with a puzzled air, for it was apparently not so easy to decipher as he had believed.

"Dictate it to me, and I will write," I urged quickly, holding up my pencil ready. The suspense was irritating. We both of us were impatient to get at the truth.

Slowly, and not without a good deal of difficulty, Staffurth reversed each three letters of the cipher, three by three, and then reading them by aid of the alphabet I had compiled, gave down the beginning of the document to me as follows—

SP HXWE HQOPHWRABEH LCWO SR MCWO AP WO
On thys twenty-first daye of Maye in ye
RSKBO CPL HXABHAOHX WOBO SR WO BCAUPO SR
foure and thirtieth yere of ye raigne of
SKB ESKNBAUPO JCLAO OJAZCFOHX YKOPO SR

our souvrigne Ladie Elizabeth Quene of
OPUJCPLO RRBCPIO CPL ABOJCPLO LOROPLOB SR
   WO
Englande Ffrance and Irelande Defender of ye
RRCAHX A FCBHXSJSMOQ LC EIXSBPS XCNO MCLO
Ffaith I Bartholomew da Schorno have made
HXWE EOIBOH BOISBL.
thys Secret Record.

Our excitement knew no bounds. It was, after all, a secret record, and without doubt it referred to the treasure! It is always interesting work to decipher an old document, but more especially so one that no man has been able to read for ages. Imagine yourself for a moment in my place, with a fortune attached to the revelation of that secret!

Old Mr. Staffurth's voice trembled, as did his thin, white hands. As a palæographist he had at times made some remarkable discoveries while delving in the dusty parchment records of bygone ages, but surely none had ever affected him like this. We were learning the place where a fortune lay hidden.

For close on two hours we worked together incessantly, slowly obtaining the right equivalents of the cipher, but very often making errors in calculation with the puzzling threes. The writing was simple after all, but at the same time difficult to decipher, requiring great care and patience. At length, however, I sat with the whole of the secret revealed before me, written down in plain English, surely one of the most interesting documents among the thousands preserved in the national archives.

The record, which we read and re-read a dozen times with breathless interest, was as follows—

ON THYS TWENTY-FIRST DAYE OF MAYE IN YE FOURE and thirtieth yere of ye Raigne of our Souvrigne Ladie Elizabeth, Quene of Englande Ffrance and Irelande, Defender of ye Ffaith, I Bartholomew da Schorno have made thys secret Record.

To EIGHT of ye men who fought wyth me on ye Great Unicorne against ye Spanysh galleon and who made covenant was ye place of ye loote knowne. In all those men dyd I place my trust. One Robert Dafte hath broken hys oath and hath reveled ye secret, for he hath tolde before hys death unto hys wyfe ye place into which we walled ye golde. Therefore it hath become necessarie in tyme to remove ye treasure which we captured from ye Spanysh and from ye Barbarians of Algiers unto a place of safetie from thieves, from conspiratiors, and from ye enemies of oure Quene.

THEREFORE be it known unto ye person who may rede thys my Record that on thys daye above written the whole of what I possess has been removed from ye priest's hole in ye Manor of Caldecott and concealed in a place more fytting and secure. The knowledge of it now remains only wyth my trusted friends Clement Wollerton and John Ffreeman, the two signatories to ye present document. Be it knowne also therefore that ye secret covenant playced in ye hand of Richard Knutton is now made by me null and voide, although my testamentary disposition of ye golde jewels and all other articles whych I Bartholomew da Schorno, noble of Ferrara, Commendatore of the Order of San Stefano, have treasured shall remain as I have before written; that is to saye that should ye Knights of Saint Stephen not require funds ye golde is to become ye sole and absolute property of ye youngest childe of ye family of Clement Wollerton, of Stybbington, in ye Countie of Huntyngedon, but without any parte or portion to go to ye familie of Richard Knutton, ye last mentioned havyng wickedly and maliciously conspyred wyth ye wyfe of ye saide Robert Dafte to steale and take possession of ye treasure during our absence on ye seas.

AND THEREFORE be it known unto ye person who gains ye secret of thys cipher that I wyth mine owne hand have written thys my record for two purposes. In ye firste playce to make it plaine unto all men that it is my ardent desire to assist ye worke of ye release of Christians in slavery in Barberie, and secondlie to reveale unto ye one who deciphers my record ye place where ye golde wyll be found. Let hym rede and marke well.

FOURE MILES from Stamforde towne on ye great roade into Scotlande and to ye left hande, is Tyckencote Laund. Within thys woode have we buried ye treasure three arms-lengths deepe, and to recover it ye directions whych

herewyth I give must be followed closely. Enter ye woode
by ye path leading through ye fieldes at ye fourth mylestone
from Stamford towne and passe ye lyne of six oakes always
facing Empinghame church until ye Three Systers are found.
Midway between ye three, at twenty-and-nyne foot-paces
from ye south, have we planted an oak sapling and beneath it
will be found hydden ye golde of ye Spanyards and ye jewels
of ye Corsairs.

(Here followed the roughly-executed plan which consisted of three
triangles at unequal distance from each other, and a crude sketch of
the tree beneath which the gold was hidden. Across the sketch was an
arrow, presumably showing the direction of the sunrise, and a second
one with the word "Empinghame" written at its barb.)

Let He Who fyndeth thys my wealthe carrie out my written
will, taking unto hymselfe one of the chests of monie as hys
recompense. But should he not give up ye remainder in full
unto ye last descendant of ye Wollertons of Stybbington
my curse shall for ever reste upon hym. That what is herein
written is true, we who alone knowe ye secret of ye saide
treasure and have taken oure oathes to keepe it untyl the
golde should be wanted by ye Knightes of Saint Stephen
have hereunto sett oure hands and seale on ye daye and yere
first above written.

Clement Wollerton
John Ffreeman
Bartholomew Da Schorno

The spot to which the treasure had been secretly removed from that
upstairs chamber in Caldecott Manor was now actually revealed to us!
But we entertained a horrible suspicion that Bennett and his friends
were equally in the possession of the secret. The suggestion that the
document sold by the dead man Knutton contained a key to the cipher
was, of course, now dismissed; but we were nevertheless filled with
fear that the quartette might, by some means or other, have solved the
problem, just as we had done.

Philip Reilly, although he had returned to his desk at the bank, had
spent his spare time down at Hammersmith, and had watched the

movements of the four men. He had once or twice told me that he believed some fresh move was being made, and he had also discovered that the fourth man, he who had charge of Dorothy on that fatal night at Kilburn—a short, dark-bearded, thick-set fellow known as Martin—was in reality a low-class solicitor named Martin Franklin, who rented a small back office in the Minories and appeared to have very few clients.

Staffurth agreed with me that we should lose no time in obeying the directions given in the document before us, therefore I drove into the city before the banks closed, and showed Philip the secret revealed. On reading it he became highly excited, as may be imagined, and, having obtained two days' leave of absence from his manager, we went out and bought several useful implements, including a saw, three shovels, pickaxes, etc. Then, having sent them to King's Cross cloak-room to await us, we drove home to Chelsea, where we informed Usher of the good news, and found him ready and anxious to render us assistance. Afterwards I went on to Dorothy and showed her the solution of the cipher. She seemed, however, apprehensive of some evil befalling me.

That night, having purchased an Ordnance map in Fleet Street, the three of us left London, travelling to the quiet, old-world town of Stamford, and putting up at that old-fashioned hostelry the Stamford Hotel. Perhaps you, my reader, know the quaint, sleepy old Lincolnshire town, with its Gothic architecture, its Elizabethan houses, its many church spires, and its noisy cobbles. Thirty years ago, before the railways came, it was a commercial centre and a busy, prosperous place; but nowadays its streets are deserted, its fine old churches seem to be tumbling to decay, and only on market days does the typically English town awaken from its lethargy. Very picturesque is its situation, lying behind the broad, fertile meadows of the Welland, with Burghley House—that magnificent palace immortalized by Tennyson—in its immediate vicinity.

It was not, however, to enjoy the pleasant peace of Stamford town that we had come there. We did not arrive until nearly ten o'clock at night, and were, of course, compelled to leave our implements at the railway station. To take them to the hotel might arouse suspicion. Therefore we ate our supper in the coffee-room—cold roast beef and ale—retired soon after, and arose early next day, after a night of sleepless impatience. In the privacy of Reilly's room we decided upon a plan of action. With Usher I was to hire a trap and drive to Tickencote village, which, we learnt, was three miles away, past Casterton, on the

Great North Road, and then dismiss the conveyance, while Reilly was to go to the station, obtain the tools, and follow us in a separate trap hired from the George. At Tickencote village we were to meet and go on together to the place indicated in the old Italian's record.

Immediately after breakfast we parted company and Reilly went out, after which we ordered a dog-cart and drove along the straight, broad highway, with its quantity of telegraph lines at the side, the great road which runs from London to York. The autumn morning was fresh, even a trifle chilly, but the season was a late one, and the leaves had not yet fallen, although the frosts had already turned them to their bright red and golden tints. Beyond Great Casterton Church we crossed a bridge at the end of the village, and a square tower among the trees in the distance was pointed out by our driver as Tickencote Church. Arrived at the village, which was just off the high road, we entered the inn.

Over a glass of ale we learnt several things we wished to know, namely, that there was Tickencote Park and Tickencote Laund. The park commenced at the junction of the high road with the short road leading up to the village, while the Laund lay back from the road behind some fields nearly a mile farther on. I learnt this by chatting with the landlady about fox-hunting. There were always foxes in Tickencote Laund, she informed me, and hounds were sure to have sport whenever they drew it.

While there it suddenly occurred to me that if Philip arrived with a collection of tools our visit would at once arouse the curiosity of the villagers. Therefore I whispered to Usher and we left the place, eventually meeting our friend on the high road a quarter of a mile away. He handed out the tools from the trap, then, jumping down, told the man to return for him at four to Tickencote village.

In order not to attract any attention we walked on, leaving Reilly to carry the picks and shovels at a short distance behind. Even there we were not safe, for we knew not whether our enemies had secretly watched our departure from London. Dorothy was always impressing upon me her suspicion that the men kept continual observation on me, while Usher knew Bennett well enough to be certain that he would not give up the chance of a fortune without some desperate effort.

Nevertheless, keeping a watchful eye everywhere, we walked along the wide muddy high road, impatient to arrive at our goal, and eager to dig at the spot indicated by the roughly-drawn plan upon that faded parchment.

# XXXIV

## Our Search at Tickencote
## and its Results

Presently we stood at an iron milestone which had, I suppose, replaced the old stone road-mark of Elizabethan days, and saw thereon the words—"Stamford, 4 miles." Then, looking across to the left, we noticed a path leading across the stubble to a long, dark wood.

At the gate leading into the field we awaited Philip, and, there being nobody in the vicinity, he quickly joined us, and we all three sped along the path beside the high thorn-hedge until we came to the border of the wood. While on the road we saw, lying in a distant hollow, a church spire which, from our map, we supposed to be that of Empingham.

The path ran along the outskirts of the wood, but we soon found a moss-grown stile, and crossing it continued along a by-path which was evidently very seldom used, for it led into the heart of the dark trees, thick undergrowth, and bracken.

"Remember the six oaks in line," Usher remarked, halting and looking round, for he was used to exploration in savage lands, and his keen eyes were everywhere.

We, however, failed to discover the trees indicated, and so ill-defined and overgrown was the path we traversed that we were very soon off it, wandering about without any landmark.

I pointed out that a line of oaks existing in Elizabeth's time would most probably have decayed or been cut down long ago. Oak is a valuable wood in these days, and during recent years the woodman has played havoc with the fine old trees that once existed in our English parks and forests. Even great forests themselves have been cut down and the roots grubbed up within our own short recollections. In more than one spot there, indeed, we discovered marks of the woodman's work—old stumps where the ivy was trying to hide their nakedness, and in two places we found a newly-felled beech awaiting the woodman's drag.

The six oaks we at last discovered—or rather two of them, both too decayed to be worthy of the timber merchant's attention. In line were four stumps, all utterly rotten and half overgrown with bindweed, moss, and ivy. Then, standing beside the last stump of the line, we saw something white in the gloom, and went forward to examine it, finding it to be a large piece of grey rock cropping up from the ground, almost covered with yellow lichen, tiny ferns growing in luxuriance in every crevice. Before us, at some distance away, gleamed two other rocks, one quite high, and the other only two feet out of the earth. There were three in all—the Three Sisters, we supposed.

"Twenty-nine paces from the south," Reilly remarked.

"That's the south, where you are standing, doctor!" Usher cried, for he had taken his bearing by the sun.

I began at once to walk forward in the direction of the two rocks before me and midway, counting the paces. There were big trees everywhere, for we were in the thickest part of the wood, therefore I could not walk in a straight line, and was compelled to judge the extra paces I took.

At last I reached the twenty-ninth, and it brought me to a stump of a giant tree that had been recently felled and carted away. Usher bent quickly to examine the wood, and declared it to be oak.

Was this the sapling planted by Bartholomew da Schorno to mark the spot where he and his two companions had buried the treasure?

Could the Spanish gold be concealed beneath those enormous roots? Was a fortune lying there hidden beneath our feet?

Excited as we all were, we did not act with any precipitation. My other two companions made measurements, each walking twenty-nine paces, and after some consultation both declared that I was correct. The stump was actually that of the oak planted by the Italian, and our next task was to remove it.

Even though the sun shone brightly, it was damp and gloomy within that lonely wood. The undergrowth and bracken were full of moisture, and already our clothes were wet through. We lost no time, however, in setting to work to dig out the enormous root beneath which we hoped to discover that of which we had so long been in search.

All three of us took off coats and waistcoats, and with our spades first dug a deep trench round the stump, and sawed through the main roots that ran deep into the ground in all directions, hoping by this to be able to remove the main portion of the wood bodily. To the uninitiated the "grubbing-up" of a tree root is a very difficult operation, and through the whole morning we worked without being able to move the big mass an inch. Having sawed off all the roots we could find we attached a rope to it and harnessed ourselves, all of us pulling our hardest. Yet it would not budge.

Of a sudden, while we sat upon the obstinate oak-root, perspiring and disappointed, a way out of the difficulty suggested itself to me. Why not dig down beside it and then drive a tunnel at right angles beneath?

I made the suggestion, and at once we commenced to suit the action to the word, first digging a big hole some eight feet deep and six across, and then driving at right angles beneath the root.

We had been at work over an hour, slowly excavating beneath the base of the root, when of a sudden my pick struck wood. My companions with their shovels quickly cleared away the earth, when there became disclosed to us a sodden, half rotten plank set up on end. The discovery showed that we had come upon something unusual, especially as the spade worked by Usher revealed a few moments later two other boards placed so closely in a line with the first that they seemed joined together.

Twenty minutes afterwards we found five thick planks, each half a foot wide, placed together in a straight line, as though it were the side of a square subterranean chamber that had been excavated and boarded up so as to prevent the earth from falling in.

All three of us were almost beside ourselves with impatience to break down that wooden barrier. I took the crowbar and inserted its curved end between two of the stout elm planks in an endeavour to break out one of them. The attempt was, however, futile.

Indeed, it took us another half-hour before we had sufficiently excavated the earth, top and bottom, to allow us to make a satisfactory attempt. At last, however, I again placed the crowbar beneath the blackened, sodden wood, and we all three jumped against it with all our might. It did not yield at first, but, working by slow degrees, we gradually loosened it, and then of a sudden the heavy bolts or fastenings within gave way with a loud crack and the plank was wrenched out, disclosing a dark cavity beyond.

Usher struck a match and held it within, but its feeble light revealed nothing. We wondered if, after all, someone had been before us, ages ago perhaps, for the chamber seemed hollow and empty.

Without loss of time we broke out three other planks from the side of the wooden wall, and then, lighting a candle, I stooped and entered the place, eager to ascertain the truth.

The moment I stepped within a loud cry involuntarily escaped my lips, for my gladdened eyes fell upon some dark objects which lay piled one upon the other in the centre of the small, close-smelling place.

I took the candle nearer, and saw that they were great, iron-bound chests—the chests which, according to the cipher record, were filled with gold!

In an instant my companions were at my side, eager and wild with excitement as myself. Each of them lit candles, and we examined the place together. It was not square but oblong, and we had entered at the end. All around were rough-hewn planks upon which were growing great fungi; the roof also being of stout oak planks and beams, one root of the great oak had grown through, twisted grotesquely, and entered the ground beneath, while the planks on the right side had been forced in by the tree's growth. The place was not quite high enough to allow us to stand upright, yet it seemed far drier than the forest earth we had excavated outside. On examining the walls I found that the planks had been soaked in tar to protect them from the ravages of insects, and that after the place had been constructed the interior had been coated with pitch to render it as water-tight as possible.

In the centre, piled together, were the huge locked chests and sacks of leather secured with big leaden seals, almost like that seal on the Italian document I found on board the *Seahorse*.

To say that we danced for joy would perhaps describe our feelings in those moments. Fortune was mine at last! Even if the heir to the treasure were found one chestful of gold was mine by right. I bent, and by aid of my candle examined the device on the leaden seals, finding it to be the familiar leopard rampant, the arms of the noble house of Da Schorno.

Eager to examine the true nature of our find, we all three of us, by dint of much exertion, managed to move one of the iron-clamped chests from the others and place it on the ground. Then we set about breaking off the lid, a difficult matter, for although the iron was rusty those locked bolts were formidable.

At length, however, we successfully accomplished it, and, raising the lid, there was disclosed to our dazzled vision a marvellous and miscellaneous collection of gold and jewels. Indeed, it was filled to the brim with almost every conceivable article of jewellery, containing nearly every gem known to the lapidary. Sight of it drew a chorus of admiration from our lips.

I took out a wonderful collar of magnificent pearls, bearing a splendid pendant set with a great blood-red ruby, the finest stone I had ever seen. Even there, in the faint light of the candles, the gem flashed crimson before our eyes, while the diamonds, sapphires, and emeralds lying heaped within the chest glittered and gleamed in the light as we held our candles over them.

Certainly, if every chest—and there were eleven of them in all, beside eight hide bags—were filled with such things, the value of the treasure was immense. In our excitement we all three of us plunged our hands in among the jewels, but Reilly withdrew his quickly, for he received a sharp cut from some old bejewelled poignard or sword. Although half-stifled in that narrow place, we opened one of the old bags of tough, untanned leather, similar to that on board the *Seahorse*, and found it also full of splendid jewels. A second contained a number of wonderful jewelled sword-hilts, some of them marvels of old Spanish workmanship, while in a third were stored jewels roughly cut and set, evidently loot from the Moors of Barbary.

A second chest we also opened, and so full was it of golden coin that as we broke open the lid the doubloons fell and scattered about the floor. I took up a handful and looked at them by the uncertain light. They were Spanish all of them, mostly of the reigns of Ferdinand and Philip II.

The sight of so much wealth must, I think, have had a curious effect on us. We scarcely spoke to each other, but with eager fingers quickly examined the marvellous jewels and cast them aside, only reflecting upon their value.

When at last I found tongue and endeavoured to calm my wildly-beating heart, I spoke to my companions regarding the best manner in which to remove the chests and bags to some place of safety.

"It must be done in absolute secrecy," I pointed out. "And we must lose no time in trying to discover the descendant of the Wollertons, otherwise the Government may seize the whole as treasure-trove."

Reilly and Usher, who were agreed that to open those remaining chests and hide bags in that place was impossible, were engaged in replacing the treasure and closing up the lids securely.

"That's so," Reilly answered. "But we shall have a difficulty, I fear, in removing all this without any one knowing. We shall require a heavy waggon, in any case," he added, recollecting the weight of those oak and iron chests even without their precious contents.

"Well," I said, much gratified at our success; "we've found the treasure, at any rate."

"And now, it seems, the difficulty will be to keep it," laughed Reilly, holding up a glittering diamond collar and admiring it.

At that instant I chanced to turn towards the hole by which we had entered and saw, silhouetted against the grey light, the dark figure of a man.

Next instant the shadow had disappeared. Someone was spying upon us! If the secret leaked out, then we should, I knew too well, lose everything!

# XXXV

## The Spy, and What He Told Us

Without a second's hesitation I drew the revolver I now habitually carried, and, dashing out through the hole, scrambled up to the surface after the intruder.

Scarcely had I gained my footing above when a shot was fired close to me, and a bullet whizzed past my head. I looked angrily around, but could see no one. The man had taken refuge behind one of the trees, while I stood before him right in the open.

My companions, alarmed by my sudden rush and the report of the pistol, were next instant beside me, and Usher's quick eyes in a few seconds distinguished a slight movement behind a bush a few yards away. He rushed forward, regardless of consequences, and then I recognized in the intruder the man Martin Franklin. Seeing that we were all armed he held up his hands, and from that action we supposed that he was alone, and that he had fired at me in order to effect his escape.

We quickly closed round him, indignantly demanding his object in spying upon us, but he only laughed and responded insolently. He was a man of about forty, dressed in rough grey tweeds and gaiters, in order, I suppose, to pass as a countryman.

Philip Reilly was furious. He had sprung upon the fellow and with a quick turn of the wrist had wrenched the weapon from his hand.

"I know you!" he shouted. "You are Martin Franklin, the man who was present on the night of the murder at Kilburn! You'll perhaps recollect that incident—eh?"

The man's face, in an instant, went pale as death.

"I—I don't know what you mean, sir!" he answered, with a vain effort to add indignation to his words.

"Well, perhaps you will when I'm called as witness against you and your three companions Bennett, Purvis, and Harding," he answered meaningly. "Where are they now?"

"In London," was the fellow's unwilling response.

Suddenly a brilliant idea occurred to me, and in a loud, threatening voice I said—

"Now, look here, Mr. Franklin. We may as well speak plainly to you, as this is no time for beating about the bush. We know sufficient about you and your scoundrelly companions to give you into the custody of the first policeman we meet. Understand that."

The fellow was a coward, we could see. Mention of the tragedy at Kilburn had sapped his courage utterly, and he now stood before us white, terror-stricken, glancing wildly around for means of escape. We were, however, three to one, and he saw how he had fallen as into a trap.

"I fired the shot in order to alarm you," he faltered, addressing me. "I had no intention of harming you."

"But you will recollect who took Miss Dorothy Drummond to that house at Kilburn, and who forced her to touch the dead man's face," Reilly interposed.

He made no response, for he saw that the secret of the murder was out.

A few minutes later, however, when he had had time for reflection, I spoke my mind further, saying—

"Now, Mr. Franklin, tell us the truth. You and your friends meant to possess yourselves of the chests we have just discovered, did you not?"

"We certainly did," was his prompt response. Then, after a short pause, he added: "I think, doctor, if you will reflect, you'll see that even you and I have certain interests in common."

"How?" I inquired.

"It is to your interest to preserve the secret of your find, eh? I heard you say so down there ten minutes ago."

"Well, I suppose it is!"

"It is also of the highest importance to you to discover the heir of Clement Wollerton?"

"Certainly."

"Well, then, I think I can assist you in both," he answered. "I am not a murderer, as you believe, although I confess to having assisted the others in their ingenious conspiracy. I know quite well that sooner or later they must fall into the hands of the police; nevertheless, if you will allow me freedom to escape and promise to take no steps against me, I will, on my part, give you a pledge of secrecy regarding your discovery of the treasure, and will also warn you of the plot against your life."

"Against my life!" I echoed. "What plot?"

"If you agree to my suggestion I will tell you," answered the black-bearded coward, who, brought to bay, was now ready to betray his friends.

I turned to Usher and Reilly, both of whom were of opinion that, secrecy being necessary, we should make the compact Franklin suggested.

Therefore the fellow took a solemn oath, and there in the dim light beneath those big forest trees, a few yards from where the treasure lay in its cunningly-constructed subterranean chamber, he related to us a very strange story, which we afterwards discovered was the actual truth.

"I am a solicitor, as you perhaps know," he began. "One day there came to my office in the Minories a sailor named Henry Harding whom I had met some three years before, and who was, I knew, a man of considerable intelligence and education. He had just come home from a round voyage in the Mediterranean, and showed me the translations of certain curious documents which had been found on board a derelict. I recognized that the treasure referred to might still exist, but that to undertake the search we should require the assistance of at least two other adventurous spirits like ourselves. Harding said he knew two men of just the stamp we required, and a couple of days later brought to my office Bennett and Purvis, the first-named a retired sea-captain and the second a bookmaker. All three were eager to set to work at once, therefore after a long consultation we decided upon a plan of action. Purvis was sent down to Caldecott to make inquiries, and, finding a man named Knutton still living there, purchased from him a parchment that had been in his family for generations. Then, recognizing that if the treasure were actually found it would be useless to us unless we knew the rightful heir as stated in the old Italian noble's will, I at once advertised for information regarding the Wollertons. Within a fortnight I received a reply from a small country solicitor, and we were very soon in communication with the heir to the property, although, of course, we preserved the secret among ourselves."

"Do you know the identity of the heir at the present moment?" I cried excitedly, for such information was of greatest importance to us, to prevent the Government claiming our find as treasure-trove.

"Yes," he answered, having grown calmer; "I will tell you everything in due course. Well, having secured the document of the Knuttons, we found it to be in cipher. Whereupon Harding recollected that in a vellum book which you took from the *Seahorse* was a cipher and key which he had not had time to copy. We were closely watching you, one or other of us, and knew all your movements; hence we were aware that the book in question was in the hands of Mr. Staffurth, the palæographist.

There seemed only one way to get possession of the book—namely, to steal it; therefore we employed a man known to Bennett, and the house at Clapham was burglariously entered, but the book was found to be locked in a safe which resisted all attempts upon it. One of the parchments—the one with the seven signatures—was, however, stolen."

"And found to be useless," I remarked laughing.

"Yes," he admitted. "But before long, after we had contrived to examine your own rooms, we saw by your movements that you had become aware that we were trying to forestall you, and that the fight for a fortune would be a hard one. Knowing this, Bennett and Purvis conceived the idea of entrapping you in a house which they took at Blackheath and—well, to put it very plainly—doing away with you. For that purpose the girl Dorothy Drummond was sent one night to the surgery at Walworth with a message regarding the illness of a fictitious brother. She knew nothing of the evil intentions of the men, but, as she afterwards confessed to me, a sudden thought occurred to her while in the cab with you, and she refused to allow you to accompany her back to the house."

"Ah!" I exclaimed. "She has told me that already."

"What?" cried the man in surprise. "Has she told you anything else?—I mean the story of the affair at Kilburn?"

"She has told me nothing of that," I answered. "I wish to hear it from you according to your promise."

"Ah, doctor," he went on, apparently much relieved by my reassuring words. "You had a narrow escape that night. She saved your life, although the thought that foul play was intended only came to her suddenly—one of those strange intuitions which sometimes come to us in moments of greatest danger. Beware of those men, for there is yet another plot against you. To-morrow, when you return to London, you will receive a telegram purporting to come from Miss Drummond. Recollect that if you keep the appointment it will mean death to you, just as it did to the unfortunate young fellow at Kilburn."

"Tell me all about that. What connexion had Dorothy Drummond with that affair?"

"Let me relate the incidents to you in their proper sequence," he urged. "Our suspicion was identical with yours, namely, that the treasure was secreted somewhere in the Manor House at Caldecott. You, however, forestalled us in buying out the tenant and obtaining possession of the house. We watched you living there day after day and working with Mr. Reilly and Captain Seal, fearing always lest you should make the discovery. If you had, then it was our intention to either raid the house during your absence and carry away all we could, or, failing that, to give information to the Treasury by which the Government would seize the whole. You see you had no idea of the whereabouts of the heir, and would, in that case, only be awarded a small sum for the discovery."

"A nice revenge! It bears the mark of Black Bennett," observed Usher.

"We had to make use of the secret passage from Bringhurst in order to enter the house, which we often did while you were absent at meals. Yet even then you got the better of us when you closed us down in the tunnel early one morning, and Purvis stumbling into the open well was nearly drowned. Then, having found nothing at the Manor, Harding turned his attention to searching at the Record Office to ascertain whether any other documents were preserved there. He found one, but it was in cipher, and utterly unintelligible. Therefore we kept a watchful eye on you, and when you came down here I was dispatched to follow you and note your movements."

"But the murder at Kilburn—how was that accomplished, and for what reason?"

"Listen, and I will tell you," the man responded. His tongue once loosened, he concealed nothing. His only object now seemed to save himself by the sacrifice of his friends. He quite realized that the game was up, and when, later, I gave him a few pearls from one of the chests that he might sell them and escape from the country in view of the coming revelations, he seemed to be perfectly satisfied. The fact that he was an arrant scoundrel could not be disguised, for he did not remain loyal to his friends in one single instance.

He paused for a few moments, as though hesitating to tell us the whole truth, but at last, with sudden resolution, he said: "When I advertised for information concerning the Wollertons I received several replies, all of which I investigated, but found the claims faulty—all save one. This latter came from a solicitor named Burrell, in Oundle, Northamptonshire, who, in confidence, wrote telling me that he could give information if paid for it.

"I therefore went to Oundle and had an interview with him. Twenty pounds was the sum agreed upon, and when I had paid it he produced some old papers which were in his dead father's handwriting, and then told me a curious story—which, later, I found borne out by the records in question. What he related was briefly this: In the year 1870 Charles Wollerton—who held documentary proof that he was the lineal descendant of Clement Wollerton who commanded one of the ships of Sir Francis Drake's fleet—was living at Weybourne, near Sheringham, in Norfolk, but, having been associated with two other men in a gigantic forgery of Turkish bonds, was convicted and sent to penal servitude. He left a wife and two children, a girl and a boy, the first aged two and the other only nine months old.

"Mrs. Wollerton, always a weakly woman, died of a broken heart three months after her husband's conviction, but before her death she had consulted Burrell, her lawyer at Oundle, regarding the bringing up of her children, expressing a wish that they should never know their proper name, fearing, of course, that the stigma as children of a convict should rest upon them. Wollerton is not a common name, and the case had excited great attention throughout the country. Therefore, on Mrs. Wollerton's decease the children, being left in the solicitor's hands, were put out to nurse, the girl being sent to a woman named Stanion, at Deenethorpe, a village about twenty miles away, while the boy was sent to Sutton Bridge, in the fen country. There was a very small estate left from the wreck of Wollerton's fortune, and out of this the people were paid for keeping the children."

"Why!" I cried, the name of Stanion recalling to my memory what old Ben Knutton had told me. "Then Dorothy Drummond is actually Miss Wollerton!"

"That is so—and, furthermore, she is the youngest descendant of Clement Wollerton, and therefore heiress to the treasure!"

"Well, I'm hanged!" gasped Philip Reilly bluntly. "But is this really true, or are you only humbugging?"

"True, every word of it," was the quick reply. "In the office of Mr. George Burrell, of Oundle, you will find the documents which prove everything I've said. Among them is Charles Wollerton's genealogical tree, properly attested, besides other family papers which will be accepted as absolute proof."

"But the boy?" I asked. "What of him?"

"Ah! About the boy there was an element of romance," was Franklin's response. "It's a curious story—very curious."

# XXXVI

## "Nine Points of the Law"

The man Franklin paused again for a few moments then, in response to my repeated question, said—

"To the boy Charles old Mr. Burrell gave the name of Wooton, the present-day corruption of Wollerton, and he was brought up by a farmer's wife at Sutton Bridge for the first ten years of his life, being afterwards sent to school at Hythe, in Kent. At the time I discovered all these facts Dorothy Wollerton, who is, of course, unaware of her real name, was twenty-two, and her brother Charles a year and three months younger—a smart young man, who had entered the office of a ship-broker in Leadenhall Street. Having obtained this information in secret, together with the whereabouts of both of them, I gave it to my companions, whereupon they at once set to work upon an ingenious plan.

"Miss Drummond—as she believed herself to be—was informed by letter from me as a solicitor that in future she would be under the guardianship of Mr. Charles Purvis, of St. Peter's Square, Hammersmith, a gentleman who had been appointed by the late Mr. Burrell before his death, while at the same time Bennett got on friendly terms with Charles Wooton. Thus, for the second time in their lives, brother and sister met at Purvis' house, and, being unaware of their relationship, fell in love with each other."

The man paused for a moment, regarding the astonishment upon the faces of all of us. Then he went on, saying—

"It must be borne in mind that Charles Wooton, being the youngest, was heir to the estate of Bartholomew da Schorno. He was a shrewd young fellow, however, and appears very soon to have entertained suspicions of Bennett and the others, while having made inquiries regarding Purvis, he found him to be scarcely the sort of man who should be guardian to Dorothy. He therefore refused to associate with us, and for some weeks we saw nothing of him. Bennett and Purvis, however, prevailed upon Dorothy to invite him one evening to the house at Kilburn, which, by the way, Bennett had taken furnished. He went there on an invitation to supper, and—well, you know the rest. He was stabbed to the heart by Bennett, while I, not knowing what was intended, escorted Dorothy to the house, where the others compelled her to touch the dead man's face, after which Bennett and Purvis pointed out to her that she had acted as accessory of the crime."

"The fiends!" I cried. "And the body—how was it disposed of?"

"It was taken in one of those zinc-lined air-tight travelling chests and left in the cloak-room at Euston, where, I believe, it will still be found. Of course, the assassination of Charles served two distinct purposes, first to conceal certain ugly facts which he had learnt about both Purvis and Bennett, and secondly his death made Dorothy heiress. It was the idea of my three companions that if the treasure were discovered Purvis should at once marry her under threats of exposure and thus obtain the money, distributing a certain portion to each of us."

"An amazingly ingenious conspiracy!" I said, utterly bewildered at the strange story he had related. "Then to this moment Dorothy is unaware that Charles was her brother?"

"After his death Bennett told her, but she is in entire ignorance that her real name is Wollerton, or that she is heiress to the Italian treasure."

A silence fell between us, but it was broken by Franklin, who, continuing, declared—

"All that I have told you is absolutely the truth. Knowing that you will keep faith with me I have attempted to conceal nothing. Purvis is aware that you are Dorothy's lover, and he and his friends also know that you carry in your pocket the decipher of the document in the Record Office. Hence their conspiracy to kill you and obtain it. Be warned," he urged. "Do not keep any appointment with Dorothy, otherwise it may prove fatal to you."

"Bennett is, I suppose, unaware that I am the man he marooned ten years ago?" remarked Usher.

"I believe so. He does not know your name," was Franklin's response.

Whereat my companion smiled grimly at thought of the revenge that was to be ours ere many days.

Martin Franklin, although an unscrupulous man, nevertheless kept his word. Probably it was because he feared lest we should give information to the police, and he believed it best to be on the side of the victors rather than the vanquished.

Before we had allowed him to go he gave us his solemn promise to hold no communication with Bennett or the others, so that they would not know of our success or of how we had been forewarned of the fresh conspiracy against me.

Leaving Reilly and Usher to guard the treasure I walked with the scoundrelly lawyer to the edge of the wood, where, with a show of politeness that I knew was feigned, he bade me good-day and left, not, however, before I had warned him in a few plain words of the consequence of any betrayal of our secret. If what he had told us were actually true, then we had now no fear of the seizure of the gold as treasure-trove. The story, however, seemed to us so romantic as to be hardly credible.

However, the removal of the chests and bags was our next consideration, and with that object I walked into Tickencote village, and there obtained a cart and drove on to Stamford. There I purchased a quantity of rope and coarse packing-canvas, conveying them to the spot where my two companions still sat on the oak stump smoking, awaiting me. Together we worked on during the whole afternoon packing both chests and bags in the canvas so that their antique nature should attract no attention.

Then, in accordance with an arrangement I had made in Stamford, a railway trolley met us on the high road at four o'clock, and we conducted its driver around the wood until we came to a drift by which the woodmen were evidently in the habit of entering with their drags. At first the man seemed rather surprised at the nature of his load, but a crisp five-pound note in his palm effectually closed his mouth, and in an hour we had the satisfaction of getting the whole mounted on the trolley, Reilly riding to Stamford Railway Station beside the carter. We had sealed the knots of the cords of each packet with black sealing-wax, which I had bought with the packing materials, therefore at the station we ordered a closed truck, saw them stowed inside for London, and, as we declared the freight to be valuable, the key was handed to me.

# XXXVII

## Contains the Conclusion

Thus far the treasure was ours. That same night we all three returned to London by the last train, the big black van containing the treasure being coupled with us at the rear, while just before two o'clock next morning I had the satisfaction of seeing the whole of it safely placed in my sitting-room at Keppel Street, much to Mrs. Richardson's wonderment as to what the heavy sealed packages could contain.

Usher constituted himself guard of the treasure, and early next morning I went to Cornwall Road and informed Dorothy of our success and of her good fortune.

"It is true, Paul, that I was fond of Charles Wooton, not knowing that he was my brother, and it is equally true that I induced him to accept the invitation to supper at Kilburn which Bennett gave him. But I never dreamed that those men intended to kill him until Martin made me enter the room against my will, and I saw the poor fellow lying dead—stabbed to the heart. But I see it all now! I see why Bennett and Purvis were constantly declaring that I was morally responsible for his death. It was because Purvis intended to compel me, by threats of exposing my secret, to marry him."

I quite agreed with her that she had been the victim of a most clever and ingenious conspiracy, which had only failed because of our constant perseverance in the pursuit of the treasure; and then, as I bent to kiss my love upon the lips, I told her what was the absolute truth, namely, that I had all along believed in her innocence.

"I love you, Dorothy," I repeated. "I have loved you ever since that night when by the intercession of Providence you saved my life. Therefore, do not think that Franklin's revelations influence me in the least."

"Ah, Paul, you are indeed generous!" she cried, springing up and clinging to me. "I—I feared that you would think ill of me—that you would believe I invited Charles there knowing that he was to be their victim."

"I am well aware that such was not a fact," I said seriously, bending to kiss her ready lips again. "You met him, but did not know he was your brother—you knew nothing of the careful and ingenious plan of that man Purvis who posed as your guardian, and who intended to marry you if occasion demanded."

"They killed my brother," she remarked reflectively, as though speaking to herself. "My poor brother, of whose very existence I was in ignorance!"

"They constituted you heiress on purpose!" I said. "But we shall be even with them before long, never fear. When did you see them last."

"I saw Bennett a week ago," was her reply. "I met him quite accidentally in St. Paul's Churchyard."

I had previously related to her all that the rascally solicitor had told me regarding the fresh plot against my life, and she now urged me to be wary.

"I am only awaiting their appointment," I said laughing. "It will be the last they will make outside a gaol."

"But do be careful, Paul," she, urged, with all a woman's solicitude for the safety of her lover. I told her, however, to have no fear.

Two hours later she was at Chelsea assisting us to open the great chests and examine their dazzling contents.

I had called at a famous dealer's in Piccadilly, and in confidence obtained the assistance of an expert, who now stood with us absolutely bewildered at the magnificence of the jewels. Some of the gems, he declared, were without equal—the finest he had ever seen.

But I may, I think, pass over that morning spent in examining our find. Let it suffice to say that the expert went back to Piccadilly, declaring that the collection was worth a very considerable sum, and hoping that his firm might have the offer of purchasing a portion, if not the whole of it.

At three o'clock, after Dorothy had lunched with Usher and myself in Mrs. Richardson's sitting-room, my own being filled to overflowing, the servant handed me a telegram, which read—

"Miss Drummond has met with accident. Wishes to see you immediately.

Clark, 76, Lavender Road,
Battersea

It was the invitation into the fatal trap! I showed it to Dorothy and to Usher, and while the former grew serious and apprehensive, the latter laughed outright.

At four o'clock, accompanied by Usher, Reilly, and two police officers in plain clothes from the Chelsea Station, I reached the corner of Lavender Road and York Road, where I took leave of my companions and went in search of No. 76. It was a small, eight-roomed house, one of a long row of similar dwellings, and when I knocked and inquired for Mr. Clark, the rough-looking lad who opened the door at once invited me inside.

The moment, however, that I stepped within the small hall I found myself seized by two men, who sprang from a room on the left; but almost before I had time to realize my situation I heard a scuffle behind, and saw that the detectives had entered behind me before the lad could close the door. An instant later Reilly and Usher were also on the scene, while Bennett and Harding, who had seized me, let go their hold and rushed to the back of the premises. It was an exciting moment.

We had taken the ruffians completely by surprise, yet Bennett, with his usual cunning, tried to make good his escape. While Harding ran out into the back yard and was captured by Reilly and Usher in the act of climbing the wall, Bennett with fierce determination rushed up to the top of the house and out on the roof, followed by the police officers.

Over the roofs he ran for a long distance as nimbly as a cat, followed closely by the detectives until they came to where two houses were divided by a narrow lane a few feet wide. Then Bennett, finding himself hard pressed and seeing the gulf before him, took a flying leap. His feet touched the gutter on the opposite side, and for a moment we thought he had escaped.

A second later, however, we heard a crack, and saw him clutch wildly at air as the gutter gave way beneath his weight, and he fell backwards to the ground, striking his skull heavily upon the paving.

The neighbourhood is thickly populated, and ere we could reach the spot a great crowd had collected. Very soon, however, the truth was plain. I examined him quickly, and found his neck broken. Death had been almost instantaneous.

Hurriedly we returned to No. 76 amid great local commotion, and found that although Purvis, who had been concealed in one of the upstair rooms, had succeeded in escaping, my friends were holding Harding prisoner. An inspection of the house showed that preparations had been made to assassinate me—indeed, there was a large air-tight travelling chest already prepared to receive my body! They evidently intended to dispose of me in the same manner as Charles Wollerton.

Harding was taken to the police station, and search among the left luggage at Euston resulted in the discovery of the trunk with its gruesome contents, as Franklin had confessed. Purvis has, up to the present, successfully eluded the police, but is believed to be abroad. Harding was eventually tried at the Old Bailey for being implicated in the murder and sentenced to ten years' penal servitude, while the last heard of Franklin was that he had been arrested a year ago in Glasgow and sent to prison on a charge of forging cheques.

As for Black Bennett, the just hand of Heaven had fallen swiftly upon him, rendering man's justice unnecessary.

Every fact that Franklin had related we discovered to be true. The proofs held by Mr. Burrell at Oundle proved most clearly that Dorothy was the youngest descendant of old Clement Wollerton, hence none could dispute her splendid inheritance.

A few days after that exciting chase in Battersea Reilly, Usher, and Mr. Staffurth assisted me to go through the treasure and check it by the long list written in the vellum book. We found, to our satisfaction, that it was intact.

Within a month, with Dorothy's authority, we had disposed of all of it save a few of the most valuable ornaments, which she kept for her own use. The firm in Piccadilly were the principal purchasers of the coins and diamonds, but much of the remainder was sold by auction at Christie's and other sale-rooms and realized very high prices, while a quantity of it has now found its way into the British Museum and other similar institutions.

The chestful of gold coins bequeathed to me as finder realized a little over £1,000, and out of this I paid for the dilapidations at Caldecott Manor—which is, by the way, now reoccupied by a highly respected gentleman and his wife—and made presents to my friends, Job Seal included, augmented, of course, by Dorothy herself.

And the rest? Need I tell you? I think not. All I shall say further is that within two months of our sudden fortune Dorothy, whom I had loved long before I knew her to be heiress of the treasure, married me at Hampstead, where we now live—in Fitzjohn's Avenue, to be exact—leading an idyllic life of peace and love. If you pass up the thoroughfare in question you will probably notice the name, "Mr. Pickering, Surgeon," upon a brass plate, for although the sum realized by the sale of the jewels has provided us with a comfortable income for life, yet I am not by any means an idle man.

So careful have we been to preserve our secret that to those who know us and may chance to read this narrative, the truth will come as an entire surprise. Our love is perfect, for surely no couple could be happier than we are. When at evening I sit at the fireside gazing at the sweet, smiling face of my devoted wife, I often reflect upon those dark days of anxiety and despair—the days of my love's thraldom and of my own desperate endeavour to solve the mystery. Before me there hang, in black frames, the parchment with the seven signatures and the ancient diploma with leaden seal which I discovered with it, and whenever I look up at them my memory runs back to the potency of that simple number three—that numeral scrawled in faded ink which revealed to us "THE TICKENCOTE TREASURE."

THE END

WILLIAM LE QUEUX

# A Note About the Author

William Le Queux (1864–1927) was an Anglo-French journalist, novelist, and radio broadcaster. Born in London to a French father and English mother, Le Queux studied art in Paris and embarked on a walking tour of Europe before finding work as a reporter for various French newspapers. Towards the end of the 1880s, he returned to London where he edited *Gossip* and *Piccadilly* before being hired as a reporter for *The Globe* in 1891. After several unhappy years, he left journalism to pursue his creative interests. Le Queux made a name for himself as a leading writer of popular fiction with such espionage thrillers as *The Great War in England in 1897* (1894) and *The Invasion of 1910* (1906). In addition to his writing, Le Queux was a notable pioneer of early aviation and radio communication, interests he maintained while publishing around 150 novels over his decades long career.

# A Note from the Publisher

Spanning many genres, from non-fiction essays to literature classics to children's books and lyric poetry, Mint Edition books showcase the master works of our time in a modern new package. The text is freshly typeset, is clean and easy to read, and features a new note about the author in each volume. Many books also include exclusive new introductory material. Every book boasts a striking new cover, which makes it as appropriate for collecting as it is for gift giving. Mint Edition books are only printed when a reader orders them, so natural resources are not wasted. We're proud that our books are never manufactured in excess and exist only in the exact quantity they need to be read and enjoyed.

# bookfinity™

## Discover more of your favorite classics with Bookfinity™.

- Track your reading with custom book lists.
- Get great book recommendations for your personalized Reader Type.
- Add reviews for your favorite books.
- AND MUCH MORE!

Visit **bookfinity.com** and take the fun Reader Type quiz to get started.

Enjoy our classic and modern companion pairings!

Classic & Modern

Printed in the USA
CPSIA information can be obtained
at www.ICGtesting.com
JSHW022328140824
68134JS00019B/1366

9 781513 280844